Why the Sky Is Blue

Susan Meissner

HARVEST HOUSE PUBLISHERS

EUGENE, OREGON

Cover by Left Coast Design, Portland, Oregon

WHY THE SKY IS BLUE

Copyright © 2004 by Susan Meissner
Published by Harvest House Publishers
Eugene, Oregon 97402
www.harvesthousepublishers.com

Library of Congress Cataloging-in-Publication Data

Meissner, Susan, 1961–
  Why the sky is blue / Susan Meissner.
    p. cm.
  ISBN 0-7369-1413-7 (pbk.)
  1. Abused women—Religious life. 2. Rape victims—Religious life. 3. Meissner, Susan, 1961–
I. Title.
  BV4596.A2M46 2004
  813'.6—dc22   2004001049

Printed in the United States of America.

04 05 06 07 08 09 10 11 /BP-KB/ 10 9 8 7 6 5 4 3 2 1

Acknowledgments

To my incredible family in Minnesota and "back home" in California, thank you for the countless ways you have encouraged me. I am blessed to be loved by you and honored to return that love. To my husband, Bob, you are my soul mate. I know I am supposed to be *your* helpmeet, but you are mine—in so many ways. To my wonderful heirs, Stephanie, Joshua, Justin, and Eric, I have learned so much by mothering you and have loved every minute of it. To my parents, Bill and Judy Horning, you gave me both roots and wings. Dad, thanks for passing on the writing gene. Here's to good books, good talks, and pullet surprises!

To the creative minds at Harvest House, thank you for sharing my vision. Nick Harrison, Carolyn McCready, and Kimberly Shumate, thank you for loving what I love—stories of ordinary people told in extraordinary ways.

To Frank Barone, my ninth-grade English teacher, thank you for watering and tending the little seed that found its way to your classroom. You fanned into flame a wonderful thing when you read aloud in class my oatmeal story. I have never been the same since.

To good friends Julie Falk, Kathy Sanders Zufelt, Tanya Siebert, and Gene Bottin, my parents, and my sister Lauren Chin, thanks for reading the early pages of the manuscript and lending your wisdom.

And finally to the God of my soul and heart, thank you for giving me a passion for storytelling. Your ways utterly amaze me. By the way, you chose a beautiful color for the sky.

*S*usan Meissner is an award winning newspaper columnist, pastor's wife, and high school journalism instructor. She lives in rural Minnesota with her husband, Bob, and their four children. *Why the Sky Is Blue* is her first novel.

for my Papa

What does little birdie say
In her nest at peep of day?
Let me fly, says little birdie,
Mother, let me fly away.
Birdie, rest a little longer,
Till thy little wings are stronger.
So she rests a little longer,
Then she flies away.

What does little baby say,
In her bed at peep of day?
Baby says, like little birdie,
Let me rise and fly away.
Baby, sleep a little longer,
Till thy little limbs are stronger.
If she sleeps a little longer,
Baby too shall fly away.

ALFRED, LORD TENNYSON

PART ONE
Claire

Prologue

I was only four and a half when my father died. I barely remember him. It was 1953, and I had awakened that May morning with a voice lingering in my ear. It was a voice that awed and frightened me at the same time. It was like God Himself had whispered to me, and the echoes of His message had shaken me awake. I could feel the words swirling inside my head—more sensation than actual sound. A father-voice had whispered *Do not be afraid.* Afraid about what, I didn't know.

I had slipped out of bed and made my way to the kitchen where my mother was making coffee. I remember asking her if Daddy was home, that I had heard his voice from my bed. A queer look had swept across her face, like she almost believed her husband was indeed only a room away instead of a world away, but then the look disappeared. She knelt down, hugged me, and told me it must have been a dream. Daddy was still in Korea. She finished with the coffee pot and began to cut a piece of toast into pieces for my little brother Matthew who was sitting in his highchair.

I remember staying in the kitchen for several minutes after she rose from her knees, pondering deep thoughts in my four-year-old head while Matthew banged the metal tray in front of him with a spatula. Had I dreamed that deep, penetrating voice? Or was it really God who had spoken to me? I remember trembling at the thought that either could be true. Even now, years later, I can remember feeling anxious that I had been able to dream up the voice of God. The only other explanation was that it actually had been the voice of the Almighty. I didn't know which one was more unsettling. Not then and not now.

I would grow up believing, however, that I had been let in on a terrible secret, because later that day men in uniform came to our door. It was late in the afternoon. Matthew was napping, and I was quietly playing with my dolls like my mother had asked. I saw a black car drive up and park in our driveway. The first man that stepped out of the car looked just like my father. He carried nothing in his hands but a white envelope. I ran to the picture window in the living room, amazed that my dad had returned from Korea without his duffel bag and brown leather suitcase. Another man got out of the car, and he sort of looked like my father too. A third one got out. He wore a little cross on his hat. He was carrying a book. A Bible.

The rest of that day is a blur. I don't remember the men telling my mother that my father's plane had been shot down. I don't remember her wailing, though years later she told me neighbors had to go looking for me when her anguish sent me running from the house.

What I remember most vividly from that day is the sound of that voice that had awakened me. That is why, thirty-three years later, when I heard it again, there was no mistaking it.

1

When I heard the voice of God for the second time in my life, I was still recovering from what everyone around me quietly called The Attack. Everyone said the words in whispers. They could have shouted it if they had wanted to. I didn't and still don't remember any of it. I cannot remember the night a man hurt me in the worst way a man can hurt a woman. I also don't remember him wrapping his big hands around my throat in a failed attempt to squeeze the life out of me. I had to be told what I had survived. A doctor informed me a couple of days later in a hospital that things would be fuzzy as I recovered. That was the word the neurologist had used. Fuzzy.

What I remember, I call The Waking Up. I woke up in a hospital bed with injuries but no idea how I got them. When I said as much to the neurologist—slightly painful for me due to bruised vocal cords—he said that was normal. I told him I didn't remember anything about that day after breakfast, even though the attack occurred sometime between eight and eight-thirty in the evening. That, too, was normal, he said.

There is nothing normal about any of this, I wanted to say to him.

"I don't remember why I love Tennyson," I said instead, feeling a tear slip down my cheek and not knowing why.

He fidgeted then. I could tell we were leaving the realm of concrete medical data regarding the brain and entering the world of the unknowable mind. It was fuzzy indeed.

In a gesture I found genuinely compassionate, he took my hand, leaned over my hospital bed, and told me that some memories would return to me, others wouldn't. There would be no way of knowing what my mind would be capable of remembering and what it wouldn't. He then gave me some rather good advice, which I failed to appreciate until later.

"If you can't remember why you loved Tennyson, then find new reasons for loving what he wrote," he said. He paused, and I could tell he was choosing his words very carefully. "You are very lucky to be alive, Mrs. Holland. I have seen other people with injuries like yours who never leave a hospital bed." In the days that followed, I tried to think of myself as being lucky, but the thought never seemed to fit the reality.

That seemed especially true that October morning, a month after I left the hospital, when I awoke with God's voice floating through my head—the same voice that stirred me awake as a child the day I heard my father had died.

I actually had two startling revelations that morning. One was from God—at least I think the message was from Him. The second discovery I came across on my own as I rose from bed contemplating the first. An unexpected wave of nausea swept over me when I stood up, and as I brought my arm to my abdomen, it brushed across my breasts. A sensation I had felt only four other times before in my life stunned me. I staggered to the toilet, lifted the lid, and began throwing up.

It was a physical response to a physical condition, and it took me only a moment to realize this. But as the seconds ticked by and I began to grasp the horrible reality before me, fresh waves of nausea gripped me; and this second round of heaving had nothing to do with morning sickness.

I was pregnant. I was pregnant with a child that I was certain had started growing in me in the quiet hours after the attack—the attack I cannot even remember. In a moment unwitnessed by anyone in the emergency room or in the quiet room on the fifth floor where I was taken later, a life had begun to shape itself within me. It was a life I already knew would tear me in two. The man who had tried to kill me—and failed—had instead, it seemed, started killing me in another way.

As the heaving subsided and I was left with only my disbelief, I lay across the cool tile of the bathroom floor and prayed that I would wake up. Surely I must be dreaming. In the fog of misery clouding my thinking, I could hear my husband, Dan, downstairs telling our eleven-year-old daughter, Katie, to make sure she turned her curling iron off. Then I heard Spencer, our six-year-old son, asking for Trix for breakfast. A quirky thought ran through my head that we didn't have any Trix. It slipped away like a lizard you're not quite sure you saw.

For a very brief moment I wished my attacker had finished the job. I'm embarrassed to admit it, but I wanted to be dead. I didn't want to be alive anymore. But the voices of the three people downstairs, whom I love deeply, drifted up to me, and that morbid thought skittered away, thankfully. However, it was replaced by a despair that surprised me by its weight.

The message God had given me that morning hovered over me as I lay curled up on the floor like a sleeping child. It was a four-word message that I would spend the next eight months trying to understand. God knew what I was about to face. He knew I would struggle to comprehend how He could have let such a thing happen to me. He knew I would seriously doubt His love, His care, His wisdom. He knew there would be many moments when I would teeter on the edge of having no faith at all.

So while I would have expected His message to be something like, "Do not give in to bitterness," or "Do not lose heart," or "Do not doubt," I was surprised that it was none of these.

His message to me was the same one He had given me the morning I learned my father had died.

Do not be afraid.

I am amazed by the strength—and fragility—of the human body. I marvel that it can do so much yet has so many limitations. Only a deity could create something so wonderful and yet so weak.

And it awes and alarms me that the body can act so independently of the soul.

My body—my brain—has never allowed me to recall what happened to me the night I was attacked. I've been annoyed by this amnesia at times. But most of the time I'm comforted by my mind's profound, benevolent refusal to remember.

When I first came home from the hospital, I was haunted by the fear I would suddenly remember everything. The specter of recollection crouched on the fringe of just about everything I did and thought. I worried it would all come rushing back in a deluge, and I also worried it would come back bit by agonizing bit, like a slow torture. I didn't know which would be worse. In the end, it didn't matter. The last thing I remember about September 9, 1985, is eating a bagel for breakfast. That day ends just after breakfast in my mind. My next memory is waking up in a hospital in the wee hours of September 10.

Now my amazing body, so valiant in its endeavor to shield me from images I should not have to relive, seemed to have turned traitor on me that morning I realized I was pregnant.

As I lay on the cool bathroom tile waiting for my world to stop spinning, I was keenly aware that my body was busily building cell upon cell inside me, growing a person like me, but not me, within the darkness of my insides. My wonderful, self-protecting brain, which had survived asphyxiation, and which then proceeded to protect my emotional state with selective amnesia, was ironically facilitating the growth of life in my womb.

The first time I learned about the human body's autonomic systems, I was in junior high school. I was intrigued to discover that we do not notice when blood vessels change size or when our hearts beat faster or when our pupils dilate. In high school I studied ancient Greek and learned that *autonomic* means "self-ruling." At the age of thirty-six, on the floor of a bathroom, I learned what that really meant: I wasn't in charge of anything.

Which is why the turmoil of my morning had done nothing to interrupt the mysterious, creative process at work within me. I rose off the floor changed forever, but inside me things were moving right along—as they had minutes before when I was still asleep and blissfully unaware.

Though completely undone emotionally and physically, I instinctively knew I needed to get up and make myself halfway presentable. It was just minutes before Becky, a good friend and our pastor's wife, would be at the house to pick up the kids for school. She had done this every morning since I had been attacked. I used to do it.

Katie and Spence would be coming upstairs to say goodbye to me. I didn't want them to know what I knew. I didn't want them to worry about me. They had already worried enough to last a lifetime.

I grabbed the marble counter to steady myself as renewed nausea teased me. I turned on the faucet and splashed water on my face, looking into the mirror to gauge if I would be able to pull it off. My eyes were puffy and red, my face ashen. The swelling on my neck had long since gone down, but the bruises that encompassed my throat like a necklace were a sick shade of pale yellow. I looked terrible.

I shut the door, put the toilet seat down, and sat on it, holding a wet washcloth to my head. I would say goodbye to my children from behind the door. I had a sinking feeling if I saw them—my own flesh and blood—I would burst into tears. There had been enough of that.

There would be no fooling Dan, however. He would never leave the house without making sure I was okay for the day. He had only just the week before begun working full time again. Dan is a veterinarian with a group practice in Minneapolis. His two partners—both alumni and good friends from the University of Minnesota—had been generous with allowing him time off, but Dan is the best small-animal surgeon in the group, and they'd missed him while he was away taking care of me. He, too, would be coming up to say goodbye. But I couldn't think about that right then.

Within moments of my shutting the bathroom door, I heard footsteps. Spencer was first.

"Mommy?" he called

"I'm in the bathroom, sweetie," I said as brightly as I could. "Can I owe you a kiss and a hug? I kind of have a tummy ache today."

" 'Kay," he said and bounded away.

Katie must have been right at the bedroom door.

"Watch it, Spencer," she said gruffly. "This is hot."

"Well, you're in the way," I heard him say, each word becoming softer as he ran out of earshot.

"Mom, I brought you a cup of coffee," Katie said to me, waiting.

"Thanks, hon," I managed. "Can you put it on the nightstand and I'll get it in a minute? I'm feeling a little under the weather, but I'll be okay in a little bit."

Despite my faked cheer, I set off an alarm.

"Do you want me to get Dad?" she said, fear thick in her voice.

"I'll be okay, sweetheart," I lied. "I'll see you this afternoon, okay? And you can tell me about your day."

She paused.

"Okay, Mom," she said. "I love you."

It was the first time she had ever said it first.

"I love you too."

I have no idea how I got the words to come out.

No one would have been able to understand this, so I told no one—not even Dan—that a tiny part of me was energized at the thought of being pregnant. It sounds so incredibly out of place, but I knew that the little sliver of elation was a remnant from those other times when Dan and I had desperately wanted children and despaired of ever having any. Or of having more than one.

I met Dan my senior year at the University of Minnesota in 1970. He was finishing up his graduate work in veterinary science. He was studying late one night in one of the carrels at the main library, and so was I. Neither of us was looking for romance. I had just broken up with a man I thought had promise at one time, but did not. Dan was consumed with completing his doctorate and finishing up his internship. I was sitting across from him, and I dropped my pencil. It hit his shoe. He bent down, picked it up, and handed it to me. It was as simple as that. We started talking and realized we were attending the same Twin Cities church. We had other things in common too. We both loved classical music, Italian food, thunderstorms, and the color blue. We laughed over the things we didn't see eye-to-eye on like sports teams, best-selling authors, and cars.

When the library closed, we went to a coffee shop and left several hours later as good friends. In a year's time, we were married, I was teaching high school literature, and he was starting a veterinary practice with two of his classmates.

We had only been married for a year, choosing to stay in Minneapolis after graduation, when we both felt ready to start our family. In hindsight I guess it wasn't that long before I became pregnant, but at the time, I thought trying for more than a year was impossibly difficult. My monthly cycles were unpredictable, so it was hard for me to tell when I was ovulating. Even my gynecologist told me mine was a frustrating case. When I finally did become pregnant with Katie, I had complications halfway into the pregnancy and had to be on bed rest until the month before she was born. I had a low-lying placenta, I was told. Toward the end of my third trimester, the placenta moved upward to the place where it should have been all along, and Katrina Noelle was born on December 21, 1973, with no complications.

I went back to teaching part-time when Katie was nine months old, and Dan and I decided to forgo using any kind of birth control because of how long it had taken to conceive Katie. In July 1976, while the nation exuberantly celebrated its bicentennial, I miscarried a little boy at fifteen weeks gestation. In 1977 I miscarried again, this time at nineteen weeks. We gave this little girl a name, Sarah—a name I still treasure and whisper from time to time.

When I became pregnant with Spencer the following year, Dan and I decided that whatever the outcome, he would get a vasectomy. We wanted this child so badly, but neither one of us could emotionally handle the death of another baby. We prayerfully committed this child to God's care, just as we had the others. I moved downstairs into the living room and literally lived on the couch for the next seven months, surrendering my teaching job. The previous miscarriages had left some uterine scarring, furthering my chances that, again, the placenta would be in the wrong place. At a little over eight months into the pregnancy, I began bleeding. We hurried to the hospital, where Spencer was delivered by Caesarean, tiny but healthy.

A month later Dan had the vasectomy, and we enjoyed a weird sense of relief that we would never have to face another difficult pregnancy or month after month of dashed hopes. When Spencer was a year old, I resumed my teaching—this time as a full-time English teacher. Our peace of mind about having completed our family pretty much carried us through the next six and a half years until it evaporated that morning when I knew the baby I was carrying couldn't possibly be Dan's.

As I waited for Dan to come up the stairs, as I knew he would when the kids were gone, this thought kept pace with my heartbeat: *It's not Dan's baby…it's not Dan's baby…it's not Dan's baby.* The accusatory tone smothered me in guilt, as if I had anything to do with any of this.

I wanted to yell out that it wasn't mine, either. But it was. It was my baby. That was the worst part about it. Just like Katie and Spencer had been created from a tiny part of me, so had this child. I was starting to feel a conflicted sense of affection for it, even though I had been aware of its presence for only fifteen minutes.

In the days and weeks ahead, a handful of people would counsel me to terminate the pregnancy. But I wouldn't even consider it. I knew I was a victim of sexual assault. And I knew pregnancies were difficult for me. But I never could have ended the life of the child inside me on my own. And it had nothing to do with politics or social agendas. It had to do with me. And what I knew was inside me—a tiny person with a beating heart. I just couldn't do it. I had longed for, loved, and lost too many unborn children. And since I was fairly certain I would miscarry this one too, I was able to convince myself that it really didn't matter.

I heard the front door open and Dan saying goodbye to Katie and Spencer. It closed, and I knew he was walking toward the stairs. Toward me.

God, help me tell him, I prayed.

As the moments that seemed like an eternity ticked by, more and more I convinced myself I would lose this child like I had lost the others. But oddly, underneath this certainty was a grain of hope that scared me because it seemed too impossible to consider. It scared me that deep down I didn't want to miscarry this child. I was already wishing the child would live.

I was standing in the bathroom with my hand on the door-knob when I heard Dan come into our bedroom.

"Claire, you want some breakfast?" he said.

I closed my eyes and leaned my forehead against the door, trying to gather strength from the solid oak, I suppose.

"Claire?"

I took a deep breath as a prayer formed on my lips that consisted of just two words: *Help me*.

I opened the door and stepped out—one of the braver things I have ever done—and looked at my husband. Dan missed nothing.

"Claire! Are you all right?"

He dashed over to me, his arm around me in an instant as I started to falter. He led me to my side of the bed and sat me down.

"What is it? What's wrong, honey?" He was beside me, strong and yet shaking. I was starting to cry again.

He thought then that he had put it all together.

"Oh, dear God, you've remembered it…" he moaned, clearly unprepared to hear what he thought was the explanation for my tears.

I shook my head and whispered, "No, no…that's not…" but I couldn't finish.

Relief was etched in his words and manner as he pulled me closer and said, "What is it then? What's the matter?"

I'm sure Dan was convinced I was worried about my safety that morning. Though my name had been kept out of the media coverage of the assault, the attacker surely knew his victim had survived. That meant he would assume I could identify him, though he would not know that was impossible. Since I was found unconscious near my own van, the police working on my case believed the attacker could have learned of my identity by going through my purse or glove compartment. The investigating detective, Mark Nordahl, told me I may have befriended the attacker or been tricked into helping him and giving him my name. Detective Nordahl also told me the attacker could have been someone I knew by name, though I found this to be very unlikely.

In any case, the month-long, round-the-clock surveillance of our house had just ended. A very sophisticated security system had been installed in its place. Dan was slow to be convinced, but he finally agreed to go back to work after I was given detailed instructions on how to work it.

He probably thought I was feeling unsure that the system would work if an intruder did try to get into the house. Actually, I never worried about that much, though I knew Dan did.

"Can you tell me what it is?" he said, smoothing my hair and kissing my forehead.

I was suddenly terrified that when I told him, Dan would stop loving me, that he would stop desiring me. I feared there would be no more romance in our marriage. I was worried that whatever passion Dan had would be spent not on loving me but on hating this unknown man who had crashed headlong into our lives.

"Dan…," I said and stopped.

"Baby, whatever it is, you can tell me," he said, sounding so sure of himself.

"I'm pregnant," I whispered. For some reason I also blushed. I couldn't look at him.

He said and did nothing for several seconds, as if waiting for the moment that had just passed to rewind.

We seemed to be on opposite sides of an abyss in that moment when I told him and the matching moment when he understood.

Then we both fell in.

"What?" he finally said, though I know he had heard what I said.

It had taken Herculean strength for me to say it once. I couldn't say it again. I just nodded my head as if to say, "What you thought I said, I said."

"Claire, how do you know this?" he said, each word laced with fear and anger. "How *can* you know this?"

"I know, Dan," I said, tears falling freely down my face. "I know this feeling. I know it."

"You could be wrong. Maybe you're wrong. You've been through a lot, Claire," he said, as if trying to convince himself, not me, that I was mistaken. "You remember what the neurologist said. Things might be confusing for a while."

Fuzzy, I wanted to say. *He said things would be fuzzy.*

It was true there were some things I couldn't remember. I couldn't remember if I had assigned *The Grapes of Wrath* or *A Farewell to Arms* to my American Lit students. And I couldn't remember the name of the new salon where I got my hair cut. And I couldn't remember what Katie had played for her piano recital three weeks before.

But I did remember what it was like to be pregnant.

"I know I am," I simply said.

He stood, and I glanced up to see him drop his head into his hands, his shoulders and back slumped by a weight I was becoming rather familiar with. But I had never seen him look quite so defeated.

I closed my eyes and let the anguish wash over me. There was no stopping it. There was no stopping anything.

We were both in the black hole, but I felt completely alone. I wondered how in the world I would get through this by myself. The road ahead looked so dark and lonely.

But the next moment, Dan gathered me in his arms. He held me tight as he cried softly, his tears falling into my hair, sliding down my neck, and finally blending with my own.

"It will be all right," he kept saying.

He was wrong.

And he was right.

I don't know how long we sat there in each other's arms, but eventually Dan whispered to me that he wanted to call Nick, our pastor. He got up, picked up the phone on his side of the bed, and went out into the hall with it. After a moment of silence I heard Dan say, "Nick, it's Dan…" And then he closed the bedroom door and walked toward the end of the hall. I think he was trying to protect me from hearing what he was going to tell Nick, but I again felt like I was alone in the abyss. His voice became muffled as he walked away.

Dan had been calling Nick a lot lately. Dan must've thought I was unaware of his frequent calls to both the church office and Nick and Becky's home, because he always returned to me after being on the phone with Nick as if he were returning from putting a load of clothes in the dryer. And I, in turn, pretended like that was just what he had been doing.

It was obvious that he was wrestling with accepting what had happened to me on a deeper level than even I was. It was silly of him to think that he was to blame, but I knew he felt he was responsible for what had happened.

I don't remember this, but apparently I had wanted to pick up his parents' anniversary gift at a nearby mall on the night I was attacked. It was a Tuesday and the mall closed at eight o'clock. There was going to be a party for his parents that Friday night. We were going to be celebrating their forty-fifth wedding anniversary, and I had ordered a gravy boat in Dan's mother's china pattern. It was something she had wanted since the day she got married. I don't remember ordering it, but I remember her wanting it. It had come in that day, and I was anxious to get it. I had asked Dan to come with me, but he declined. It was no big deal. I had been to the mall dozens of times alone. This was the only time that it mattered. I don't recall asking him to come with me, and he cannot forget that I did.

So I went. The police found the gravy boat in my van, still in the box and bag it came in, so I obviously had made it to the mall. A clerk remembered me buying it, but she didn't look at the clock, of course. She estimated it was sometime between seven fifteen and seven forty-five.

I was found at eight thirty, lying next to my van in the back alley of a used-car lot four blocks away. The couple that found me had been lost and were in their car, turning around in the alley, when the wife saw me crumpled by my van in the glare of their headlights.

Neither she nor her elderly husband knew what to do with me. Both of them thought I was dead. They agonized over what to do. After several panicked moments, the man sent his wife out to the street to flag down a passing car while he stayed with me.

The police arrived first, and the first cop to reach me detected a pulse, which greatly relieved the elderly couple. But I guess my breathing was shallow. And I was bleeding from two sizeable head wounds. My clothes were a mess, and I had been deposited in a puddle of muddy water.

By eight forty-five I was in an ambulance on my way to Abbot-Northwestern Hospital, and one of the three squad cars that had sped to the scene was on its way to my house to inform Dan I had been the victim of an apparent assault. They didn't know it was a sexual assault then, though I think they had already guessed. My purse, which was still in my van, was untouched. Seventy-five dollars was still tucked inside it, along with several major credit cards.

Even though all of this actually happened to me, it may as well have happened to someone else. I remember none of it, which frustrated the police to no end, and later, Mark Nordahl. I could give them nothing to go on.

When I regained consciousness, I was in the emergency room, but I don't remember this. The doctor treating me told me I tried to speak but couldn't. I kept reaching for my throat, and they had to restrain my arms. Dan was in the room then. He told me later he kept telling me he was there, though he had to stand off to the side.

When I woke up again, my head was pounding, and it felt like there was a bucket of bricks on my neck. I reached up to remove them, but of course there was nothing there. Dan was at my side. I was in a semidark room. Two IVs were poking out of my left wrist. My wedding ring was off my finger.

"Claire, honey, I'm here…" Dan said gently, stroking my ring-less hand.

"My ring…" I tried to say, but nothing came out except rasps of air.

"Shhh," he said. "Don't try to talk, hon." Two tears were at the corners of his eyes. I watched as they tumbled over the edge of his eyelids and slid unchecked down his cheek.

I had never felt more confused in my life. I knew I had to be in a hospital, but I didn't know how I had gotten there, or why.

"What happened?" I whispered.

His wet eyes got very large.

"You don't…you don't remember?" he said.

I shook my head. It hurt.

I found out later that was the third time that night I'd asked that question. Dan had to tell me three times I'd been attacked and nearly strangled. He left out the part about the sexual assault, and I guess I don't blame him. I kept asking about my ring. Dan assured me over and over that he had it in his pocket. He kept taking it out and showing it to me. I only recall his doing it once.

It wasn't until the afternoon of the following day that a doctor told me my would-be killer was also a rapist. He urged me to be tested for every sexually transmitted disease in the book. He also asked when my last period was. I told him I didn't know. It had nothing to do with my short-term memory loss. I really didn't keep track anymore since we weren't going to have more children. My cycles had never been regular. I managed to squeak this out through swollen vocal cords. I also told him it took well over a year for me to get pregnant the four times I did conceive.

That was the last time I thought about the possibility this assault would lead to a pregnancy. Actually, I hadn't even thought of it then. The doctor had. I knew better. Or so I thought.

4

$\mathcal{J}$ was dressed and had run a brush through my hair when Dan returned to our bedroom. I could tell breaking the news to Nick had been hard on him. I took a sip of the coffee Katie had brought me and winced. It was stone cold.

"They're coming over," he said, as he put the phone back on his nightstand. "I hope that's all right."

I nodded.

He came to me and we embraced. Neither of us said anything for several minutes.

"Claire, I think you should see a doctor before we do anything else," he finally said. "I...I just think we need to know for sure."

Again, I nodded.

Nick and Becky arrived not long after that, and though I appreciated their presence and prayers, I hated being the pitied center of attention. Again. After five weeks of it already, it now seemed it would never end.

Becky, too, felt it imperative I get to a doctor, that day if possible. She asked for the name of my gynecologist and used the kitchen phone to call his office. I actually hadn't been to see Dr.

Chapman in several years. Dr. Fremmer, who had seen me through the births of Katie and Spence, both miscarriages, and every infertile month of my early childbearing years, had retired not long after Spencer was born. That, coupled with my disappointing retirement from babymaking, left me with no great desire to step into an OB/GYN office of any kind. I'd had just one exam in the past five years. I had been told five weeks ago at the hospital to make an appointment with my own gynecologist. But I hadn't. It really didn't seem like I needed to. I just wanted to get back to my normal, day-to-day life.

Becky was gone for several minutes, longer than it would have taken Dr. Chapman's receptionist to tell her there wasn't an opening until the following month. I knew she was talking them into seeing me that day. That meant she was telling them why. More people to pity me. Her bargaining must have worked. She came back into the room and knelt by me.

"Dr. Chapman can see you at eleven thirty, Claire," she said. "There's been a cancellation and they're giving you the slot."

"Okay," I mumbled.

"I'll come with you if you want," she said.

I looked over to Dan.

"It's okay, Becky, I can take her," he said, sort of to both of us.

Nick and Becky stayed a little while longer, and I was actually sad to see them go. Nick prayed for us before he left, pleading with God to give us wisdom and peace. Interesting choice of words. Wisdom and peace would turn out to be exactly what we needed most and utterly lacked.

The ride to the clinic was a quiet one for Dan and me. I hadn't been in the van since the attack, but I'm sure Dan didn't think of that or he would have grabbed the keys to his Bronco instead.

The van had been impounded for several days during the initial investigation as Mark Nordahl and a team of forensic experts combed it inside and out searching for clues. I don't think they found much. They believed the attacker somehow tricked or forced his way into the passenger side, probably in the mall parking lot. The door handle was wiped clean. There weren't even any prints from Katie or Spence, and they both had used that door handle several times that day.

There was no evidence inside the van. No signs of struggle. No blood. Whatever happened to me had happened somewhere else, most likely in the alley. Doctors at the hospital believed the two gashes on my head were the first wounds I received. One, delivered by my own steering-wheel locking device, knocked me to the ground, perhaps while I was trying to run away. The second one was caused by my subsequent fall to the ground, I was told. Scrapes to my left arm, side, and hip were contaminated with mud, tiny stones, and asphalt from the alley. Everything else happened while I was unconscious.

It sounds so much worse than it actually was, at least for me. Patty, the victim counselor recommended to me by the hospital, was a little unsure what to make of me. I had none of the usual posttrauma disorders, not even anxiety. There were times when I believed she wished I did. But I wasn't fearful of my attacker because I didn't even remember meeting him or having been afraid of him before. Patty no doubt believed the memories locked inside my brain would one day spill out and she wouldn't be around to help me mop them up.

We arrived at the clinic in plenty of time for my appointment but still sat until nearly noon in a waiting room full of women with protruding tummies. Finally when my name was called, I stood, and Dan started to rise to his feet too.

"Want me to come?" he asked.

"Not really," I said, displaying the tiniest of grins. It was my first attempt at humor in weeks.

I think Dan truly appreciated it. He grinned too. It was a wonderful two seconds.

"I'll be right here, then," he said and sat back down.

By the time I had given a urine sample, a vial of my blood, and been weighed, it was after noon, and my stomach was beginning to growl. The morning nausea was gone, and I was ravenous.

Dr. Chapman came into the room where I sat clothed in a blue dressing gown.

"Mrs. Holland, it's been awhile," he said in a neighborly tone that was nearly devoid of chastisement, but not quite.

"Sorry about that," I said meekly. "I didn't realize it had been this long. You can call me Claire."

He smiled, and then the whole countenance of his face changed. It became stern and soft at the same time. It's hard to describe.

"I have your results," he said.

I nodded and felt tears welling.

"The tests are positive. You are pregnant," he said.

I nodded again and tried brushing the tears away. Fresh ones replaced them. He reached behind his stool to a box of tissues, grabbed the box, and placed it in my lap.

"I'm sorry to have to tell you this, Mrs. Holland. I understand you were the victim of an assault," he continued.

Again, all I could do was nod. I yanked a tissue out and savagely wiped my eyes. I was so sick of crying.

"You do have some options," he went on. "It would be a very simple procedure to terminate the pregnancy."

Still the tears came. My nose started running as well.

I shook my head.

"I…that's not an option for me," I managed.

"It's an option for all women," he said gently.

"I mean, I couldn't do it," I said. "I couldn't let you…I couldn't…What happened to me isn't the child's fault," I finally eked out.

Dr. Chapman paused for a moment and then tenderly said, "It's not your fault either."

He was right. But so was I. There was no escaping it—both statements were true.

"I will probably lose it anyway," I whispered.

"Perhaps," Dr. Chapman said as he looked at my patient file. "But you have had two second-trimester miscarriages, Mrs. Holland. It could be three or four months before this pregnancy is naturally terminated, if indeed you miscarry. Or you could possibly carry to term. There is also some risk for you, personally, in letting the pregnancy continue."

"I know," I said and sighed. "That never seemed to matter before…," I continued absently.

"The situation was different then, Mrs. Holland. You were carrying children you wanted," Dr. Chapman said. "That's understandable."

"I never said I didn't want this child," I said in return, hardly believing the words that came out of my mouth.

Dr. Chapman was silent as he processed this, and so was I. I was finally beginning to understand the depth of my sorrow. The tears that kept springing fresh from my eyes that day were tears not just of grief over a pregnancy I didn't want but also over a child I couldn't have. I wasn't grieving for what I had, but what I didn't have. And couldn't.

I left the office with a due date, a prescription for prenatal vitamins, and the resolve that I wouldn't come back to this clinic. It was too full of little memories my selective amnesia hadn't stolen from me, like listening with joy to the steady, brisk cadence of my infants' heartbeats. I also felt like Dr. Chapman thought I was somewhat foolish. He didn't say this. Maybe he actually thought I was brave. But I couldn't tell which. And that mattered to me.

Dan knew when he saw me emerge from the clinic's back rooms that what I had told him earlier that day in our bedroom was true. As I passed by the reception desk, I heard a kind voice ask if I would like to set up another appointment. I said I didn't and continued walking. The front-desk clerk watched me go with a quizzical look on her face, her pencil still poised above the appointment book, as if she hadn't quite heard me correctly. Or perhaps she thought *I* hadn't quite heard correctly. *That woman does know she's pregnant, doesn't she?* I could almost hear her say to the medical assistant next to her.

"June third," I said simply to Dan as he started to ease the van out of the clinic parking lot.

He hesitated for a moment and then turned left, instead of right. Away from home, instead of toward it.

*I*t seemed like Dan was driving with no clear destination in mind. He made several turns onto roads I was unfamiliar with, often at the last moment. But soon we were on a bridge that spanned the Mississippi River, and then in St. Paul, and I knew where he was headed.

Dan had proposed to me along the bank of the river at a park where he used to play Frisbee and touch football with his U of M buddies. It was a place full of wonderful memories for both of us. And it was captivatingly beautiful in October.

He surprised me by asking me nonchalantly if I was hungry, and of course I was. He turned into a drive-through burger place that he and I had eaten at dozens of times and ordered us cheeseburgers, fries, and chocolate shakes. Just like old times.

We drove to our favorite spot, grabbed our food, and headed to a shaded table.

"I love this place in the fall," he said.

And I told him I did too. And it wasn't just small talk. We were both soothing ourselves with the calm beauty of a place where so many dreams and hopes had been shared between us.

When I think about it, I am immensely thankful the only memories I lost were ones from the few months before the attack.

It scares me to think I could have awakened from my ordeal not knowing who I was or who I loved. Or who loved me. It was comforting to be where Dan had told me he loved me and wanted to marry me and that I remembered it vividly.

Patty, my therapist, had once asked me how I felt about the memories I had lost, and I told her it was difficult to feel a sense of loss at all. I didn't feel like I was missing anything. It was just time that had been taken from me. And I had been granted more of it, so what was the big deal?

She asked me on more than one occasion if I missed my students. School had only been in session for a week when I was attacked. I had eighty kids on my class lists and knew hardly any of them. Was I supposed to miss them? She also asked if I was feeling anxious about going back. I didn't feel anxious, I told her. I didn't feel ready. She asked why. I told her I wasn't going to go back until every trace of the bruising on my neck was gone. She nodded and wrote something down. Probably something like "Still in denial." But I wasn't in denial. I just didn't want to provoke curiosity or pity regarding something that was no one's business but my own.

It dawned on me then that when she learned I was pregnant, Patty was probably going to double her efforts to guarantee I was not on a path to suicide. It wearied me to think about it. I began to twirl my straw in my shake as I contemplated her likely response. I looked up to see Dan pushing his straw up and down in his shake and looking at me.

"We need to talk about this," he said.

"I know," I said, and waited for him to say it.

"I can't raise this child," he said softly. "If you don't...if you carry this baby to term, we need to have a plan of what we're going to do."

I nodded.

"Do you understand where I am coming from, Claire?" he continued. "I know how much we both wanted more children, but I can't pretend this child is mine. I would never be able to love it."

He stopped then, unable to continue.

It was probably my turn to say something, but nothing seemed appropriate. I wondered what Patty would say if she were included in this conversation. *Claire, how do you feel about what Dan just told you?*

"It wouldn't be fair to the child," Dan added, when I said nothing in response.

I knew he was right, but it was not what I needed to hear.

"For Pete's sake, Dan, let's not talk about what's fair," I almost growled.

We sat there playing with our straws, pondering the problem of evil and our powerlessness to tame it.

"I'm sorry," he said.

"No, I'm sorry," I replied. "I shouldn't have snapped at you."

Several minutes of silence followed.

"I'm afraid of what would happen to us if we kept it," he said, his eyes growing misty.

"I'm not afraid," I replied, remembering a message from heaven delivered to me just hours before that I suddenly wished I had told Dan about.

"You want to keep this baby?" he asked, and I could sense the apprehension in his voice.

I knew that scenario was impossible. I knew the best thing for this baby was for it to be placed into a home with two parents who desperately wanted it. I knew this child, like any child, deserved the love of both a mother and a father. This child would not be like Katie and Spence, not to Dan. And really not to me either. I knew what was best. But knowing it wasn't a comfort to me.

"From the moment this ordeal began, it hasn't been about what I want," I said, as tears began to roll down my cheeks. "You ask me if I want to keep this baby. I know I can't. Should we give it up for adoption? I know we should. But it's not about what I want, Dan. It will never be about what I want."

He slipped off the bench on his side of the table and came to mine, scooting in beside me.

We were quiet for several minutes as I gathered my composure and stemmed the flow of tears.

"God, I wish this had never happened," he said. And it really was a prayer.

"What are we going to tell the kids?" I moaned.

"We'll find a way," he whispered.

We stayed at our special place for a little while longer and then got back into the van for the ride home. The kids would be coming home from school in less than an hour. They were expecting me to be there. Both Dan and I wanted to get home before they did.

On the way, I asked Dan if we could hold off telling anyone for a while. I think he was thinking the same thing. Both of us were supposing that in a few months' time, there would be no troubling news to break to the kids. I dreaded the thought of another miscarriage, though I felt it would be best. I think Dan, on the other hand, was anticipating it, though he never did admit it.

I also told Dan on the way home that I was going to ask the school board for an extended leave of absence. A long-term substitute was already handling all my classes anyway, so I was certain that wouldn't be a problem. He agreed that was a good idea.

Dan never asked me why I didn't make another appointment nor did he ask if I wanted to stop and fill my prescription for the prenatal vitamins. To borrow from Patty's vocabulary, I think he was in a state of denial. And I actually didn't mind. I didn't want to validate this doomed pregnancy with vitamins and doctor visits. I wanted the next few months to pass quietly, without anyone knowing a thing.

The morning sickness would last another month and then go away. After that I would feel fine until the fourth or fifth month. Then I would notice drops of blood on the bed sheets or my underwear. I would call Dan. We would go to the hospital. My low-lying placenta would be expelled first, followed by a tiny body. I would cry. Dan would hold me.

Then it would be over.

I wasn't afraid.

6

an and I made it home just minutes before Katie and Spencer. Becky, a true friend, simply dropped the kids off like she usually did. I knew she would call me later when the kids were in bed.

Spencer's "Dad! You're home!" was in stark contrast to Katie's "Dad, how come you're home?" I think they had both been relieved when Dan went back to work the week before, the unmarked blue car across the street disappeared, and our home life took on a familiar shade of normalcy. They weren't expecting Dan to be home at three fifteen that day, and yet there he was.

Dan stole a glance at me sitting at the dining-room table with the day's mail and thought up a quick half truth.

"I just thought I'd spend the afternoon with you guys today," he said.

"Too many dogs in a bad mood!" Spencer said with a laugh— his and Dan's private reason for anytime Dan was home early from the vet clinic.

"That's right," Dan said, ruffling Spencer's sandy blond hair as he headed into the kitchen with him. Snack time.

Katie dropped her book bag by the stairs and then started for the kitchen too. She stopped where the kitchen and the dining room met and looked at me.

Why the Sky Is Blue 41

"Are you feeling better, Mom?" she asked.

It took me a moment to remember that when she left that morning—a pocket of time that already seemed ripe with age to me—I had been throwing up in the bathroom.

"I am," I said and smiled. Not exactly a lie.

"You look a little tired," she said, cocking her head in worry.

"I'll be fine, Kate, really," I said. "So how was your day?"

She came and sat in a chair across from me and told me about the math test she took, what the cafeteria had for lunch that day, and that Shelley Gifford had let a boy kiss her behind the gym. She was properly disgusted, and I couldn't help but smile. And feel relieved, if only for a moment. Her innocence and naiveté were so soothing to me. I hated her knowing and understanding what had happened to me. I didn't want her to know I was pregnant on top of everything else.

The phone rang then, and Dan poked his head around the doorway.

"It's your mom," he said, communicating with his eyes a reminder of what we had agreed to on the way home: Tell no one. I could tell he was wondering if that meant our parents too. I didn't know what to communicate back to him with my own eyes. How could I know? We were making this up as we went along.

"I'll take it upstairs," I said, leaving him to hang up the other end and wonder.

My mom had called almost every day since the attack. She and my stepdad, Stuart, had been on an archaeological dig in Egypt when they got word that I had been hurt. They both wanted to drop everything and come to Minnesota, but I had insisted they stay at the excavation and finish. Just the week before, they had returned to their home in Ann Arbor, Michigan.

"Claire, it's Mom," she said like she always does. I've always thought that funny. Like she thought I wouldn't know her voice.

"Hey Mom, how's it going?" I said, stretching out on Dan's side of the bed in our bedroom.

"Well, that's what I was going to ask you," she said, like she was disappointed I had asked her first.

"I'm doing okay, Mom," I said.

"We've got everything settled here at the University. We don't have to go back out in the field for a while," she said. "Why don't we come up and see you kids?"

It wasn't that I didn't want to see her. I did. I just didn't want company. Not yet. And that's what Stu was to me. I was fond of Stu, but he was a part of my mother's life after me. She met him when I was away from home as a freshman in college, and they were married that same year. Stuart was incredibly smart and funny and a gifted archaeologist, but he still felt more like a gentlehearted, next-door neighbor than a stepdad. I didn't want him in the inner circle of those who knew the worst about what happened, even though I knew he already was. We were good friends. I thought having them visit me for the sole purpose of sharing my trauma would alter that.

"Mom, I'm doing fine. Really I am," I answered. "You're coming at Thanksgiving, and the kids will be out of school then. There really isn't a whole lot to do, what with Dan at work all day and the kids in school."

"We wouldn't be coming up to *do* things, Claire," she said, a bit miffed. "We would be coming up to be *with* you."

"Mom, I just want my life to get back to the way it was," I said with a sigh. "I need for it to. And so do Dan and the kids. I need for things to be normal. It isn't normal for you to come in October."

"I feel like we've done nothing to help you," she said after a pause. "I hate being this far away when there's trouble."

She was sniffling. And no doubt remembering the miscarriages and that she had been in Israel and Cyprus with Stuart at some of my darkest hours.

"I know, Mom," I said. "I don't like it either."

"Why don't you come here for a few days?" she said. "You could just watch the leaves fall and not think about anything."

I had to admit that was the first thing she had said that sounded tempting.

"I'll think about it, Mom," I said. "I promise I will."

"You could bring Katie. It could be just us girls. We could send Stu and Matt on a dig in Tibet."

I couldn't help smiling. She was joking, of course, but the funny part was that both Stuart and Matt would've jumped at the invitation. My brother, Matthew, had taken to Stu like a duck to water. He had always loved looking at Stu's artifacts and digging around in the buried remains of a four-thousand-year-old hut. He didn't remember our father at all, and by the time my mom met Stu, Matt was fifteen and starving for a father figure. Matt was now a professor of ancient cultures at the University of Michigan, the same place where Stuart taught budding archaeologists. To be truthful, I was probably a little jealous of their close relationship. Matt called Stu "Dad," and I still just called him "Stu," even though he was never anything but kind and gracious to me.

"Let me think about it, okay, Mom?" I said.

"You're not back at school, are you?" she suddenly asked.

"No, Mom. I'm still on leave. And I will talk to Dan about Kate and me coming out."

"All right," she replied and then felt the urge to add: "Claire, you should just take a break from teaching this year. You really should. You've been through so much."

"I am, Mom. Dan and I talked about it today."

"Well, there you go," she said. "I think that's wise. Well, I better be off. Matt is coming over for supper, and I don't have a thing in the house."

"Not even a date for him?" I said, sitting up on the bed and feeling content that I could share this long-standing joke that my mom was a persistent, though unsuccessful, matchmaker for my thirty-four-year-old single brother.

"Oh, Claire, that's not funny," she said, but I knew she was grinning. "If I could just bury an intelligent girl in the sand, and he could dig her up, all my dreams would come true."

We both giggled.

"So you *do* remember little things like that, Claire?" she said. "You haven't forgotten our special family jokes?"

"It's just stuff from the last couple of months that I can't remember, Mom," I reassured her.

"And you…you still don't remember anything about…what happened?" she asked carefully.

"No, I don't."

"But something else is bothering you, Claire. Are you sure you're all right?"

For a second her intuitiveness tested my resolve. I almost let it all spill out. I probably should have. But then the moment passed.

"Yeah, I'm all right," I said, rubbing my forehead.

"I'll call you this weekend."

"Sounds good," I replied. "Bye, Mom. I love you."

"I love you too."

By the time the kids were in bed, I was exhausted. Becky called about nine thirty, and I told her that Dan and I decided to just keep our news to ourselves for the time being. I knew I could trust her and Nick to do the same.

"So what exactly did the doctor tell you?" she asked.

"He told me what I already know—that I'm pregnant. He said I'm due in June."

"So when's your next doctor's appointment?" she asked.

"I didn't make another appointment," I said.

"You didn't?"

"I don't want to go back to that clinic."

"Why not?"

I chose to make a little joke, hoping Becky would get it and not think I was having an irrational, posttrauma moment. "Dr. Chapman wouldn't call me by my first name."

"Claire, c'mon. What's up?"

"Too many memories," I said after a moment's pause. "Good ones and bad ones. I don't want to be in a place I'm familiar with."

"Do you want to try my doctor, Claire?" she said. "He's a great guy. Very personable."

"Maybe," I said. "I don't want to decide on doctors right now, Becky. I'll probably miscarry anyway."

"Well, isn't that all the more reason to be under the care of one?" she asked.

She was probably right. But at that moment, it just didn't motivate me.

"I won't wait too long, Beck. I promise."

"I'm going to keep you to that," she said. "You sound tired. I'll hang up and let you get to bed."

At that moment, I suddenly needed reassurance from another woman—someone I trusted to give me a straight answer—that I wasn't being a fool.

"Becky, if you were me…if this were happening to you, what would you do?"

She was quiet for a moment.

"All day long I've been asking myself that very question, Claire," she finally said. "I know what I believe about when life begins, and I know what I'd like to *think* I would do. I'd like to think I would be as brave as you."

"I'm not so brave," I said. "I'm counting on a miscarriage."

"Yes, you *are* brave, Claire," she said emphatically. "Because you know you may not have a miscarriage. I know you know it. That's why you asked me what I would do. It takes tremendous courage to do what you believe is right when you know many others would choose to do something different, Claire."

"Then why do I feel foolish?" I said, in not much more than a whisper.

"Maybe it's not foolishness you feel. Maybe you just feel alone," she said. "But you're not alone, Claire. You do know that, don't you?"

At that moment, my two messages from God, in spite of the thirty-four years between them, merged in a way that is difficult to describe.

The day my dad died, God had somehow communicated to me that He didn't want me to be afraid. On an October morning three decades later, He had told me the same thing. The first message, which I cannot remember in words but rather in sensation, traveled through time to the moment I was on the phone with Becky, and the second one, the one I had been given that morning, touched it. And together they folded me into their embrace:

I was not alone, and I did not need to fear the future.

When I was still a child, I used to imagine that my father had not been killed in a war in Korea, but that he had just gotten lost there. I had a hard time imagining the place where he had been, and I actually had a hard time remembering *him*. I could not picture him or his surroundings in any colors except black and white. In fact, I could only picture him one way: immobile and in shades of gray, like the photograph of him I had on my dresser.

I would mentally place him on a dusty road along a river's edge, looking for his way home. His black and white body, face frozen in a careful grin, moved along the path in my mind like I moved my dolls across the floor of my room. Sometimes I pictured him stopping to rest or ask for directions. I often imagined him kissing me good night, bending over my bed with his black and white face. Even now I can only see my dad's face in black and white.

I really only remember snatches of the day my father died, mere snapshots. I remember the morning I woke up with heavenly whispers in my ear. I remember Matt in his highchair, eating little rectangles of buttered toast; I can recall the picture window in our living room, the black car pulling into our driveway, and the man who looked like my dad but wasn't my dad and who carried no duffel bag. I don't remember our move from Los Angeles to Minnesota the week after my father's funeral.

My next memories are of kindergarten in a Saint Cloud classroom, a broken wrist when I was six, and my lingering daydream that Daddy was lost somewhere in Korea.

Later I would learn that my dad had died just weeks before the war ended. This would explain much about why it took my mother so long to get over his death. It seemed so terribly unfair. Another few weeks and he would have been on his way home. And she was deeply in love with him. It would be nearly fourteen years before she would even look at another man.

My father died in May 1953, and the Korean War ended in July. There was talk of an armistice in the months before he died, but nothing had been settled. My dad was part of a strategy to bomb irrigation dams so that floodwaters would destroy critical rail and road networks. His bomber was shot down on this maneuver, though all the dams were successfully destroyed. I suppose that's why I always pictured him near water when I imagined him trying to find his way home.

In Minnesota we lived with my mother's sister, Elizabeth, and her husband, Gene. Aunt Elizabeth and Uncle Gene lived in a suburb of Saint Cloud, in an older house in need of repair but sprawling with extra rooms. Uncle Gene worked part-time for a company that made hoses and fittings, but he and Aunt Elizabeth spent most of their waking hours caring for kids in need of a safe place to live for short periods of time. They were foster parents for the county we lived in but only took kids for the short-term—until a permanent home could be found or conditions at their own homes improved.

Matt and I grew up in that house with dozens of foster kids, none of whom stayed longer than a few months. Aunt Elizabeth always cried when they left, and Uncle Gene always told her they would remember her for the rest of their lives. I learned early not to get too attached to any of them, especially the girls, because they always left.

For quite some time I thought my mother had been amazingly composed during our move. I pictured her summoning a quiet strength from within and then bravely selling our house in California and moving with her two youngsters to Minnesota, a place where she had never lived before.

Actually, my mother was close to being hospitalized because of the intensity of her grief. It was Gene and Elizabeth who took care of everything, including the sale of our house, the move, and getting us settled in the third story of their house.

In hindsight, I suppose it was the best thing for us. My grandparents on my father's side had offered to take us in too, but they were also awash in grief. And they lived on a farm in Kansas with no neighbors for several miles. That thought alone scared my mother, I'm sure. My mother's parents, who lived several hours away in Fresno, offered to find us an apartment close to them, but they were going through a tough time of their own. A few years later they divorced.

I guess I don't have any regrets about leaving California and growing up instead in Minnesota, but I wondered, and still do, how my life would have been different if we had stayed in California.

My mom had no professional skills, though she was an avid reader and knew something about just about everything. For nearly a year after our move, however, she read nothing except the Psalms. Then, a few days before the first anniversary of my father's death, she began reading other things again. She started bringing books home from the library. Lots of them. I don't remember this; I was only five. But I know she was still doing it when I was seven, when she started taking me to the library with her. And then she brought Matt. Then she started bringing the foster kids. We would all come home with piles of books. In the evenings we would lose ourselves in the pages of every kind of book imaginable. Sometimes my mother would read aloud to Matt and me and as many as five foster kids. Other times she would pull me into her lap and read to me alone. And sometimes she would pull me into her lap and she would read her book and I would read mine.

Most people would later attribute my choice to become a teacher, especially a high-school literature teacher, to my mother and her devotion to books. And in some ways that's true. But the older I became, the more I realized she and I devoured books for the same reason. Not for entertainment or even enlightenment. It was for escape. She dealt with the loss of her husband and her own home by escaping into books, and I dealt with the loss of my father and that same home the same way.

Not that there was anything wrong with medicating ourselves with books, but I think knowing it made it seem less a weakness and more like a comfort.

My mother always read more than one book at a time. There were usually five or six on her bedside table or on the coffee table in the living room. Each one was bookmarked, most of the time with coupons for things we didn't use, like cat food, baby powder, and denture cleaner. The books were never about the same thing. One book might be a biography; another, about the Civil War; another, a classic by Dickens or one of the Bronte sisters; and another, the current bestseller. She usually had a Bible nearby, also bookmarked, but never with a coupon. And there was never more than one bookmark in any of her Bibles.

My mother is the only person I know who reads the Bible cover to cover. She never decides to read Romans or start a study of Ecclesiastes. She always reads it from page one in Genesis to the last page in the Revelation of John. Sometimes reading it takes her six months; sometimes, a year; sometimes, two years. I wouldn't call my mother a religious person, though I know others do. She has what I call a simple faith in a God who is both powerful and personal. Apparently my dad had the same kind of uncomplicated faith.

She told me once that of all the books she has ever read, she has found the Bible to be the most spectacular book ever written. I suppose she approaches it like it's great literature, in addition to being the Creator's inspired word, and that's why she has always read it from beginning to end. It surprised me, then, to learn that when she was grieving for my father, she read only the Psalms. She told me this when I was eleven.

"I wasn't actually reading them," she said when I asked her why. "I was praying them."

I told her I didn't understand what she meant.

She told me that because she was so sad, she couldn't pray her usual way but felt a crushing need to pour out her heart to God. She told me she had to keep talking to Him so that she wouldn't start to blame Him for what happened. So she read the Psalms for a whole year, and they were her prayers.

I remember asking her if it worked. She didn't understand what I meant.

"You never blamed God for what happened?" I asked by way of explanation.

She considered my question for a moment, no doubt weighing its significance to my blossoming understanding of God.

"I know God could have stopped it from happening," she said. "He could have kept Daddy safe that day, like He had all the

other days of the war. But it *was* war. We knew he was in danger.
The world is not a safe place, Claire; only heaven is. This is not
heaven. And we cannot expect it to be like it."

Then she told me something that I found utterly remarkable.

"If God had come to me before I met your daddy and told me
I was going to marry a wonderful man who would love me com-
pletely, that we would have two precious, beautiful children, that
I would experience unequaled joy, but that this good man would
be taken from me after only eight years, I would have told Him
I still want to meet him; I still want to marry him."

"Why?" I had asked.

"Because," she said, drawing me close. "When I look at you
and Matthew, I know I would have wanted Him to change
nothing."

I was amazed at her insight and awed by her love for Matthew
and me.

"But you were so sad when Daddy died."

"I missed him so much, Claire," she said. "And I still do. And
it's okay for us to miss him."

"But don't you wonder why God let it happen?" I asked.

Again, I can remember her taking her time choosing what
she would say next. I would remember her next words always.

"For a long time I did want to know why," she finally said. "It
seemed to me I deserved an answer. Your daddy was a good man
and a good father. And he loved God. But deep down, I knew
that sometimes God's reasons for doing things or not doing things
are as deep as His character. Being supplied with a reason when
maybe I wouldn't have been able to understand it might have
made it worse for me."

She drew me even closer and cuddled me so that my head
rested in the special place between her neck and chin. "Sometimes asking God for a reason for something is like asking Him

why the sky is blue. There is a complex, scientific reason for it, Claire, but most children, including you, are content with knowing it is blue because it is. If we understood everything about everything, we would have no need for faith."

I never looked at the sky the same way after that. There would be many times over the course of my life when I would wonder what in the world God was up to. Sometimes I would look at the abused, neglected, and unloved children that found their way to my aunt and uncle's house and wonder if God saw their pain, why He did nothing. I asked my uncle this once, and he said, "Why, Claire, He's brought them here to us," like it was the easiest thing in the world to see.

But I knew there were many other kids who had no safe place to go to escape suffering. It didn't seem fair, and I knew what I really wanted was a heaven on earth, where no one suffered at all. Ever. But after that day, whenever I wrestled with why people suffered, I always thought of my mother and the sky, and I learned to comfort myself with the knowledge that when the question is complex, the answer is too. I learned to be at peace with a sky that is blue for no given reason at all.

In the coming months people would assume this was the question that troubled me most: Why? Why had God let this happen to me? Well-meaning friends would feel compelled to say, "We know God has a good reason for this," or "God must have a wonderful reason for allowing this to happen." And while I didn't doubt their sincerity, I did wonder if they had stopped to think before they spoke. Obviously they had never stopped to consider if God had a wonderful and good reason for making the sky blue instead of red.

I wasn't overly perplexed by the "why." What awoke me in the middle of the night, disrupted my thoughts when I tried to read a bedtime story to Spence, and haunted my quiet moments alone in the house was the "what."

What was to become of my marriage, my family, and me when this was over? What would I be like at the end of the journey? What would I see in the mirror a year, two years, ten years from now? What did I *want* to see? Those were the questions for which there did not seem to be any answers.

$\mathcal{T}$he next few days felt like I was preparing for a long trip, like I was organizing my affairs for a long journey, and time was of the essence. For the first time since I got home from the hospital, I began to set my alarm so I would be up before the kids, up even before Dan. The first ten minutes of my day I spent hugging the toilet in the master bathroom until the morning sickness subsided. It was how I oriented myself to the reality of each new day. The morning sickness daily reminded me of what was in store for me, and after I threw up and showered, I read the Psalms. I even set my alarm on Saturday, so that I would be through with the morning bathroom routine before anyone else was awake.

The kids were thrilled to have me back in their morning routine, and Spence told me—after the first day—that he didn't even mind that I made peanut butter and jelly for his lunch when he told me back in August that he was tired of it. I began taking Katie, Spencer, plus Nick and Becky's twin boys to school again in the mornings. Becky insisted she bring them home since that had been our previous arrangement. I started to pay the bills again and do the grocery shopping and run errands.

Dan was pensive about my "jumping back into things," as he liked to call it. He made me promise to call Patty and get her opinion on my resuming day-to-day responsibilities. He didn't ask me to tell her about the pregnancy, though, which surprised me, because that very thing was what had motivated me to reclaim—as much as possible—my normal life.

I called the superintendent of the high school where I had been teaching and told him I had a letter for the school board asking if I might have an extended leave of absence due to medical reasons. He was very understanding. He assured me that surviving a violent attack on my life was more than sufficient cause for a year's leave. He told me to send him the letter and not to worry a moment over it. So I did.

I attended a church service for the first time since the attack the following Sunday, wearing a favorite turtleneck so that the pale yellow bruising on my neck wouldn't startle anyone. People were genuinely glad to see me, several hugged me with tears in their eyes, and I wondered how much Nick had told them. The police had been careful to keep my name out of the papers and news reports, but many of these people were friends, and I'm sure they knew the unnamed woman abducted from a mall parking lot, nearly strangled, and left for dead, was me.

That same Sunday afternoon, my mother called and again offered to come out. This time without Stuart.

"No, Mom," I pleaded. "I wouldn't have you do that to Stu."

"He's okay about it," she insisted.

"But I'm not," I said. "I want you both to come. At Thanksgiving. Like we had planned."

"What about your coming out here for a few days? Did you and Dan talk about it?"

We had. Dan didn't seem to mind, but I knew he was wondering what Patty would want me to do. Or what Nick would suggest. He was afraid to trust any gut feeling of his own. I imagine he was still blaming himself for not going with me the night I went to the mall. I also wondered if he'd had some sort of feeling before I went that night that I would be better off if he came and had shrugged off the hunch. But of course I couldn't ask him that.

"We're still trying to decide, Mom," I said.

"Matthew really wants to see you," she added.

We ended up leaving it that I would let her know by the next Sunday. It was actually Thursday that I called her back and told her I was coming.

~ ~ ~

It wasn't a horrible week, but it was one that left me feeling like a fish out of water. On Monday, after the kids left for school, Dan had left for work, and the security system was properly switched on, I began to feel a compulsion to clean. Part of me was at a loss as to what to do with myself with a Monday morning all to myself with no kids, no students, and no husband to occupy my time. The other part of me was still grappling with the enormity of the situation facing me. It wasn't the first time in my life I had cleaned instead of pacing the floor in frustration.

I started with the bathrooms, then moved on to the linen closet. Next, I attacked a hall closet simply known to everyone in the house as my closet. In it I kept dozens of boxes of things that were either precious to me or that I had been unable to throw away. The kids' first shoes, their baby books, and boxes of their artwork were in there, as was the top from my wedding cake, letters my dad wrote to my mom from Korea, and my set of first-edition Nancy Drew books. But there were also notes from all my college courses, past issues of cooking magazines, and several boxes of old Christmas cards.

I don't know why I had kept the cards, but I had—for the past eight years. Each bundle contained dozens of old cards that I hadn't looked at since the day I had gathered them up and tied them up with used gift ribbon. I don't recall why I suddenly decided keeping them was utter nonsense, but it just struck me what a waste of time and energy it was to hang on to them. I sat down on the floor, pulled out the boxes, and untied the ribbons. I opened each card and checked for a photo. If there was one, I set it aside, having decided to keep them. The cards, including any outdated Christmas letters, went into a garbage bag.

Dan decided to come home for lunch that day and found me fully engrossed in this task. He came up the stairs and, his surprise evident, surveyed the scene, mouth kind of open, eyes taking it all in. Finally he said, "Claire, what are you doing?"

It seemed pretty obvious to me what I was doing, and it annoyed me that he asked.

"I'm throwing these out," I said, trying not to sound flippant.

"Why?" he said, incredulous.

"Because I don't want them anymore," I answered, tossing a few cards from five years before into the trash bag.

He again studied my project—assessing it, evaluating me.

"But you've had these for years," he said, his voice softening a little.

"I know," I replied, in a gentler tone as well. "But I don't want them anymore."

He was silent for a moment, and as I reached for the bundle of 1981 Christmas cards, he knelt beside me and touched my shoulder.

"Claire," he said, in a different tone of voice altogether. "I really don't think this is a good time to throw stuff out that you've kept for years."

"But they're just old Christmas cards," I said, and then I giggled, which was a huge mistake because I saw a wave of worry rush over Dan's face.

But I couldn't help it. He had said that very same thing to me about a year earlier when *he* wanted to throw the cards out. He had even said it the same way. I thought it was funny that he and I were having the same conversation in reverse roles.

My ill-timed giggle really threw him, though. I could see in his eyes that he was replaying in his mind the information Patty had given us about how assault victims deal with the trauma afterward. She had told both of us that mood swings and irrational behaviors were common. We could also expect me to have episodes of anxiety, even rage. Patty had told Dan to let me vent my own way as long as I didn't hurt myself or anyone else. She also said some destructive behavior was common too. She thought it would be a great idea if we got a punching bag, just in case. We didn't even consider it. I could see Dan was now wishing we had. He was wishing he had come home to find me gloved and busily thrashing a therapist-approved punching bag instead of throwing out my precious, outdated Christmas cards.

"Dan, it's not what you think," I said reassuringly. "I'm not flipping out on you. I've been thinking about doing this for a long time."

That was a lie. I had just thought of it that morning. I don't know why I said that. I guess it was to reassure Dan that I wasn't having one of Patty's predicted irrational moments. And maybe I was trying to convince myself of that too.

Dan let me continue with my campaign to rid the house of old Christmas cards, but contrary to what he told me, the garbage bag full of cards was not put out with the rest of the trash later that week. He hid the bag in the garage. I found it several weeks later.

I know he thought he was protecting me from my spontaneous decision he assumed I would later regret, but finding that
bag hurt me.

But that emotional wound was nothing compared to finding
a box of Katie's and Spence's earliest crayon drawings stashed in
the back of Dan's closet on the evening of the Christmas-card
purge. That box had been in my hall closet. He had hidden it.
From me.

That he thought me capable of tossing out Katie's and
Spencer's masterpieces like they were old, forgotten Christmas
cards was a blow that would take me several days to get over.
Patty should have told me Dan would have some posttrauma of
his own; that he also might exhibit irrational behavior. I was
beginning to realize that the more I kept hidden from Dan, the
less he would worry about me. He couldn't handle knowing
everything, and I couldn't handle his worry.

Two days later I got a call from Mark Nordahl, the detective
assigned to my case. He asked if Dan and I could come to the
police station. There had been a new development. I was totally
unprepared for this call and found myself shaking as I called the
vet clinic and asked to speak to Dan. He cancelled a routine
surgery, and we headed over to the police station just after lunch.
We could think of nothing to say to each other on the drive over.

Detective Nordahl was a gentle and compassionate police
officer. It always surprised me when he would take off his coat,
revealing his shoulder holster and the handle of the gun inside it.
At the station the holster was always empty but it still seemed out
of place for him. I couldn't imagine him reaching for a gun, let

alone aiming at or shooting someone. On the few occasions he came to the house, he left his coat on. If he reached for anything though, even a pencil on the coffee table, I would see that dark brown holster on his white-striped shirt, and I would also see that it wasn't empty.

Detective Nordahl greeted us warmly but professionally when we got to the station and ushered us into a small conference room. After asking us if we wanted coffee, he dispensed with any more small talk, as was his custom, and got right down to business.

"Did you two happen to watch the news or read a newspaper this morning?" he asked.

Dan and I exchanged glances.

"No," we both said.

"There was an attack the night before last not unlike yours, Mrs. Holland," he said. "Same general location, same time of day, same M.O."

Neither Dan nor I said a word. Dan reached for my hand and squeezed it.

The detective continued.

"The victim, a thirty-nine-year-old woman named Carol Wells, was on her way home from the same mall as you, was traveling alone, and was found around midnight two blocks away from where you were found, with roughly the same injuries."

"Is she okay?" I managed to say.

"Before I tell you anything else, I want you to know we got him," Mark said. "I *know* we got him."

"What are you saying?" Dan said.

"The man that killed this woman is the same man that attacked your wife, Mr. Holland. I am sure of it. And we got him."

Killed this woman.

I felt the room getting very warm. I asked for a glass of water. It was there in an instant.

"So, she died?" I finally asked.

Detective Nordahl nodded.

"Her husband has admitted to killing her," he continued. "And he has admitted to assaulting a woman matching your description near the same mall on the night of September ninth. He never knew your name."

"Why?" Dan was asking, but I was having a hard time concentrating on the conversation in the room. "Why did he do it?"

Detective Nordahl told us that Philip Wells had massive gambling debts and wanted to cash in on his wife's million-dollar life-insurance policy. The first attack on me was meant to pave the way for the second attack and make it seem like a serial killer was on the loose. He made mistakes when he committed the second assault, however. He didn't wipe the passenger door handle clean, and the blows to the head were made after his wife was already dead. He was very nervous when questioned about his own whereabouts at the time of his wife's attack. The detective said he and the other officers became suspicious during questioning and asked him about his whereabouts on the night of September ninth. Wells broke down within minutes, the detective said, confessing to attacking me. He apparently also told them he was sorry for what he did to me and was relieved he had not killed me like he thought he had. So much for an apology.

"He is in custody, Mrs. Holland. We have his confession," Detective Nordahl assured me. "Wells is not going anywhere."

I just nodded my head. I liked it better when the attacker had no name.

Dan asked if he could take me home. The detective said if I wanted to see Wells in a lineup, it could be arranged in minutes, though he admitted he didn't need me to identify Wells to put him away. Confessing to his wife's murder was, thankfully, enough. I had no desire to see this man. I was content that I could not remember and had no yearning to go poking around looking for lost memories.

We were also told that Wells would likely get a life sentence.

"You will keep Claire's name out of this?" Dan asked as we prepared to leave, and the detective said he would do his best.

Then we left.

The rest of that day was surreal. Dan, the kids, and I raked leaves when school got out, and Dan ordered pizza for supper, making the evening as relaxing as he could, but he and I barely spoke to each other. Afterward, I helped Katie with her homework. The phone rang once, about nine. It was my mother. I told Dan to go into our room and tell her what had happened at the police station. I would call her the next day.

That night as Dan and I lay in bed, I couldn't get the image of this other woman out of my mind. I kept picturing her the way I had been told I had been found. It haunted me. What I really wanted was a way to flush it all away—the image of her, the name Philip Wells, and everything else I knew about that night. I wanted to find the secret file where my brain had hidden the rest of it, dump these new contents inside, and close the lid forever.

But that was impossible.

Instead, I found myself feeling oddly grateful that Wells wasn't some maniacal, sadistic beast; he was just completely overcome with greed. Avarice—nasty as it is—was a motive I could handle. There were so many others I could not.

Especially when I considered the life that was growing within me and who had helped create it.

I made the mistake of trying to share this with Dan as we lay there together in the darkness of our bedroom. But he was repulsed by any notion that Wells wasn't a brutal murderer. What I said made no sense to him at all.

"How could you think he is anything but a monster, Claire?" he said, clearly disappointed in me.

It was evident to me then that though Dan and I had fallen headlong into a swirling blackness that neither one of us knew how to navigate, we weren't struggling arm in arm in the abyss. The episode with the Christmas cards and the isolated relief I felt about Wells not being a psychopath convinced me I was in one abyss and Dan was in another one entirely.

9

$\mathcal{K}$atie and I left for Ann Arbor the third week in October, on a chilly Thursday. Spencer had at first been melancholy about our going, but I managed to convince him that having four days alone with his dad was going to be wonderful. Thursday and Friday might be a little boring for him, but he would be able to go with Dan to the clinic on Saturday, which Spence loved to do. He coddled and cared for the dogs and cats in the kennels like they were his own, or like he was the kind doctor making them well. I promised him that Katie and I would be home early Sunday evening.

Dan drove us to the airport an hour before our six thirty flight, and since Spence was asleep in the back seat, he dropped us off curbside in the predawn darkness. Katie wasn't going to miss any school since her teachers were off that Thursday and Friday for a state convention. Nevertheless, she was unable to contain her excitement about our four-day excursion. It was the first time she and I had done anything special together for longer than a couple of hours.

I was prepared to field questions from her on the relatively short flight, but I was hoping they would be easy ones with concrete answers. I had a suspicion that being seated next to me on the plane with no other real distractions for either one of us would prompt her to take care of any lingering questions about the last seven weeks. She only asked me two questions actually. The first was if I was afraid to be alone or go anywhere by myself. I guess she thought I had brought her with me to keep me company or to ward off a potential threat. I assured her I was not afraid. Then she asked if I thought the police would ever catch the man who had hurt me.

Dan and I hadn't really discussed what to tell the kids about Philip Wells. I decided to tell her what the police told me, hoping it would allay any fears that my life was still in danger.

Her eyes widened as I explained as vaguely but truthfully as I could about Philip Wells and his unfortunate wife.

"How could he have done such a thing?" Katie said, shaking her head. "He didn't even know you."

I told her not to dwell on it, that I was not dwelling on it. I told her to be glad he confessed. And that he would never be able to hurt anyone again.

Seeing that she was troubled, I wondered if I should have said nothing except that the police did catch him and then left it at that. But I wanted Katie to know Philip Wells had felt remorse and that he had been relieved I had not died. It softened my attacker's wickedness. I desperately needed this less sinister image in my head if I was going to carry the child in my body and not go crazy. And I knew if I didn't miscarry, Katie would eventually have to be told I was pregnant. I would want her to know this about Wells if it came to that.

Seeing my mom at the airport waiting expectantly for us and smiling from ear to ear triggered something inside me—some latent, postcrisis response—and I began to cry even before I reached her arms. I was stupid not to have let her come when she wanted to.

She just hugged me tight and didn't let up until I began to pull away first, many moments later. Katie and Stu had long since ended their embrace and were standing there watching the tearful exchange between wounded daughter and compassionate mother.

"Hey, Stu…" I finally said to my stepdad, in a weepy voice that I hated to be displaying in front of him.

As he folded me into his arms, I again found myself in an embrace that I did not wish to end. I began to cry again. I couldn't believe it. In fact, I was crying harder wrapped up in Stu's big arms and wide chest than I had been within my mother's petite frame. Stuart was stroking my hair and patting my back and saying all the things fathers say to their little girls when they're hurt, like "It's all right, honey," and "It's over now, sweetie," and "You're my brave girl," and "I am so proud of you."

I finally pulled away and began apologizing profusely, which neither one of them was interested in hearing. I had upset Katie, something I had not wanted to do, and as we started to walk away, I saw tears in her eyes. When my mom put her arm around her, she laid her head on her grandmother's shoulder for a brief moment; I couldn't hold in a shudder. Stu noticed this too and squeezed my shoulder.

By the time we reached their home, I had recovered and thankfully so, because Matt was waiting at the house for us.

"I heard Mom had made a great lunch, and I didn't want to miss out on a free meal," he said as he and I hugged on the front porch. It was really good to see him again. I was reminded of simpler times when we were young and the world seemed big and inviting, not bizarre and dangerous.

After lunch, Matt headed back to the university with a promise to be back for supper. We decided to have some ice cream in Stuart's study among his scores of books and magazines, every classical music recording ever made—so it seemed, and Stu's trinkets from the ancient past.

I sat in the chair my mom usually occupied, noticing that four books with bookmarks were arranged on the table next to it. Off to the side was her current Bible, open to the book of Amos.

I love Stu's study, I really do. It's more like a museum to me than anything else. It's slightly disorganized, at least it usually looks that way to me, but Stu remarkably knows where everything is. The floor-to-ceiling bookshelves are not only lined with books but also with old spoons, vases, and necklaces from his many digs. Rocks, stones, and fragments of pottery are scattered everywhere.

Even though it has never been my home, I feel comfortable in my mom and stepdad's house. And I'm glad that my mom met Stu and that he fell in love with her. They met at a lecture he was giving on ancient Mediterranean cultures at the University of Minnesota during my freshman year there. She had gone because she had read his book on the topic, and after the lecture, she had approached Stu to have him sign it. Ten minutes after they met, he asked her out for coffee. They dated for six months—mostly by phone and mail since Stuart lived in Michigan—before he asked her to marry him. Actually Stu approached Matt first, who was fifteen and still living at home, and asked for our mother's hand in marriage. Matt, who gave his approval in a matter of seconds, was the best man at their wedding. I was the maid of honor. I didn't know Stu as well as Matt did when they married, but I could tell Stuart was a gentleman. And that he loved my mother very much. I loved seeing her so happy, even though I was sad to see her and Matt leave Minnesota to join Stu in Ann Arbor.

It really didn't surprise me that after fourteen years of being a widow, my mother would suddenly fall for another man. Stu was her soul mate. His love for history and the past resonated with my mom. Her penchant for books never included works of science fiction or speculation about the future. She always read books about people—fictional and otherwise—and where they had been and what they saw and did while they were there. That's why Stu always brought my mother on his field trips all over the Middle East and the Mediterranean. First, because he loved her, and second, because she loved what he loved: the past.

After lunch, I asked to see Stu's photos of their recent trip to Egypt, and at some point while he was showing me pictures of the burial ground he had been excavating, my mom and Katie left the room. I found out later my mom had brought something back from Egypt for Katie and was giving it to her.

When we had finished looking at the last set of photos, I wasn't quite sure what to do with myself. I felt awkward being alone in the room with Stu. And I felt awkward about feeling awkward. Why would I be anxious about being alone with Stu in his study? That question led to the next, which was, why had I completely fallen apart at the airport when I hugged him? It finally dawned on me that Stu had always been more a father to me than my biological father. I could barely remember my real dad. I had less than five years with him, none of which I could recall. Stu had been my mother's husband and my stepfather for nearly two decades. He was wise and good and was the perfect person to "father" me through my crisis.

And I was both afraid he would and afraid he wouldn't.

I had already lost one father and was realizing that I was purposely keeping Stu at a distance. If anything ever happened to him, it would not feel like the death of a parent, but rather the loss of a good friend. I could almost hear Patty's flannel-soft voice telling me this, revealing to me the inner workings of my troubled subconscious.

I felt sad as this understanding crept over me. And I must have looked like I felt.

"What is it, Claire?" Stu said, so gently.

Who knows what part of my brain was in control the next moment, because I looked straight at him and said it.

"Stu, I'm pregnant."

My mom and Katie came back into the room as Stuart digested my news. He said nothing.

Katie was jabbering about the necklace my mother had given her, and my mother was completely engrossed in her grand-daughter's joy. I knew neither one had heard what I had said to Stu.

He looked at me and suggested we all visit the University's Nichols Arboretum for the afternoon. I nodded, looking straight back at him.

"I think that's a great idea," I said, though my mom had to ask if Katie and I felt like an outing after getting up so early that morning. I knew Stu was expertly filling the time until Katie went to bed that night and I could talk to my mom—privately—for as long as I wanted and in whatever emotional shape that fell over me.

The afternoon passed pleasantly as did the early evening hours. After supper Matt and Stu told story after story of my mother's latest matchmaking efforts on Matt's behalf. Katie and I hadn't laughed that hard in weeks.

Matt left when Katie started yawning. I sent her up to the guest bedroom that she and I were sharing.

After I had settled her in, I made my way slowly down the stairs, feeling reluctant to disturb the lighthearted atmosphere that still permeated the downstairs rooms.

"Why don't you two go on into the study, and I'll bring in some hot apple cider," my mom said as she switched on the dishwasher and a low hum filled the kitchen.

I followed Stu into the study and eased into one of the overstuffed couches. He sat at his desk and absently picked up a fragment of a Roman water jug.

"I will be happy to leave the room, if you want," he said softly. "I can say I'm tired and that I want to go to bed early. I have class tomorrow, Claire. It would seem natural."

I was beginning to understand and feel comfortable with my deepening appreciation for Stu and learning to fear it less, so I think I surprised him when I asked him to stay, when I told him it would be easier for me if he was there.

He looked away as my mother came into the room bearing a tray, and I saw him reach up to his face and flick away a tear.

My mom didn't know it at the time, but she made it easy for me to tell her. She handed me a mug of cider and asked me pointedly but tenderly what was bothering me. She knew there was something more than just the attack itself weighing on my mind.

For some reason, telling her about the pregnancy with Stu already knowing about it was soothing to me, though I didn't want her to know that Stuart knew before she did, and he never let on that he did.

Mom began to cry softly when I was finished, and I had to look away from her for a few moments.

"I just don't understand," she said, shaking her head. Then she said it again.

She didn't say it to me or to Stu. She just spoke the words into the quiet room, addressing no one. It was the closest she dared go toward demanding a good explanation from a God who could have intervened. It was the closest any of us dared to go. Then, in spite of the heaviness of such incomprehensible matters, my mother came to me, wrapped me in her arms, and held me close. This much she *did* understand: I needed her.

It was after midnight before we all headed upstairs to bed, exhausted and deep in thought.

The next three days were incredibly special to me, and I look back on them now as days that significantly prepared me for the difficult journey that lay ahead, even though the pregnancy was never mentioned again until my mom was kissing me goodbye at the airport. And even then, she just whispered in my ear as we hugged goodbye, "I am here for you. And I can be there for you. In a heartbeat, I can be there."

10

When Katie and I returned from Michigan, I was strangely at peace. Dan seemed alternately glad and worried that I was so calm and collected. He didn't think it was normal. He urged me to call Patty and tell her the latest news, meaning the pregnancy and Philip Wells's arrest. He had decided it wasn't wise to keep her uninformed of such significant developments. I didn't say this, but I wanted to tell *him* to call Patty. He was apparently the one struggling to deal with emotional overload.

But I called her and told her everything. She wanted to see me. I thanked her but told her I was feeling fine, that I was working through my feelings of disappointment and relief in "positive and affirming ways." Those were her exact words to me several weeks before. I don't think she liked being quoted.

"Well, we can talk about other things, then," she had offered.

For what possible purpose, I wanted to say, but didn't.

"I'll think about it, Patty," I said. "Right now coming in to see you seems rather pointless. I'm sure you're a great therapist, but I don't need any therapy at the moment."

There was silence on the other end. I hadn't remembered ever being so blatantly honest before. I wondered if my head injuries had flipped a switch in my brain that had never been "on" until then. We hung up shortly after that.

That night after supper, Dan asked me if I had called Patty. "What did she say?" he asked when I told him I had.

I told him instead what I had said.

"Claire, why don't you just go see her? It can't hurt just to talk with her," he said.

"Dan, I am not going to see her just so you can feel better," I replied. "That's like my putting on a sweater because you're cold."

And then I added what I hadn't earlier and shouldn't have then. I guess the flipped switch was still humming along in my brain: "If you're having trouble dealing with what has happened, by all means, call her up."

I regretted saying it the moment the words left my mouth. I apologized, but as is always the case, spoken words cannot be unheard, even though they can be forgiven.

I promised Dan that I would go to Nick the moment I felt emotionally unstable or unsure. I reminded him that that was what he was doing. And he seemed to relax after that. But we were so obviously at different poles in our still-black abyss. He struggled to see my perspective on so many things just as I struggled to see his. We struggled in every area of communication, including our most intimate moments in our bedroom. It was nearly the end of November before Dan felt brave enough to approach the topic of lovemaking. We stumbled through our first night of intimacy after the attack like newlyweds in an arranged marriage.

"When this is all over, it will be different," Dan said afterward, in the darkness of our bedroom. "It will be the way it was."

I convinced myself that he had to be right. My attacker would steal—at the very most—nine months from me. But only nine months. The rest of my life belonged to me. And the rest of our marriage belonged to Dan and me.

By Thanksgiving, the morning sickness had ceased, and I felt particularly well. Hormones, I'm sure. My parents and Matt flew out for the long Thanksgiving weekend, and we had a wonderful time. I only had a few moments alone with my mom, just long enough to confirm to her that I was still pregnant. She asked if I had been back to a doctor, and I guiltily told her I hadn't. Becky had been bugging me for several weeks to set up an appointment with her doctor, but I hadn't felt shamed about not doing it until my mother asked me why I hadn't.

"Claire, you must know that you may not have a miscarriage," she told me gently.

She was right. I did know it. But I didn't want to think about giving birth to this child. And I figured if I held off going to a doctor, I wouldn't have to. I was pretty sure I would know one way or the other by the fourth or fifth month of the pregnancy. All a doctor would do between now and then is feed me vitamins, measure my abdomen, and listen to the staccato sounds of an infant heart beating. I had no interest in those things.

We celebrated my birthday before my family left, though I wouldn't officially be thirty-seven until December first, and then the wonderful weekend ended. The day after my mom, Stu, and Matt returned to Michigan, the first winter storm rolled in, instantly transforming the barren Minnesota landscape into a stunning and elegant scene.

I spent the rest of December preparing the house for Christmas and putting off making a doctor's appointment. Both were easy to do.

We had a slumber party on the night of December twenty-first for Katie's twelfth birthday and it was two in the morning before the house was finally quiet and Dan and I fell exhausted into bed.

Outside, a gentle snow was falling, and the house was peculiarly silent after having been so noisy. I was lying on my side, near enough to Dan to feel his chest rising and falling against my back. The house was warm and cozy and the scent of evergreen from the freshly cut Douglas fir standing in the living room wafted up the stairs.

In the serene quietness of that moment, just as I was drifting off to sleep, I became aware of the slightest flutter inside me, like the airy movement of butterfly wings. My eyes snapped open. I felt it again. The child was moving inside me.

It was as if a fairy princess was making those tender, flawless movements within me. I think I knew at that moment that the baby growing inside me was a girl. Those perfect movements just inches below my heart were remarkably feminine.

The next half minute was equally split into fifteen seconds of wonder and fifteen seconds of despair. I had nearly shaken Dan awake to tell him when I suddenly realized I could share this incredible moment with no one. Especially not him.

So despite the coziness of the house, the gently falling snow, and my husband's warm nearness once again, I felt alone in the dark place I had been in for weeks.

I couldn't stop the tears from slipping out of my eyes and onto my pillow, so I tried very hard to lie still and just let them come. But every now and then a stifled sob would ripple through my ribcage and cause me to move with its rhythm. And each time, my movement was answered by the matched shifting of the tiny one inside me, like echoes across a moonlit valley.

It wasn't until mid-January that I finally called Becky's doctor and made an appointment. By then I was wearing the baggiest sweaters I could find in my closet and pants with an elastic waistband. I had only gained five pounds but my waist had disappeared, and a thick, elongated lump had replaced it. I was nearly halfway through the pregnancy. It would soon be difficult to hide.

Dan offered to go with me to that first appointment, but I really didn't want him to go, and I could tell he really didn't want to go, either. Becky offered to come too, but I really didn't need anyone to hold my hand.

Dr. Whitestone was indeed as personable as Becky had promised. He had every right to scold me for waiting until I was four months pregnant to see a doctor, but he said nothing about it. Becky had made it easy for me by telling him my circumstances, for which I was very grateful. It was a sad story I didn't care to share with anybody. But I was glad he knew.

He wanted to do an ultrasound, which I figured would be the case. As I lay there with my stomach bare in the dimly lit room, he quietly asked me if I wanted him to turn the screen away from me and turn the volume off. I was touched by his consideration. I thought about it for a moment and decided I wanted to see for myself the child I was carrying. We both watched as he moved the sensor across my middle. The heartbeat was clear, steady, and unmistakable. And it wasn't as painful to hear as I thought it was going to be. It actually calmed me to hear it, though I don't think I could ever explain why. There were shapes on the screen that I couldn't quite make out, but Dr. Whitestone pointed to them and said, "Here's the skull," and "Here's the spinal cord."

I then saw a tiny rod with a bloom on the end of it, like Tinkerbell's wand, propel itself away from the center of the screen. It was a tiny arm, graced with tiny fingers. I was in awe.

"The placenta's in a pretty good place, a little low," he was saying, and I was instantly struggling to reconcile the awe I felt with the news that my placenta wasn't causing any trouble.

"How low?" I asked.

"Well, it's not in the ideal place, but it's not in the danger zone, either," Dr. Whitestone said. "We'll have to watch it. As the baby grows, the placenta might move upward or it might slip down farther than is safe."

"I know all about that," I said with a sigh.

"It's a little early to think the worst, Mrs. Holland."

I just sighed and asked him to please call me Claire.

That evening, I told Dan I thought we should tell Katie about the baby. Maybe Spencer too. He didn't agree at all.

I began to think I should have brought him to the doctor's office after all so he could have seen what I saw, heard what I heard. He was still pretending none of this was real, that I would miscarry before he had to deal with any visual evidence that I was pregnant. He didn't want to deal with it verbally, either.

"Dan, I'm starting to show," I said as softly as I could, because I knew he would wince at hearing it. And he did. "The doctor said the placenta's not in the danger zone. It's just a little low. It could be many more weeks before anything happens. I could be six or seven months pregnant by then, Dan. Katie will know. She will be able to see it. Everybody will."

He almost put his hands over his ears—that's how frustrated he was. But there was no easy way to make him understand.

I said nothing for a few minutes as he wrestled with the reality of that which he wanted to believe was only a nightmare, just a bad dream he would soon awaken from.

"I've dealt with not having protected you from this happening, but, by God, I was going to protect them from knowing," he finally said, hoarse with anger. "They shouldn't have to deal with this. They're just children."

"I know, Dan. But I don't think we can wait much longer," I whispered.

He didn't want me to be right about this, but he knew I was. He just nodded and then started to walk away.

"I want to make sure we do it right," he said.

"Yes," I said in response, hardly knowing how we would do it at all.

We told them that night after supper. Dan got a fire going in the family room, and I made hot chocolate. We gathered on the couch, the four of us in a row. It was a blistering cold evening, and a frigid wind was howling around the eaves of the house. It felt snug and warm in the house.

It was difficult to tell them both at the same time because Katie, at twelve, knew a great deal more about life than Spencer at nearly seven. While she understood all too well how this baby had started growing in me, Spencer was full of questions that we hadn't planned on getting into for a couple more years. We tried to keep it simple, but it kept getting more complex.

"But how did the bad man give you the baby?" he kept asking me, even after Dan and I had tried twice to vaguely explain that the father of the baby wasn't Dan.

"It doesn't matter how he did it. It just matters that Daddy didn't give it to her," Katie snapped, surprising Dan and me with her abruptness.

In any case, it satisfied Spencer for the moment.

"So what are we supposed to do with the baby?" he asked next.

Although Dan and I had never talked specifically about giving the baby up for adoption, we both knew that it seemed like the only option we could both live with.

"If I don't have any trouble, and the baby is born okay, then we will find a good home for it," I said, shaking a little as I said it. "There are many people who want very much to have children and can't."

"Why can't they?" Spencer asked, ever the inquisitor.

"Stop asking so many questions, Spencer!" Katie snapped, again. I could tell I was going to have to spend some time alone with her. She was terribly angry.

"So it's not going to be our baby?" he continued.

"They don't want it. Can't you understand anything?" Katie exclaimed, glaring at her little brother. She was slipping into as dark a mood as I had ever seen her in. It scared me. It also occurred to me that we weren't "doing it right."

"Look, kids," Dan ventured. "Your mom has had lots of trouble with her pregnancies. She may have trouble with this one, and then it won't matter."

"But what if she doesn't?" Katie retorted. "What if she doesn't have trouble?"

Dan was quiet for a moment and then he shared something from the depths of his wounded heart that I hoped Katie and Spencer would always remember.

"Kate, you and Spencer mean the world to me," he began. "I would walk through fire for you. I would do anything to keep you safe. That's how much I love you both. I have loved you like this since before you were born, since the day Mom and I knew she was expecting. Every child deserves a love like that from its father. Every child."

He was close to tears, and Katie was crying freely. Spencer had climbed into my lap, and as he rested his head on my shoulder, my own tears fell onto his blond curls.

"But why can't you love this baby?" Katie said, her voice softening. "I could."

I think I could too floated across my brain, but I did not say it. Dan wiped his eyes and cleared his throat.

"Do you remember the night when the policeman came to our house?" he said. Katie and Spencer both nodded their heads.

"I told you when I left for the hospital that Mommy had been hurt but that she was going to be okay. Do you remember that?"

They nodded their heads, but I was hearing this for the first time.

"But I didn't know if she was going to be okay," he said, and his eyes filled with fresh tears, his voice beginning to tremble. "The policeman wouldn't tell me. I kept asking, 'Is she okay? Is she okay?' but he wouldn't answer me. He kept saying I would need to ask the doctor at the hospital. He wouldn't answer me."

Dan wiped his eyes again, and we all did the same.

"So when I got to the hospital, I thought they were going to tell me Mommy was…that she was in heaven," he continued, acutely aware of Spencer's wide-eyed stare. "Nobody would tell me anything. So I thought, that's it. She's gone. I don't have my best friend anymore. I don't have my wife. My kids don't have their mother."

I could hardly bear to hear this. I had no idea this had happened to Dan. I felt so bad about all the times I had been short with him the past few months. No wonder he acted and felt the way he did. It was all making sense.

"When the doctor finally came out to talk to me, he didn't smile. He didn't look happy. And I was so scared," Dan said, choking back a sob. "He made me sit down and he wouldn't say right away if Mommy was still alive. He started telling me where she had been hurt and how badly, and it seemed like a long time before he said she wasn't dead."

Dan stopped for a moment and gathered his thoughts. There wasn't a sound in the room except an occasional snap from the wood in the fireplace and the wind outside.

"So when I think of how scared I was," he finally said, "and how close I was to losing Mommy, how much I already had begun to miss her, I know I cannot love a baby given to her by a man who hurt her so badly she almost died."

He was completely spent, and I don't think he could have uttered another word if he had wanted to.

Katie said nothing, but her face was wet with tears, and she no longer looked angry. Spencer put his arms around me.

The four of us huddled together on the couch for what seemed like hours. The fire dwindled away to nothing, and the swirling wind threw yesterday's snowfall against the window-panes, but nobody seemed to notice or care.

11

After we told Katie and Spencer about the baby, the circle of those who knew the truth widened further to include my brother Matt, Dan's parents, his sister Karin, and her husband, Kent.

None of them knew quite what to say to me or to Dan, and since we told them by phone, I couldn't judge their reactions by their faces. It was silly of me to think this, but I felt like I had brought a sense of disgrace to Dan's side of the family. I was itching to have the whole thing behind me.

About a week later, Becky came by the house with a big cardboard box. She had gathered maternity clothes for me from women in the church. The clothes had all been freshly washed and ironed and smelled faintly of Downy. I had kept none of my maternity clothes after Dan's vasectomy and had no desire to shop for new ones. Becky didn't make a big deal about the clothes, which I was grateful for. She just brought the box in, set it on the floor, and told me when I was done with them, just to give the box back to her and she would get the clothes back to those who owned them.

Later, as we sat in the kitchen enjoying a cup of late-morning coffee, Becky asked me if Dan and I had contacted an adoption service. She and Nick both knew we weren't going to keep the baby. I wasn't thinking much beyond one day at a time. I told her no.

"There's a couple that some friends of ours know. They're American missionaries to Ecuador," Becky said. "From what I hear, they're wonderful people, Claire. And they've never been able to have children."

I was a little unprepared to have this conversation, so I just sat there playing with the handle of my coffee mug as Becky continued.

"They tried adopting a little girl from Argentina once, but it fell through. They lost a lot of money, and I'm told it broke their hearts. They had wanted that little girl very much. I think they would give this baby a loving home, Claire—just the kind you have been telling me you want for it."

I took a deep breath. Talking about handing over my child made my head ache and my throat feel funny.

"How do you know they would want this baby?" I asked.

"Because I called them last night," Becky said simply. "I got their number from my friends in Wisconsin and called them."

"What? You called them in Ecuador?" I said, laughing a little.

"No, I called them in Duluth. They have family near there and are on furlough for a year. Claire, they want to talk to you and Dan."

It seemed to be happening way too fast.

"I think it's a little early for that," I managed. "A lot could happen in the next month or two."

"I know," Becky said, but she was really saying, "But what if nothing goes wrong?"

I took a sip of my coffee. What if nothing did?

"Who are they? What are their names?" I asked.

"Ed and Rosemary Prentiss," Becky replied.

"They sound old," I said quickly, hardly thinking.

"They aren't that much older than us. He just turned forty-five. She's forty-two. She's only five years older than you, Claire."

I didn't want to talk about it anymore.

"I'll think about it, Becky," I finally said.

"Talk to Dan," she said, picking up her coffee cup and taking it to the sink.

"I will," I said, but I must not have sounded very convincing.

"It would take a tremendous burden off of you, Claire, knowing there's a family waiting to raise this child. You wouldn't have to give it another thought."

I didn't know how to tell her that was precisely what troubled me. I was terrified of being expected not to give this child another thought. How could I not give it another thought? How would I ever be able to forget I had borne a child I wasn't supposed to love and couldn't hate?

It was several days later that I finally asked Dan about it. I had seen Becky at church and, sure enough, she asked me what Dan had thought. I told her I would ask him that day. When the kids went sledding with some friends in the afternoon, I took advantage of the time alone to tell him.

I should have guessed Dan would think it was a great idea. I knew he didn't love this child, but I also knew he didn't want it to suffer or be harmed in any way. He wanted it to have a good home to grow up in. And the little I knew of the Prentisses, he liked.

"Let's call them up," he said.

"Can we wait until at least the fifth month is over, Dan? They've been disappointed before," I said.

He thought about it and then agreed.

We decided to hold out until the first of March. If there was no change in my condition, then we would get the phone number from Becky and call them.

~ ~ ~

The last two weeks of February passed quietly and without incident. Katie was still moody and quiet, and I wasn't sure how much of that was due to her own puberty and how much was due to my pregnancy.

She was aloof around me, detached in a way that I recognized as a tool to protect herself from hurt. I imagine that watching my abdomen swell with a baby she would have loved to have welcomed home—but would not be able to—was hard on her. So she kept her distance. I let her and prayed to God that was the right thing to do.

I saw Dr. Whitestone on the last day of February. The ultrasound revealed a growing baby and a placenta that had not budged up or down. It was still low, but not causing any trouble. I was beginning my seventh month; the last trimester.

I knew that when I told Dan this, he would want to call Ed and Rosemary and begin making the legal arrangements. I hated making the call. Not because I didn't think they would make great parents. For some reason I was sure they would. I just didn't want to put the wheels in motion. I knew it was the beginning of saying goodbye, and I dreaded it.

Rosemary Prentiss was kind and composed when I called her the next day. It was almost as if she knew I would call her, as if she had been expecting it. She told me she and Ed would love to drive down so we could meet them. She suggested the following Saturday. Dan and I decided to arrange for the kids to spend the day with his parents—they lived an hour away—so that we could talk openly with Ed and Rosemary. There was still plenty of snow on the ground, and we knew the kids loved riding with their grandpa on his snowmobile. An overnight trip to go snow-mobiling would be a real treat for them. Spencer didn't think twice about it, but Katie seemed suspicious that we were purposely getting them out of the house. I hoped she would forget about it. I found out later that she didn't.

We took them to Red Wing the night before and enjoyed a nice meal with Dan's family. I couldn't help but notice that Dan's mother used her everyday stoneware, not the china she usually used when we were all together for a meal. And there was absolutely no sign of the gravy boat. I wondered what Dan had done with it.

After supper, Katie and her eleven-year-old cousin, Allison—Karin and Kent's oldest—disappeared into the TV room. Spencer and Jennifer, Allison's younger sister, followed them, were chased out, and finally ended up with Dan's dad at the kitchen table playing Chinese checkers.

We said goodbye, and Nina, Dan's mom, walked out to the van with us. Dan told her the little we knew about Ed and Rosemary.

"They sound like nice people," Nina said as we hugged goodbye. "I hope they're the right family. I really do."

I could only nod and thank her for a wonderful evening.

Dan had asked Ed and Rosemary to meet us at our house at eleven that Saturday, then he wanted us all to go to lunch. I just let him call all the shots. It was easier for me that way.

Our doorbell rang at five to eleven, and I found myself strangely nervous, as if I were the one about to come under inspection. Dan welcomed Ed and Rosemary into the house and brought them into the living room, where I was waiting.

My first impression was not what I had been expecting. They were such charming people, so relaxed and friendly. I guess I had expected them to be anxious and overly eager to please. But they were calm and collected, and it wasn't but a few minutes that they felt like old friends.

They both bore the marks of people who had spent years in the sun, though six months in Minnesota had caused their South American tans to fade a bit. Rosemary's long brown hair was French braided at the back and fell past her waist. Strands of gray covered the crown of her head like a tiara. She had an easy smile, the bluest eyes I had ever seen, and delicate hands. She was slim, a little shorter than I am, and looked the picture of health. Ed was tall, a little overweight, and nearly bald. But he had a full, silvery gray beard and sparkling gray eyes. His eyebrows were still very dark, and I imagined that when he was younger, he had been strikingly handsome. He reminded me of Stuart for some reason, and that immediately relaxed me.

After we talked about their drive down, the weather, and Katie and Spence—they were both disappointed the kids weren't there—Dan decided it was time to talk about the real reason they had driven two and half hours to see us.

"This has been a difficult time for my wife and me," Dan began. "And we both want this next step to be as painless as possible for everyone. We both want this child to have a home like this one to grow up in, with a mother and father who will love this child with all their hearts."

"Of course you do," Rosemary said softly, which Dan drew strength from, I could tell.

"We just want to know this child will grow up loved and wanted," he continued.

Ed and Rosemary then told us about their work in South America, how they had spent the past twenty years teaching Ecuadorian children to read and write and how to blossom despite difficult circumstances. They also assured us that a child they raised as their own would grow up in a home where God was honored, where love abounded, and where faith was lived out. Hearing this had a soothing effect on me.

Yet I felt Ed and Rosemary should know why Philip Wells had done what he did, that although he was not a madman, he was still a despicable brute who had killed for money. So I told them. I told them a greedy, violent man who had murdered his wife had fathered the baby. It was the first time I had actually said it out loud like that. It made me shudder.

Ed looked down for a moment, and at first I thought he was weighing what I had just said, but he was really weighing how best to say what he would say next.

"Without talking to Mr. Wells, it's hard to know why he did what he did," Ed said. "I know it was technically for money, but surely there were other things at work. It takes more than just ordinary greed for a man to do such horrific things."

He paused for a moment and then continued. "I believe that when God says he can make all things new, that includes people with hearts as dark as Mr. Wells'. I don't think virtue or the lack of it is hereditary. Actually, I wouldn't be at all surprised to learn that Mr. Wells grew up thinking he wasn't worth anything, so he sought to prove his worth his own way, a horrible way. On the other hand, a child who is loved without condition and who is sure of his or her incalculable worth has nothing to prove. I don't know how much genes play a role. I do know how much love does."

I suddenly felt a tremendous rush of allegiance to the child, and with it came a powerful compulsion to make certain that this baby—my baby—would be loved like this—unconditionally and lavishly. I also felt the tiniest inkling of disappointment that Dan could not love the child like this—like he loved Katie and Spencer—but I pushed it away because I didn't like thinking about it. It seemed purposeless to dream about what it might be like to keep this child. I knew it was hopeless. The baby could never be ours. Could never be mine.

We enjoyed a nice lunch later at a restaurant, but I couldn't concentrate on the small talk. Rosemary sensed this and found little ways to let me know she understood. She would squeeze my hand, or look at me a certain way, and I would know she knew. She knew the mother part of me was already aching.

We had told Ed and Rosemary before leaving for the restaurant that I had miscarried before and that it was possible I might miscarry again. Just talking about that possibility made me uneasy, so I had withdrawn from the conversation. I think Rosemary somehow knew I was no longer fearful that I wouldn't miscarry, but that I was now fearful I would. I think she knew I no longer wanted this child to live because I believed it had a right to life, but because I loved it. Her.

I loved her.

*T*hough Ed and Rosemary had met our every expectation, they insisted we pray about the adoption over the next week. They would do the same. I had no doubt God wanted them to raise my child. I knew Dan felt the same way.

Even after knowing them for only a short while, it was hard to say goodbye that afternoon. Part of me wished for more time just to be with them, and part of me wondered if the next time I saw them would be when I'd be giving them a piece of my very soul. As it turned out, I saw them on two other occasions over the next couple of months.

As we stood in the restaurant parking lot, Dan and Ed began discussing the legal documents that would have to be drawn up. I heard Dan tell Ed he would contact our lawyer and the county courthouse. I turned away. I wanted nothing to do with the logistics of this transaction. Rosemary put her arm around me and steered me away from their conversation.

"Can I call you from time to time?" she asked me.

I nodded.

"Sometimes we need someone to just listen to us think out loud, you know?" she continued.

Oh, how I knew.

"Sometimes it's hard to talk with Dan about how I feel," I spontaneously confided in her, immediately aware that I had told no one else this. And I had only known Rosemary for a few hours.

"Yes," she said, like she already knew. "His anguish over this is different from yours."

"I don't think he knows *how* different," I said quietly.

She was thoughtful for a moment.

"And how about your kids? Especially your daughter. How does she feel?" Rosemary asked.

To be completely honest, I didn't know exactly what Katie was thinking or feeling. I knew she was disappointed and maybe still a little angry. I didn't know if she was mad at me or Dan or God or all three of us. I explained this to Rosemary.

"You might want to talk to her about it," she said gently. "You know what it's like to feel as if you're alone in your troubles. Perhaps she feels the same way. Maybe Ed and I should come down again and meet your children."

"I don't know if that's necessary," I said quickly. Too quickly.

"Oh, it certainly isn't necessary for us to meet them," Rosemary said. "But it might be necessary for them to meet us. They may have feelings for this baby you're unaware of."

I didn't have time to answer her and wasn't sure how to anyway. Ed and Dan joined us at the Prentisses' car.

"Claire and I were wondering if maybe we should come again sometime, Ed. Maybe next month?" Rosemary said.

"That's probably a good idea," Dan said. "There might be some paperwork we can take care of by then."

I tried not to sigh aloud. Oh yes, by all means let's take care of the paperwork.

Rosemary gave my shoulder a squeeze.

"I'll call you," she said more to me than to Dan.

"Great," Dan said and began shaking Ed's hand. "Well, I hope you have a safe journey back. We'll be in touch."

Goodbyes were said all around. As Rosemary hugged me, she whispered in my ear: "Don't lose heart."

As I watched them drive away, I realized I was strangely jealous of them.

Dan was feeling as confident as I had ever seen him as we drove home. I guess he felt like he was back in control of things. I didn't know it then, but he was making all kinds of other plans for our future, and it was all beginning to gel for him that first part of March. Finding Ed and Rosemary was just one item on his list of things to do, and now he could cross it off. About a month later I would find out what else he had on his list.

We headed straight for Dan's parents' house after lunch to pick up the kids. They were out on the sleds with Dan's dad and Kent when we arrived, giving us a few minutes alone with Nina and her many questions about the Prentisses. I let Dan do all the answering. I knew I would have the same conversation with my mom and again with Becky.

When the kids came back from sledding, we packed up the car with their overnight things, said goodbye, and headed for home. We hadn't been on the road for ten minutes when Katie asked what Dan and I had done while they were gone.

There was a momentary pause in the front seat as Dan and I silently volleyed who would give the response.

"Well, we met with a couple interested in adopting the baby," I blurted out, suddenly feeling a need to be completely honest with her. I guess the switch in my brain was still in the "on" position.

Dan glanced my way.

"You did?" Katie sounded unsure, like she was trying to decide if I was telling the truth. But why would I tease her about something like that? She knew instantly that I wouldn't. "You did that without us?" Now she was irritated.

"We didn't know what they were going to be like, Katie," Dan said quickly. "We thought we should see them first so we could see if there's any point in having you and Spencer meet them."

"Well, is there?" she said flatly.

"Is there what?" Dan said, trying to look at her in the rearview mirror.

"Is there any point in having me and Spencer meet them?" This was not going well at all.

"They're very nice people, Kate," I said. "They're wonderful people, actually. They want to meet you and Spencer."

There was silence in the backseat.

"We're going to get together with them next month, and you can meet them," Dan said and then hastily added, "and then you can let us know what you think."

"What difference does it make what *I* think," Katie said under her breath. But I heard it. I was sure Dan did too.

"Well, who are they?" Spence said, his first comment in this conversation.

"Their names are Ed and Rosemary Prentiss," Dan said. "They're living in Minnesota for the year, but they usually live in Ecuador. They're missionaries."

Dan was trying to make it sound like they were very lively, interesting people, but it occurred to me in a new and painful way that Ecuador was thousands of miles away. And that's where this child would be taken, if I didn't miscarry. Katie picked up on this right away. I wish I had.

"Ecuador. You're letting them take the baby to Ecuador?" Katie said angrily.

Yes. I thought miserably. *Yes it's true. I'm letting them take my baby to the uttermost ends of the earth where I can't feel it, see it, or even sense it.*

I don't think Dan had given the "where" of this arrangement much thought at all. That aspect wasn't on his list.

"Well, Katie, that's where they live," Dan said. "Ed and Rosemary run a wonderful school in a place called Otavalo. It's a school where they teach kids of other missionaries as well as Ecuadorian children. They do tremendous work there."

Katie said nothing.

"Where's Ecuador?" Spencer asked.

"It's in South America, Spence," Dan said.

"So it's far away?"

Katie said something else under her breath. This time I couldn't hear her.

"Yeah, it's far away," Dan replied.

"So we won't get to see the baby very much," Spencer said.

Dan swallowed. I don't think he had envisioned this conversation taking place like this at all. I'm sure he thought we would all see the situation like he did—like it needed to be dealt with carefully and then forgotten.

"No, we won't see the baby," he said, to Spencer conversationally, but in reality, to Katie and me as well. "The baby will have a family of its own, Spence. A really great family, just like ours."

"Oh yeah, just like ours…" Katie mumbled.

"Kate, you're going to have to trust us on this one," Dan said forcefully, trying to make eye contact with our daughter in the rearview mirror. "I am *asking* you to please trust us on this."

Katie was quiet for a moment.

"You shouldn't have sent us away today," she finally said.

"I'm sorry we did, really I am," I said as I turned to look at her. "We've never had to do anything like this before, Kate. This is all new to us. We're not always sure we're making the right decisions."

"My point exactly," she said softly, astounding me with the depth of her perception.

I could say nothing in response to this, so I just apologized again. She nodded her head, and we rode the rest of the way home in silence.

The next few days were rather awkward for us as a family. Katie spent most of her time upstairs in her room or in the living room playing her piano recital piece over and over—well past the point of memorization. On the few occasions I tried to talk with her about our situation, she put up a wall of feigned indifference. She was pretending she didn't care what we did with the baby, but it was so obvious that she did.

One morning late in the week I came downstairs in some of the maternity clothes Becky had brought. Katie looked up at me as I came into the kitchen and stared. She had never seen the clothes before, and I could see it was on the tip of her tongue to ask me about them. I suppose since it had to do with the baby, she opted not to.

"Becky brought over some clothes for me," I said simply, wanting her to know I knew how she felt.

She just put another spoonful of cereal into her mouth without saying a word. I couldn't tell if she was relieved I had sensed her interest or perturbed.

By the week's end, Dan was resolved to call Ed and Rosemary and tell them we had made our decision.

"So you've prayed about it?" I said, since this was what Ed and Rosemary had expected of us.

"Several times a day," he said. "This is the right thing to do, Claire. Don't you agree?"

I didn't know how to tell him that nothing felt "right" to me. There was nothing "right" about any of this. But since I knew it made the most sense, I nodded.

"Did you pray about it too?" he asked me, and I could tell he was afraid I might announce I had received a different answer to our predicament.

"Yes," I said softly and then added, "Psalm 20."

All he heard was "yes." I don't think he knew or was concerned I was still "psalming" my way through my prayer life. Dan had always been private about his prayers. He never prayed out loud and he didn't expect me to. If I wanted to pray Psalm 20 every day for the rest of my life, I knew Dan believed that was between me and God and no one else.

"So you agree with me?" he asked cautiously.

"We can call them," I said.

On Saturday I made pancakes for breakfast, and while we ate, Dan told Kate and Spencer we were going to invite Ed and Rosemary down so they could meet them.

"So, they're going to get the baby," Spencer said, not so much a question as a plea for confirmation.

"We think they will be wonderful parents. They want this baby very much," Dan replied.

I expected Katie to say nothing, and she did not surprise me.

Dan called the Prentisses later that day, and the three of them made plans for all of us to get together the Saturday before Easter. Dan even asked them to stay overnight and to come with us to Easter services the following day. Ed had apparently said something about getting a hotel room, but I overheard Dan insist they stay with us. It surprised me that Dan was including them in such a traditional family event. It wasn't that I minded. I just found it odd.

I called my mom that night and told her Dan and I had finalized our decision, that Ed and Rosemary would be adopting the baby. The possibility of my miscarrying was slipping further and further away. It didn't even seem there was a chance of that anymore. When I thought of the future, I saw Rosemary holding a tiny bundle, not me delivering a tiny, lifeless body.

"So how do you feel about that?" my mother asked.

I shrugged, not caring she could not see it.

"It seems to be the best I can expect," I said truthfully. "I really like Ed and Rosemary. And I know they will love this baby."

"Love is everything to a child," my mom said, and I knew she was not trying to be condescending. She was just reminding me of a truth I had to hold on to.

"I know, Mom," I said as a tear escaped one eye.

"Don't forget you're doing what you must because of love," she said.

We were both quiet for a few moments. A thought occurred to me that I had never told her what had happened to me on the morning this journey really began. I felt a need to tell her.

"Mom, do you remember the day Daddy died and I came into the kitchen and told you I thought I heard Daddy's voice?"

She paused. "Yes, Claire. I remember."

"I think it was really God trying to tell me something. I think He was telling me not to be afraid. He knew that day was going to be terrible."

I waited for a moment, and she said nothing. I wondered too late what it might be like for her to be called upon to remember that day. I didn't want to stop to think maybe I should have said nothing.

"On the morning I knew I was pregnant, I heard Him speak to me again, Mom. It was the first time since that other day."

She was silent for a moment. Then she said: "What did you hear?"

"The same thing. I heard the same thing. 'Do not be afraid.' "

Again, she was silent.

"Are you, Claire?" she said finally, gently. "Are you afraid?"

I hesitited for a moment even though I knew I felt no fear among the mix of emotions rolling around inside me.

"No, I'm not," I answered. "I'm not afraid. I'm sad, but I'm not afraid. But I honestly thought *not* being afraid would make it easier to say goodbye. I think it's going to make it harder, Mom. I really do."

I was not mistaken.

We celebrated Spencer's seventh birthday the Saturday before Palm Sunday, taking him and six of his friends to a movie and then out for pizza afterward. It was a weird kind of day. I know Spencer had a good time, but I didn't. I didn't mind the movie, but it was made for adolescent boys and people who like to think like adolescent boys. The jokes were silly, sometimes crude. I realized I was feeling very much like I was nearing my forties and feeling far too old for immature nonsense.

Then at the pizza restaurant one of Spencer's little friends looked at my abdomen, which I tried to conceal with a baggy sweater, and said, "So you're having a baby?"

Dan was involved in pouring glasses of root beer at the other end of the table and hadn't heard it. I wasn't sure what to say. If I said "yes," this kid would no doubt expect to see me at some future event with a baby in my arms.

I was formulating an answer when Spencer said, "Yeah, but we're not keeping it." And then he took a bite of his pizza.

The kid whirled around and looked at me like either my son was nuts or I was from another planet.

I felt like I *was* from another planet. I wanted to look at that wide-eyed kid and say, "Yep, I'm from Mars. We only keep babies born in December and March."

"How about some more pizza, Kyle?" I said, though his plate was full of pizza. He looked at his plate and then back at me. I guess he decided Spence and I were both nuts.

I was anxious for the day to end and tried hiding my middle from then on anytime I stood up. I insisted on carrying all of Spence's presents out to the van, even though Dan kept pestering to help. I didn't want his help. I wanted camouflage.

That night when I tucked Spencer into bed, I asked him if he'd had a fun day, and he was all smiles.

"Yeah, it was great," he said.

"I'm glad," I said and brushed a stray hair off his forehead. "Say, Spencer," I continued, like I had just thought of something when actually I had been rehearsing what I would say next all evening. "People may not understand why we aren't keeping the baby, so it would be better not to tell them. It's kind of a private thing that I don't want to have to explain to people."

"You want me to tell people we're keeping it?" he said, incredulous that I would ask him to lie for me.

"No, no," I said quickly. "You don't need to say anything, hon. You don't need to even mention that I'm pregnant or that we aren't keeping the baby. If someone asks you if I'm having a baby, you can tell them the truth. You can say "yes." But you don't need to say anything else. Okay?"

"But what if later they ask where the baby is?" he asked.

It suddenly occurred to me that everybody who knew me and could see that I was pregnant would wonder where the baby was. There seemed to be no end of uncomfortable circumstances looming ahead.

I wanted to say, "Tell them the baby died." But I couldn't tell my son to say that. I knew I couldn't say it. It was a lie. I decided I needed time to think about what we could say to little seven-year-old boys and everyone else.

"Let me think about it and get back to you on that. Okay?" I said.

"All right," he said, cuddling down into his blanket.

I told Dan that night as we got ready for bed about the little problem I had at the pizza restaurant and what I had told Spencer.

"What are we going to tell people when they ask, Dan?" I said. "Only a handful of family and friends know the truth. What are we supposed to say?"

I could tell Dan had already given this a lot of thought.

"I'm working on it," he said.

"What?" I said, though I had heard what he said.

"I am working on it."

He wouldn't say anything else. I was tired after the long day with seven little boys, so I let it go.

Katie's piano recital was held at her school on Palm Sunday afternoon. She played flawlessly. Practicing her piece relentlessly the previous few weeks had definitely paid off, but she had grown to hate the piece, I think. She never played it again.

Two days before Ed and Rosemary came down for the second time, I had another doctor's visit. I was nearing the end of the seventh month.

An ultrasound revealed the placenta was still in the same place, perhaps a little higher.

"At this point, I would say you could possibly deliver this child naturally, Claire. A lot depends on these last two months," Dr. Whitestone told me. "The weight of the baby often pushes the placenta upward, where it's supposed to be.

That's what happened with your first child. Other than that, everything looks fine."

"I really don't want another Cesarean," I told him as I sat up on the table and covered my stomach.

"I know you don't," he said gently. It was like he and I both wordlessly agreed I shouldn't have to bear that burden along with everything else.

The picture of my child was still on the ultrasound screen, frozen in time as Dr. Whitestone printed the image.

"Do you know if it's a boy or a girl?" I asked him out of the blue, suddenly wanting confirmation of what I already knew in my heart.

He looked up from the printer and studied me for a moment.

"I do," he said.

I nodded. So he knew.

"Do you want to know?" he asked.

"Yes, I do," I said. There didn't seem to be any point in not knowing for sure. This was not like being pregnant with Katie and Spence or even Sarah—the child I miscarried and we named. I thought for a second that perhaps it would be helpful for Ed and Rosemary to know. Maybe it mattered to them. I quickly dismissed that thought. I knew it would not matter to them. It would not matter to them if the child was male or female, one-legged, blind, or anything else.

"It's a girl," he said and turned away from me so I could process this information privately.

"You're sure?"

He turned around and smiled just a little. "Ninety-nine percent sure," he said.

So was I.

I left with instructions to take it easy. Keep stair-climbing to a minimum. No jogging or jumping, neither of which I had done in years. Dr. Whitestone also wanted to see me in two weeks, not four, to see if there had been any change.

I didn't want to go home right away. It was early in the day yet, and the kids wouldn't be home from school for a few hours. I stopped for lunch at a Taco Bell and then drove to the nearest Target. It was the Thursday before Easter, and the department store was decked out in pastel colors from floor to ceiling.

I shouldn't have done it, but I purposely strolled over to the baby section, and for a long time I just stood there and stared at the display of Easter dresses for baby girls. I was overcome with a tide of memories of dressing Katie in frilly pink and purple dresses, of stuffing her chubby baby legs into white tights with ruffles on the seat, and trying to keep a bonnet festooned with ribbons and rosebuds on her head. It didn't seem that long ago that she spent most of her waking hours in my arms. A peculiar sense of longing crept over me as I stood there in a sea of rosy pink, lavender, and pale yellow.

I don't know how long I stood there. Long enough to attract attention, I suppose. I came out of my reverie to the sound of a woman asking me if she could help me find something. Her tone suggested she had already asked me several times and had gotten no answer.

"No, no," I stammered.

I attempted a smile, thanked her, and walked away. I headed back to my van and drove home, wildly frustrated and wishing I still had boxes of old Christmas cards to sort through.

Instead I called my mother.

She wasn't home, but I poured out my heart to Stuart, unaware that the kids had come in through the kitchen door and that Katie had probably heard everything I said. Stu told me he would have my mom call the minute she got in.

When I hung up, I saw Katie standing there, arms folded across her chest and leaning against the arched doorway between the living room, where I was, and the dining room.

I felt foolish for not having looked at the clock before making the call and for being so absorbed in it I didn't hear the kids come in.

"Katie. You're home," I said. A really dumb thing to say, but I was completely taken by surprise at seeing her.

"It's a girl," she said to me in a tone of resignation that didn't suit her but was becoming commonplace for her.

"Yes," I said. I didn't take my eyes off her.

She stood there for a few more seconds and then headed up the stairs, slowly, one at a time and with no lift in her step.

I found Spencer in the kitchen eating Oreos and watching cartoons on the little televison on the breakfast bar. He appeared to have heard nothing.

"Hey, Spencer. How's it going?" I said as cheerfully as I could. "Did you have a good day?"

"Yep," he said, twisting open a cookie and scraping off the filling with his front teeth.

I grabbed some cookies, poured a glass of milk, and headed up the stairs myself. I knocked on Katie's door and waited for her to answer.

"What?" she said.

"May I come in?" I said.

There was a pause.

"Yeah."

She was on her bed looking at a catalog, her head propped up on an elbow.

"I brought you a snack," I said.

"I'm not really hungry."

"Well, maybe you'll want it later," I said, setting the cookies and milk on her dresser. She said nothing and turned a page in her catalog.

"Katie, can we talk about this?" I said.

She was silent for a moment. I could tell she was considering my request, but she turned another page in the catalog in a way to suggest she wasn't.

"Talking about it isn't going to change anything," she finally said.

"No, it won't," I said as I sat down next to her. "But not talking about it is changing *us*. Can't you feel it?"

"I don't feel *anything*," she said softly.

I stroked her head and she amazed me by letting me.

"Sometimes I don't feel anything, either," I said. "And sometimes I feel way too much."

She looked up at me, surprised, I think, that she hadn't shocked me by saying that she felt nothing. If she didn't want to tell me what was going through her head, then I was going to tell her what was going through mine.

"After my doctor's appointment," I said to her, "I went to Target and just stood in the baby-girl section, looking at all the dresses and bonnets and thinking how wonderful it is to be your mother. I was remembering when you were a baby and how much fun it was dressing you up at Easter. One year you wouldn't keep your bonnet on. Not even for one picture. You were sixteen months old, and in all the photos we have of you, you're holding your bonnet in your chubby little hands."

We both smiled—me at the memory, she at the image.

"I just don't see why we can't keep her," she said.

I knew she needed something grand and persuasive to get her through this, just like I did. I prayed a quick prayer for wisdom and charged ahead with what I hoped made sense.

"This baby is not a possession we can keep, like an heirloom or even a precious stone. She is a person, and she didn't choose her circumstances anymore than I did," I said. "Most of the time I think I could love her just like I love you, but the truth is, Kate, I'm unsure. And your dad…well, he is sure he cannot."

"But what if he's wrong. What if he can and he just doesn't know it?"

Katie had unknowingly asked the one question that pestered me daily. I knew there was a possibility that Dan's feelings for the child could change. But we both knew it was too much of a risk with the child's emotional welfare at stake.

"But if he is right, and he cannot love her, it could destroy this little girl and probably the four of us as well," I said. "That would be worse than this."

We were both quiet for a moment.

"I don't want her going to Ecuador," Katie said.

"I really don't either, Kate," I said. "But where she lives won't be up to us."

It was several long minutes before I rose from her bed and left Kate alone with her thoughts. And feelings she said she didn't have.

With Katie's aversion to the baby's living in Ecuador, I was afraid Ed and Rosemary would find her unapproachable on Saturday. But to my surprise, she was polite, though not overly friendly. Rosemary and Ed would think she was just shy, I thought. Actually Rosemary was able to sense Katie's displeasure for exactly what it was. At one point on Saturday afternoon the two of them disappeared. I learned later that they had sat on the deck even though it was forty degrees outside, talking about choices, circumstances, and trust.

I could tell that Spencer liked Ed and Rosemary very much. I heard him tell Ed that if they ever needed help in Ecuador, he could come over and lend a hand. He was serious. Ed smiled and said how wonderful that would be. I knew he was serious too.

I had told Dan earlier that when he wanted to talk legal matters over with Ed, I wanted to be out of the room. I could tell he was a little startled, but he said nothing.

I hated the mountain of paperwork we were already wading through. Private adoptions weren't legal in Minnesota. Since Ed and Rosemary weren't blood relatives, we had to get connected with a licensed child-placement agency so that the adoption would have state oversight. I had nothing against the agency Dan found; the people were more than kind—to us and to Ed and Rosemary. But the legalities felt like a dehumanization of my predicament. The adoption would take place inside a county courthouse in front of a judge, a complete stranger. Legally that's how the adoption would appear to take place. But it wouldn't be that way for me. The adoption of my child—the surrender of my child—would take place inside my wounded heart.

Dan took advantage of the time I was preparing supper to go over with Ed a few details our lawyer had advised Dan about. Rosemary came into the kitchen to help me and told me she had spent some time alone with Katie. Actually it was more like a confession.

Rosemary was worried she had overstepped her bounds by speaking to Katie about the adoption without Dan or me there.

I told her I trusted her with Kate. And it was true. I did.

"Did you have a good talk with her?" I said.

"I think so," Rosemary replied as she tore up romaine lettuce for a salad. "I feel badly we'll be living so far away. I think maybe Katie was hoping she would be able to watch the baby grow up."

"Maybe it's better this way," I said absently.

"Maybe. It is hard to know, isn't it?" Rosemary said.

"Very," I agreed, then added, "did Katie tell you it's a girl?" I could not help smiling as I said it.

"Yes, she did," Rosemary said, smiling herself. "But she told me not to say anything in case you wanted to be the one to tell me. She was looking out for you. She loves you very much."

I smiled again.

We finished supper preparations and then enjoyed a nice meal featuring my mom's stroganoff recipe. It occurred to me that I should have invited my parents. They would have flown out if I had asked them. I hoped there would be another time.

We passed the evening by looking at slides from our family vacations and just getting to know one another better.

On Sunday morning, Rosemary and I hid eggs all over the downstairs for Kate and Spencer—there was still some snow on the ground—while Ed and Dan made French toast.

After church, it was time to say goodbye again.

"Call me anytime," Rosemary said as we hugged goodbye. She had called me twice in the three weeks we had been apart. It was nice to be invited to do the same.

We had Easter dinner at Dan's parents' house with Karin, Kent, and the cousins. Nina used her good china and served the gravy for the ham in a soup bowl.

April was one of the wettest months in years, and it seemed that spring would never come. The changing season—or lack of it—really didn't make a difference to me. I didn't feel the eager expectancy that long Minnesota winters typically create for those who must bear them. I was already keenly aware that new life waited just around the bend; I didn't need the spring thaw or protruding tulip tips to remind me of that.

My mid-April doctor's appointment was encouraging, at least from the standpoint of labor and delivery. I wasn't looking forward to either one, especially since there would be no joyful homecoming to follow. But I didn't want to have the baby delivered by Cesarean. I wanted to physically recover from this as quickly as possible. I wanted no stitches, no searing pain, no scar. Dr. Whitestone said the placenta seemed to be inching its way upward, but he still wanted me to watch my physical activity. He didn't want me going into labor—or worse, starting to bleed—this early and at this stage.

So I did what came natural to me. I went to the library and checked out piles of books. I also dug around in the house for old favorites, especially my volume of Tennyson's poetry, which I read twice.

Spending so much time taking it easy at home actually provided me with a good reason not to be out and about, exposing myself as pregnant. It also gave me time to find new reasons for loving Tennyson, like the neurologist had advised me to do seven months before, which I did.

On one day in the middle of that wet and dreary month, Dan came home early from work with a manila envelope in his hands and a childish smile on his face. He was up to something.

"Claire, I have something I want to show you," he said, coming to sit by me on the living room couch. He swept away the books and magazines I had on the coffee table and set the envelope on the bare surface. He reached in and pulled out half a dozen color photographs. One was of a white, two-story house with a porch and gabled windows. Another was of a barn—red with white trim. A third was of a ravine with a brook running through it. The rest were interior shots of a house, presumably the white one. The rooms were spacious and empty. Hardwood floors. Cherry fireplace. Kitchen cabinets painted sky blue.

"What do you think?" Dan said, excitedly.

"I think they're pictures," I said, a little dumbfounded. Was he thinking what I thought he was thinking?

"But what do you think of them?"

I looked at the photos, picked up a couple, and declared it looked like a nice place.

"I think we should buy it," he said, almost breathlessly.

"You mean buy it to live in?"

"It would be great! Look at all the room. And there's a barn. We can finally get the kids some pets. Maybe a horse or something. At least a dog. Do you know how weird it is to be a veterinarian who has no pets?"

"Dan, what are you saying?" I asked, my head spinning. I could tell this was what he had been "working on" when he had been thinking about our immediate future. This was what he'd had at the top of his list. He wanted us out of Minneapolis.

"Claire, I think we should move," he said, locking his eyes onto mine. "I've been thinking about it for a long time. Even before you got hurt, I was thinking about it. I'm tired of fighting traffic, tired of city life, tired of spending my days spaying cats and clipping dog ears."

And then he said what was really motivating him to do this.

"And I think it would be good for us to have a fresh start. We both know there will be questions when you come home from the hospital without a baby. I don't want you or the kids to have to deal with that. We could begin a new life without the past haunting us at every turn."

I didn't know what to think. It felt like we would be running away. I told Dan this. He said indeed we *would* be running away; we would be running away from congested city life, high crime rates, long commutes, a hectic pace, and, first and foremost, too many painful memories. We would be running to a simpler life, with a new beginning and a new home free of a painful past.

I looked at the pictures again. It looked like a charming place, but it also looked very foreign to me. I had never lived anywhere but in a city. City life was what I knew. This place looked like it could be almost anywhere, but definitely not in the Twin Cities suburbs.

"Where is it?" I asked.

"It's a couple miles outside a town called Blue Prairie, about two hours south of here."

Two hours away. What Dan was suggesting was extreme. It would mean changing jobs, schools, our church. Everything.

"What about your practice?" I said.

"This is the best part," he said, breaking into a wide smile. "Remember Wes Gerrity? He was a year ahead of me at the U? He has a practice there with four other veterinarians. One of them is retiring, and he wants me to join them. He specifically asked me to join them, Claire. I didn't even have to go looking. And I will finally have a chance to do more than just take care of overweight dogs and cats. It's a big practice, Claire. They handle cattle, dairy herds, swine, sheep—the works. It would be a great career move for me."

He was practically there already. I was still trying to imagine a life other than the one I knew.

"You're afraid of the big animals," I said meekly, trying to buy time and come up with a real response.

Dan laughed. "Not afraid. Just inexperienced, Claire."

"But what about our friends? And my job at the school?" I said.

"We'll make new friends," he said confidently. Then he pointed out that Blue Prairie had a high school, too. He also reminded me that neither one of us had cartloads of friends we would miss. I had a few acquaintances in the English department at the high school where I taught, but I hadn't seen them since Christmas and hadn't even missed them. And Becky, my closest non-work-related friend, was a friend to countless others. It was her nature to be on emotionally intimate terms with dozens of other women in the church. She was the personification of the perfect pastor's wife.

"Did you already tell Wes you would come?" I asked.

"I told him I wanted the job. He knows I need to talk to you first."

"And this house?" I said, picking up the photo of the white house.

"It's half the price we'll get for the house we're living in right now, Claire. And it includes four acres and three outbuildings. It's been on the market for nearly a year. The owners are anxious to sell."

"Is there a white picket fence around it?" I said, partly in jest and partly not. I was weary of the burdens I was carrying, figuratively and actually. I wanted the fairy tale ending. I wanted us to live happily ever after.

"There will be if you want there to be," he said, drawing me into his embrace.

He took the stillness of that moment as a "yes."

A few minutes before the kids got home from school, Dan called the realtor, and the two of them made arrangements for us to come down and look at the house that Saturday.

I dreaded telling the kids what we were considering. Well, actually, I dreaded telling Katie. The circumstances that had fallen on us as a family were already testing the limits of her blossoming adulthood. This would come as another blow. I imagined her storming upstairs to her room and refusing to speak to us after we told her what we were thinking of doing. I began mentally preparing myself for accusations of how unfair we were.

But Katie surprised me by her response. She barely said anything. Spence loved the thought of living on a little farm and finally getting a big dog. He couldn't wait for Saturday to come so we could go see the place. Katie sat there absorbing it all but giving no indication of how she really felt. I actually found myself wishing she had exploded. That would have been normal. Her disinterest didn't seem appropriate.

I didn't know if Dan sensed this also, but somehow I managed to communicate to him without saying a word that I wanted to be alone with Katie. He announced he needed to take care of some things back at the clinic before it closed and invited Spence to come along.

The excitement of perhaps an upcoming move followed Dan and Spencer out of the kitchen like a loyal dog, and Katie and I were left in a room with no aura of anything in it.

She was on the verge of rising out of her chair, and it felt like if I didn't stop her, she would disappear into her room and maybe disappear altogether.

"Katie, please tell me what you're thinking," I said.

She had her hands on the table like she was going to get up and I had interrupted a shift she had been looking forward to completing. Her hands fell to her lap in defeat. She looked at me. Her eyes met my eyes in a way that made me feel uncomfortable. Perhaps she was considering how could I *not* know what she was thinking. Was I supposed to know? Would a good mother have known? I decided to tell her the truth, that I had expected her to resist.

She looked away then, and I wasn't sure if it was because I had said the right thing or the wrong thing.

"It wouldn't change anything," she said, looking at the stove for no reason at all. "If I put up a fight, it would change nothing. If you and Dad decide we're moving, then we're moving."

It pained me to realize she was right. I also realized that even if *I* had put up a fight, Dan was determined to do this. He had already told Wes he wanted the job. He had already contacted a realtor. Maybe he even had a moving date picked. And he had done all of it on his own.

But I trusted him. I knew Dan was motivated by love—for me and for our kids. Dan and I were still on different paths, but despite the isolation I felt, I still trusted him. Somehow I had to communicate this to Katie. Suddenly I knew how I could.

"Kate, when my dad died and Grandma moved us to Minnesota, it was a huge step for her, and for me and Uncle Matt," I said. "It was really hard for her to know what was the best thing to do. Uncle Gene and Aunt Elizabeth stepped in for her and made choices that changed everything for us, but in the end, it all worked out for the best. She had to trust that the people who loved her would know the right thing to do."

Katie continued to stare at the stove. A tear slipped from her left eye. I thought this was a good sign. I waited for her to speak next. It seemed like a long time before she did.

"But how do you and Dad know this is the right thing to do?" she finally said.

How indeed? How do we ever know what is the right thing to do? She was asking the question that sooner or later everyone who believes in a sovereign God asks. Assuming God is the God of right things, how do you know the right thing from the wrong thing when both choices seem practical? Does it matter to God which one you choose? Has He chosen already for you but waits to see if you agree with His choice? Then when you choose, does He thwart the plan He will not bless? Or does He allow you to make a choice you will later regret so that you will become wiser by experience?

I can think of times when my mother let me make a mistake so I could learn from it. I also know there were times when she forbade me to do something that was inappropriate for the same reason. But I also know having faith in a wise God is as simple as that and as complicated as any puzzle dreamed up by man. What I know of God is that He is above being completely figured out. I know I will never be able to say, "Now I understand how God works." I actually don't want to. A teeny God who could be fathomed in His entirety seems a pitiful thing to me.

As I sat there with my daughter, I knew Dan and I had to live by this faith, using the knowledge we had at the time, and daily make it our goal to do the "right thing."

I suddenly felt empowered to pray something other than a psalm.

But first, I wanted to bring Katie up to where I was. Or at least as close as I could.

"Does it seem like the wrong thing to you?" I asked, in response to her question.

She sat very still, her eyes still on the stove, but I could tell she was not seeing it. Then she looked down at her feet, like she had seen something else, something meant for only her to see.

She turned her head and looked at me.

"No," she said. "It doesn't seem like the wrong thing..."

Our drive to Blue Prairie was a wet affair, and I prayed the whole way down that the rain and sleet would stop when we got there. By the time we reached the little town of four thousand, the skies had brightened a little, but there was mud and water everywhere.

The town's main street was the kind of quaint avenue that now only exists in small towns blessed with entrepreneurial shop-keepers who know how to thrive in tiny, dying Midwest towns. There were two grocery stores, two drug stores, a hardware store, and a county courthouse that looked like Sleeping Beauty's castle. There were also numerous specialty and gift shops, a fairly up-to-date, twenty-bed hospital, two nursing homes, and several restaurants.

Mel Houghlin, the realtor, was eager to show us the farm site, but drove us around the town first, showing us the high school, the elementary school, the community center, the city's two parks, and the town's self-proclaimed highlight: the two bed-and-breakfast establishments—side by side Victorian mansions owned by twin sisters. One was painted blue with white trim; the other, white with blue trim.

He drove by Wes's vet clinic too, which Dan pretended to be seeing for the first time. I got the impression he had seen it before. I was going to ask him if he had come here by himself to look at it first, but I decided it didn't matter.

We headed down the main road out of town for maybe two miles and took a left turn onto a tar road. On either side of us were barren fields. Mel told us they would be planted with corn and soybeans as soon as the weather cooperated. After a couple more miles, we turned onto a winding, dirt driveway that seemed to end in a clump of trees. As we neared a bend, the white house I had seen in the photo came into view. Nearby were the red barn, an old chicken coop, and a greenhouse. There was a tire swing swaying from a heavy oak limb on a tree whose leafless form towered above the house. I nearly expected a couple of dogs to come bounding off the porch, scattering chickens and announcing our arrival.

But it was still and silent, as if the whole place was awaiting our approval. Mel was saying how beautiful it was when the grass was green and the hydrangeas were in bloom, but I didn't have any trouble picturing any of it. I knew before we even stepped inside the empty house that this was going to be my home, that this was the place where I would finally be at peace.

This would be the place where no anchor to the past existed for me.

I didn't even want to linger in any of the rooms. I wanted this house to have no attachment to the child I was carrying. I hurried through the tour of the house, rushing Mel, and behaving like someone who just wanted to leave.

When I could bear it no longer, I hurried out the front door, holding my breath so I would not inhale any more of the house's newness.

"She doesn't like the house?" I heard Mel say to Dan.

"No, I think she likes it very much," Dan said, watching me leave.

I was glad he understood this about me. It would have been hard to explain in words.

15

Two weeks after we put our Minneapolis house on the market, it was sold to a young couple with a new baby. It was only the end of April. We weren't expecting to move to Blue Prairie until just after the baby was born, presumably the first part of June. But the couple was anxious to take possession, and asked if we could be out by the end of May.

My due date was June 3, the same day as the last day of school. If we were out of the house by the end of May, we would likely only have to spend a week at a hotel suite. I refused two offers to stay with different friends from church. I wasn't trying to be rude. Nick and Becky understood, I think. I just knew it would be a very difficult time for me. I wanted solitude.

Three other significant events occurred in April—all on the same day, April 25. My teaching contract for the 1986/87 school year arrived from the high school where I was on leave. I sent it back the same day, unsigned, with a note asking for the board to accept my resignation. When I mailed it, I realized I did not want to go back into teaching at all. It was a funny feeling, not exactly one of relief, but I felt very satisfied making the decision not to pursue a teaching job in our new county. Not then and not ever.

Later that day, I had an appointment with Dr. Whitestone. The ultrasound I had that day revealed a placenta high in my uterus, where it should be, and a baby in a likewise proper position, down low. Barring any unforeseen complications, I would be able to deliver this little girl naturally and leave the hospital the next day, as I had asked. Dr. Whitestone then reminded me that there was a daylong childbirth class the following Saturday that I should attend. He told me there was still room in the class for me and a labor coach, if I wanted to have one. I told him I didn't. But I would come alone.

Just after supper that night, the third event etched itself into the day. My mother called in tears from Michigan. Uncle Gene had died that afternoon. The funeral would be in three days.

I lay awake that night after everyone was asleep, unable to relax. The baby was restless as well, kicking and prodding, and I was uncomfortable with the extra weight. The three events of the day kept playing themselves in my mind as I lay there, willing me to ponder them.

I had never had any career other than that as a teacher. The thought of not having an answer if someone asked me "What do you do?" began to needle me. I had always been quick to say I was a teacher. Now I wasn't a teacher. And I was pretty sure I didn't want to be. So what was I? And what did I want to do? Dan hadn't been too concerned when I told him that when we moved I didn't want to look for a teaching job, although for a moment he had that maybe-you-should-call-Patty look in his eye. He quickly dismissed it, I think, when he pictured me redecorating our new home, fixing up the greenhouse, and planting a garden.

But I knew I wanted to do something else besides plant tomatoes and stencil the kitchen. I just didn't know what.

Then I wrestled with knowing the delivery of this child was only a month away. It had been twelve years since I had naturally given birth, but I remembered the peculiar pain of labor like it was yesterday. The pain had been tolerable knowing that my child, who I longed for, waited on the other side of it. But I winced at the thought of the depth of that certain distress with no bright hope at the end.

Vying for my thoughts was lastly the death of my uncle, the only father figure I can remember from my childhood. I hadn't seen my aunt and uncle in many years, not since they retired from foster parenting and began traveling around the country in a motor home. Every Father's Day I sent two cards—one to Stuart and one to Gene. He was a remarkable man, and I knew I had failed to truly appreciate him and to let him know what I thought of him. Regret over this, worry over the pain to come, and anxiety over not knowing what to do with myself careerwise kept me awake until after three o'clock.

Dan was a gem the next morning and got the kids ready for school so I could catch up on the sleep I lost. I finally got out of bed at ten o'clock, made a fresh pot of coffee, and sat down with my Bible. Seeking comfort, I turned to that which was familiar, the Psalms. I felt marginally refreshed twenty minutes later. I needed something else. I needed someone—someone of flesh and bone—who would let me think out loud. I called Rosemary.

She was genuinely happy for me that the doctor's appointment had gone so well. And I don't think it was just because it meant the baby was also doing well. She also offered to be my labor coach and drive down the next Saturday to attend class with me. I had already mentally prepared myself to be alone in the delivery room. It was what I wanted. I wanted to be alone with my daughter when she was born. I didn't even want my own mother in the room with me. I thanked Rosemary, but told her the truth. I knew she would understand. I had already told Ed and Rosemary they could be right outside the delivery room and that Dan would probably need their company, since I told him he didn't have to come in with me. I was comfortable with these arrangements.

I then told Rosemary about my Uncle Gene. For ten minutes I told her what a terrific father he had been and how I wish I had told him so when I had the chance. She told me I should share these things at his funeral, which, surprisingly, had not occurred to me.

As I told her that was a good idea, I realized my Uncle Gene's funeral was the most opportune time for my family and Dan's to meet Ed and Rosemary. The conditions weren't the best, but there would not be another time when we would be all together like this.

"Would you come to my uncle's funeral in Saint Cloud?" I asked her.

"Would you like us to be there?" she replied.

"I would."

"Then we'll be there."

Mom, Stu, and Matt made their way directly to Aunt Elizabeth's the same day Gene had died. Dan and I took the kids out of school on Monday, the twenty-eighth, and together with Dan's parents and his sister and family, we caravanned up to Saint Cloud. The church where Gene's funeral was held was the same one I grew up in. Even twenty years after I had left it for college and my own life, it looked and smelled the same, except that the sanctuary was now a sea of flowers. I knew Gene had touched many people in his life, dozens of them young kids. I had no idea so many of them would grow up remembering fondly the few short months they had spent at my aunt and uncle's house. Half the flowers were from people who had met my uncle at one of the lowest points in their lives.

Aunt Elizabeth looked tired, like a ship without a sail. She was seventy-three, but looked older, weighed down by grief, I think. I found it remarkable that my mother was now caring for her sister like Aunt Elizabeth had cared for her under the exact same circumstances. My mother had enjoyed only eight years of marriage with my dad. Elizabeth had forty-nine years with Gene. But grief is grief.

I was glad someone video-taped the service for Aunt Elizabeth, because I don't know if she truly heard everything people said about the man she had shared her life with. Even when I got up to speak, she merely nodded once as she looked at me, like she was thinking, "Oh, there's Claire," and then she retreated to her secret place of sorrow.

After the interment, we gathered for refreshments at the home of Gene and Elizabeth's best friends, the Talbots, since my aunt and uncle had sold their big house when they retired. Ed and Rosemary had stayed in the background until then, not coming forward to speak with me until the day was half over. I appreciated that about them, that they had such an impeccable sense of timing.

As I had imagined, Stuart and Ed became fast friends, and spent nearly an hour talking about South American digs Ed had been on just for fun. Rosemary, my mom, and Nina also got on well together, which was no surprise to me. I was beginning to think there was no one Rosemary couldn't get along with. While making sure the coffee pots stayed filled and guests were properly thanked for coming, I lost track of Ed and Rosemary. When the house was nearly empty of guests except for immediate family, I found Ed chatting with one of the last kids Uncle Gene had under his care, now a grown man, and Rosemary sitting in a quiet spot, holding Aunt Elizabeth's hand and talking softly to her. Aunt Elizabeth was crying—the first tears I had seen her shed that day.

I left them and went into the kitchen where my mom, Nina, and Karin had begun helping with the dishes.

When it was time to head for home, Aunt Elizabeth looked weary but not despondent. She hugged Rosemary goodbye.

My mom took me aside and told me she was going to stay with Elizabeth until I was ready to deliver. Then she was going to come to me. She didn't ask. She just said she'd be there, on the other side of the door, in case I needed her.

As we gathered at the front entry to say our goodbyes, I was struck by the incredible bond that families share. I laid my hand on my abdomen, feeling the child that had been a part of this day though she would never know it, and inwardly mourned that she would not know this family. She wouldn't know how we cared for one another, how we shouldered one another's burdens. Ed and Rosemary had no other children, and they had no relatives with children. Rosemary had a brother in Florida who had never married and Ed was an only child. Of their parents, only Ed's mother was still alive, and she was apparently in frail health.

I prayed to God that a life with two obviously gifted people would be enough for my daughter. I prayed that her life as a child of missionaries would give her a family of others just like her, that she would know what it was like to be surrounded by a cluster of people who loved her without hesitation.

Stuart and Matt came home with us and stayed overnight. In the morning, Dan took them to the Minneapolis airport for their flight home. The kids had left for school already, so I tagged along. As we dropped them off at curbside, I gave them both hugs, feeling that when I saw them the next time, everything would be different. I would be different. Nothing was going to be the same.

"Matt and I are going to come help you move into your new place," Stu said as he picked up his bag and started to walk away. "We're going to drive out, so we'll see you in a few weeks!"

Dan began to protest, but Stu just waved and smiled.

"It's all arranged," he yelled over his shoulder as he and Matt crossed the threshold of the entrance and disappeared inside.

Spring finally arrived the second week in May. I took little notice as I spent most of my days sifting through all that Dan and I had accumulated in fourteen years of marriage. Professional movers were coming for the big pieces of furniture, but I wanted to pack the smaller things myself. Dr. Whitestone had lifted the earlier restrictions on physical activity, and I needed to stay busy. So what I didn't throw out I packed and labeled. Dan worried that I was doing too much and told me not to pick up any of the boxes I filled. I tried to oblige.

On the twenty-fourth of May, Katie had an end-of-the-school-year soccer game that Dan and I went to. It was a warm Saturday afternoon, the sun was shining, and the game was going well. As I sat there on the bleachers, I could feel things happening inside me. I didn't want to cry wolf so I said nothing, but I couldn't sleep that night. I felt like I was on the edge of my pregnancy, like I had climbed up to the rim of the abyss and would soon be free of it. Finally, a few hours before dawn, I fell asleep. When I awoke at eight o'clock on Sunday, I knew. Labor had begun.

Dan wanted to call Nick and Becky and have them take the kids right then. I told him to wait. The contractions were too far apart. It was way too soon to go to the hospital.

When Katie awoke a few minutes later, I heard Dan telling her we were skipping church, that it looked like the baby might come. She came into my room and sat on the edge of my bed as I put a few things in an overnight bag. I smiled at her and asked her to hand me the hairbrush lying next to her.

"I want to see her," she said softly as she placed the brush in my hand.

This did not surprise me, but I still hesitated before answering her.

"It might make it harder for you to say goodbye," I said.

"I want to see her," she said again, this time a little more forcefully.

I sat down next to Katie and told her I didn't want her to be hurt any more than she already was. I was afraid seeing the baby would tear her in two. I told her that.

Katie swiveled her head to look at me and said in a plea that began to tear *me* in two, "Please, Mom. I am begging you. Let me see her. *She is my sister.*"

I nodded, and she stood up and left me.

When Dan came into the room to get dressed, I told him what Katie had said to me. I told him I agreed to let her see the baby. He looked up from what he was doing but did not look at me.

"Are you sure that's wise?" he said.

"Dan, she begged me."

He sighed.

"I think it will be more than she can handle," he said.

"I agree it will be hard, Dan," I said, "but I don't think she will ever forgive us if we don't let her. *That* will be more than any of us can handle."

He was quiet for a moment.

"When it's all over, I'll bring her."

16

What stands out above all the aspects of that day of birth is not the pain, though there was plenty of that, and not the waiting, though it seemed to take forever. What rests just on the edge of this present moment is an overwhelming feeling of emptiness, like I had been completely poured out. When she slipped out of my body, I instantly felt naked and unnamed— like I was the one who had been born, not the one who had just given birth.

It was like the timeline of my existence—the one that began December 1, 1948—stopped and a new one commenced. I felt young and old at the same time, like I knew everything and I knew nothing.

I felt empty—not in an aching way—that is, not in the way I thought I would. I felt raw. Exposed. As tender and weak as a new blade of grass.

On Sunday, when I awoke with labor pains, I was still in my old, full life. The day ticked by slowly, much too slowly, and tried everyone's patience. My mom was at our house by noon, and Rosemary and Ed arrived an hour later. I was still at home, pacing the rooms, trying to speed up the contractions that never seemed to settle into a routine. Even though my due date was a week away, the hospital wanted to see me when the contractions were five minutes apart. By five o'clock everyone was hungry, bored, and agitated. I had no appetite, but my mom made spaghetti for everyone. I went for a long walk.

When I returned, I went to the kitchen for a glass of water. As I stood there sipping it, the contractions slipped into a quickened rhythm. I waited half an hour before telling anyone. When I finally told Dan, the contractions were four minutes apart, and we got ready to leave for the hospital. Nick and Becky came and got Katie and Spence. They took along things to stay the night just in case. Katie hugged me goodbye and whispered to me, "You promised," as though I might forget.

"See you soon," I said.

It was very strange watching my family stare after me as I was ushered into a labor and delivery room. I suppose my mom and Rosemary were especially wishing I would change my mind and allow them to join me. Dan would have come with me in a heartbeat if I had asked him. But I knew he would have only done it for me and wouldn't have enjoyed a moment of it.

"You send someone out for me if you change your mind, Claire," my mother called after me.

I gave her the thumbs-up sign. I knew I wouldn't change my mind. This was going to be my grand moment alone with my daughter. I would share it with no one.

The two nurses assigned to my care were polite but aghast at my refusal to have anyone in the room with me. Twice they encouraged me to at least let my husband come in.

In between contractions and while they were both in the room I said, "Look, I was assaulted. This is not my husband's child. The couple in the waiting room are adopting this baby. And I want to be alone."

Then I was thrown into a spasm of pain that left me dizzy, and I shut my eyes, missing their reaction. When I opened my eyes after the pain subsided, I was alone in the room.

For the next few hours I labored, half-sitting, half-lying; working out the greatest and most mystifying of human phenomena. Every so often, a nurse would come and check on my progress, ask me if I wanted something for the pain—which I did not—and offer me a word of encouragement. I saw Dr. Whitestone once, around ten o'clock. He told me it might be a while.

It was a few minutes after midnight when I sensed that the pain was changing, that labor was shifting rapidly into delivery. I could feel the urgency of my body to grant my daughter her freedom.

"I have to push," I said through my teeth.

"It's way too soon, Mrs. Holland," one of my nurses said, and lifted the sheet draped over my legs. Then her voice doubled in decibels as she yelled to the other nurse. "Oh, good heavens! Wendy, she's crowning! Mrs. Holland, don't push yet!"

The nurse who had yelled grabbed a stool on wheels and tried to pull out surgical gloves from a box at the same time. She couldn't do it. The gloves wouldn't come and the stool scooted past me. I heard the other nurse yell for someone to get Dr. Whitestone.

"Don't push! Don't push!" the first nurse was saying as the other one hurriedly wheeled an infant warmer into the room. But I could not stop this child from coming.

The fluttering princess began to slip from me into my own hands as I reached down and held her head.

"Don't touch the baby, Mrs. Holland!" cried the one nurse who at last had her gloves on.

What a stupid thing to say, I thought, ignoring her. *I cannot harm her. I am her mother.* Another contraction came and I felt my hands being shooed away from my daughter's head as the rest of her body glided into the world of light and shadows.

For the first few seconds after the birth, there was such a flurry of activity it nearly seemed comical. A third nurse had joined us, and all three were shouting instructions to one another. Then Dr. Whitestone rushed into the room, and there was more chatter. Then the baby began to squeal, and that became the only sound I heard.

"I want to hold her," I said when the chaos subsided.

The baby was soon wrapped in a blanket and placed in my arms.

"What are they going to name her?" one of the nurses said to me as she looked at the tiny infant in my arms.

"I don't know," I said, because at that moment I didn't.

I held her for several minutes while Dr. Whitestone delivered the placenta and made me otherwise presentable.

I said nothing as I looked at my baby, not wanting another soul to know what I would say to this child. So I talked to her with my eyes.

She in turn gazed at me, hearing every word, it seemed. The little stocking cap they placed on her head popped off, and I saw a head of dark hair that was as smooth and fine as silk. Katie and Spence had golden halos of blond hair at birth. This child looked nothing like them.

She blinked at me as if she knew I had noticed.

The nurses took her then to measure her and put an anklet on her, putting my last name on it. I guess in the eyes of the law, she was still mine. But I was glad they did all this in the same room I was in. It had not been this way in 1973 when Katie was born.

They handed her back to me and said immediate family could come take a quick peek before I went to a regular room and the baby went to the nursery for a little while.

"Everyone out there is immediate family," I said.

"How about two at a time, then?" the nurse said. "And just for a few minutes."

I asked if she would tell my mom and Dan they could come first.

A few minutes later my mom came alone.

"Dan wants to wait and see her when he brings Katie. He just left to go get her," my mom said. "Katie has been calling, wanting to know, Claire. I don't think she will be able to sleep tonight until she sees her."

My mom had reached my side and leaned down to look at her granddaughter. She pulled the stocking cap off, and I saw her eyes widen.

"She doesn't look much like Katie and Spencer, does she?" I said.

My mom didn't say anything at first. She looked like she had just remembered something that filled her with joy and yet also left her feeling sad.

"No, she doesn't. She looks like Matthew."

Rosemary and Ed could not control their tears when they came in next. I lifted the baby to them as I expected I should, but

Rosemary said she could wait. She came to me and, as best she could, hugged me, though I was sitting upright in bed.

"It's all right, Rosemary. You can hold her," I said. "I think you should."

She hesitated and then reached down, but she didn't take the baby from me. She entwined her arms with mine and bent her face close to me.

"Let's just hold her together for a few minutes."

Ed came and stood next to us, kissing first Rosemary on the forehead and then me. Then he placed his hand on the baby's head as he led us in a prayer of blessing. I don't remember what he said, but I do remember thinking everyone's life should start out that way.

When he was done, I was aware that my cheeks were wet.

"What will you name her?" I said, wiping them with a free hand.

"We'd like to name her after my mom, actually," Rosemary said, resting her head next to mine. "Her name was Lara."

I loved the way the name rolled off Rosemary's tongue. *Lara.* It rhymed with the "star" if you added the "a" at the end. It sounded like music.

"That's so beautiful," I said.

Rosemary smiled. "My mother was a remarkable woman. I wish you could have known her."

"Do you have a middle name for her?" I asked.

Rosemary hesitated for a moment, not because she had forgotten the name or had decided to suddenly come up with one. I think she was gauging what my reaction would be because she didn't want to cause me any additional heartache. She must have judged me wisely, for when I heard it, I felt peace, not pain.

"Claire," she said.

By the time Dan arrived with Katie it was after one o'clock in the morning. I had been shown to a room of my own, but I was not in the bed they had prepared for me. Instead, I was sitting with my mom in the open waiting area by the nursery. Ed and Rosemary were at the huge plate-glass window watching Lara being poked, bathed, and diapered.

Dan and Katie's footsteps were the only sound in the hall as they made their way to me, both of them glancing at the window as they walked for a glimpse of the baby. I could see Katie was torn between wanting to come to me and wanting to head straight for the window. I decided to stand up and join her so she wouldn't have to choose. I winced as I rose, and my mom reached out to steady me as she got up also.

Dan enveloped me in his arms, and I could sense he was feeling many other things besides relief that it was over and I was safe. He held me tight.

I was still coming to terms with the raw emptiness I felt and broke away from him first. His touch was too much for me at that moment. I felt as fragile as crystal.

I led him to the window where Katie was and put my arm around her shoulder. Rosemary was next to her and she had an arm around Katie's waist.

The neonatal nurse taking care of Lara noticed the audience at the window and smiled. Then she quickly finished, wrapped Lara in a receiving blanket, and walked over to the window. She held her up for us. Lara blinked at the overhead lights.

"Her hair is so dark," Katie said softly.

Dan, I think, noticed this too. I was looking at him when the nurse brought Lara to the window, and I saw a wave of needed assurance wash over him: There had been no quirky twist of fate, no reversal of what had been done to Dan's body. There didn't seem to be any way that little girl could be biologically his.

We stood there for probably half an hour before my mom convinced me to go back to my room and the rest of us to go home and get some sleep.

"You'll be so tired tomorrow," I said to Katie as I hugged her goodbye.

"It *is* tomorrow," she said. "Besides, there's no school. It's Memorial Day."

Memorial Day.

Even if I wanted to try and forget everything that had happened to me those nine months of my life, I knew it would be impossible. Lara had been born on Memorial Day.

I would never be able to forget.

And I don't think I'm meant to.

I left the hospital at noon. But I did not go home.

I made the spontaneous decision to spend a week recuperating with my mom and Aunt Elizabeth in Saint Cloud. I didn't want to go back to my house. I didn't want to sleep in it or eat in it or be in it. I had been given a fresh start. I wasn't about to destroy it by plunging into the dregs of my old life.

There wasn't much left to do there. The movers were coming on Wednesday anyway.

I asked Katie if she wanted to come with me when she, Spencer, and Dan came for me that morning. She asked to hold Lara for a while when the two of us were alone in my room. Spencer—after we had asked him if he wanted to—had taken one casual but contented look at Lara and then announced he wanted to see the cafeteria.

"I would miss the last week of school," Katie said, holding Lara close to her heart and not taking her eyes off her.

"I think that would be okay," I said with a smile. "I don't think anyone will make you repeat sixth grade if you miss the last week."

She was thoughtful for a moment.

"I have to be there. I have to say goodbye to my friends," she said, still not looking at me.

"I see," I replied.

"Don't you have friends to say goodbye to?" she asked. I think she wanted me to know this move was going to be harder for her than it would be for me. She knew I was a bit of a loner. Both Dan and I were. It was one of the things I planned to change about my new life.

"I'm sorry you have to say goodbye to your friends, Kate. I really am," I said, not really answering her question. "I want you to know we can have them down to the farm as often as you want this summer. They can even stay for a few days or a week. You know, Dad thought maybe you and he could start looking for a horse right away. Maybe Ashley or Lisa would like to come down and help you find one."

She just nodded her head without raising it to look at me.

"Can I be alone with her for a little bit?" she said.

This was a request that frightened me, yet I knew from where in her heart the desire had sprung. I knew what it was like to want to be alone with Lara.

"Sure," I said and rose to leave. "Kate, you *do* understand why we're doing this?" I said as I turned to go. "You understand why Ed and Rosemary are adopting her?"

She kept her eyes on Lara while I waited for her answer.

"I understand your reasons," she said and then lifted her face to look at me. "But I don't agree with you."

She looked back down at Lara, and I left her because I didn't know what to say in response.

There was no medical reason for Lara to remain in the hospital another day. I signed for her release. I hated doing what we had to do next, but I did not want to prolong it either. Technically, I was under no obligation to hand over my infant daughter until seventy-two hours after her birth. But I didn't want to wait that long.

It didn't seem right to say goodbye to Lara and Ed and Rosemary in the hospital parking lot, and I didn't want to go to the house.

In the end Dan did an amazing thing. He loaned me our special park in Saint Paul for my farewell to my old life and my new daughter.

Rosemary and Ed followed us across the river in their own car. They offered to let us borrow the infant seat they had bought for Lara so she and Katie could ride together with Dan, my mom, and me. Spence wanted to ride with Ed and Rosemary. We let him.

The park was crisp and green and full of new things—as beautiful as it was that autumn day Dan and I had come there to set in motion this plan that would reshape all of our lives, but it was an altogether different kind of beauty.

Katie gently removed a sleeping Lara from her infant seat and carried her to the quiet place by the river that Dan had chosen. We gathered in a circle. A few teenagers were playing Frisbee nearby. They stared. I didn't care.

We joined hands, except for Kate, who still held the baby. Ed and Dan put their arms around her.

Ed began to pray.

I don't know why I can never remember Ed's prayers. The few that I have heard have left me breathless, including that one. I was glad Katie was there to hear it. At least I hope she heard it.

When he was done, he and Rosemary backed away and gave us a few moments alone. Dan and Spencer both kissed Lara's forehead, Spencer following Dan's lead. It surprised me that Dan did that. I asked him about it later.

"She is half yours," he had said.

Katie was crying as she handed Lara to me, and together we walked over to Ed and Rosemary. I kissed my little girl and placed her in Rosemary's arms.

"You know you are welcome to be as much a part of her life as you want," Rosemary said, tears streaming down her face. "I will send you pictures; I will send you anything you want. Whenever we come home on furlough, we will come visit you, or we can send Lara to you alone when she's older. Just tell us what you want, Claire."

I want to be free is what I thought. *That's what I want.* But I did not say this.

"I don't think I want to say goodbye to her more than once," I whispered. "It would kill me a little more every time, and I have to live."

"They should just take her and go," Katie said softly, surprising me. "I don't want to see her anymore."

"You let us know if you ever change your mind," Ed said gently.

I nodded.

Katie placed her hand on Lara's head and rested it there for a moment, then she turned and walked past Dan and Spence and got into our van.

I leaned down and brushed my cheek against Lara's. It was softer than down. She didn't look like me. She didn't look like Kate or Spencer. I was glad she didn't.

"When we have the court hearing to make this final," I said, tucking Lara's blanket around her legs, "please don't bring her."

Ed and Rosemary promised they would not.

Lara slept through the exchange. She was as much unaware of the moment she passed from my life into Ed and Rosemary's as I was aware of it. It was a moment that scraped my newness like a razor.

I could not help but flinch as they drove away.

$\sim\quad\sim\quad\sim$

The following day, I left Dan, Katie, and Spence in Minneapolis and drove with my mom back to Saint Cloud, back to the place where I grew up. Back to the place where I had flown for cover once before, though I cannot remember it.

Elizabeth's motor home was spacious enough for the three of us, but the closeness of the walls began suffocating me within moments of our arrival. My mother was quick to pick up on this. The motor home was parked in the driveway of the house where Gene's funeral reception had been held, so my mom hastily made arrangements for me to stay inside the house with Leo and Margaret Talbot. I remembered them vaguely from my childhood as being good friends of my aunt and uncle, but they seemed like strangers to me, even after having spent a day with them the month before when my uncle died.

I liked it that way. I liked it that they barely knew me and I barely knew them.

Dan had asked me to call him when we got there, which I did. I talked with Spencer for a little while and with Katie for only a few minutes.

When Dan got back on the phone, he asked how I was doing. Did I want him to come get me?

I didn't know how to say that if he came right then, I would come, and if he didn't, I wouldn't care. The truth was, nothing seemed right. Being in that strange house didn't seem right and going back to Minneapolis didn't seem right, even if we did stay in a hotel instead of at the house.

"I'll be all right. Eventually." I said to him. I figured that much was probably true.

I couldn't sleep when I finally went to bed. I was sore physically and emotionally, and I was restless. I got up.

The house was dark, and the Talbots were fast asleep as I made my way downstairs into their living room, which seemed strange and uninviting to me.

I went into the kitchen and to a back door, which led to a screened porch. Pale cushions on a set of wicker furniture glowed like pearls in the moonlight. I sat down on one of the chairs, and it squeaked a greeting.

I didn't have my Bible with me, and there was no light, so I couldn't escape into the Psalms like I suddenly wanted to do.

I was alone with my pain and my God. Both overwhelmed me.

For the first time since I had been attacked and left for dead, since I learned I was pregnant and knew we could not keep the child, I sank to my knees in supplication.

I suppose I had been afraid to be completely and brutally honest with God, to truly lay my heart bare before Him in my own words, because I knew it would reveal to me my displeasure with Him. And that scared me to death. I didn't want to acknowledge that I was mad at the God of the universe.

And I was deeply afraid to admit I had grown to hate Philip Wells for what he did to me, what he had done to my marriage, and how he had come between Katie and me.

I don't know how long I cried out to God. I just know that I awoke at six o'clock on the sunroom floor stiff, sore, and utterly drained. I thought I had been emptied before, in those hours after Lara was born, but that emptying had only been at surface level. During the night of prayer I had gone deeper. I had poured out the last ounce of my tortured being.

I felt exhausted and refreshed at the same time. It seemed like something untouched and unblemished was beckoning me after the long night of sorrows. I stepped out of the porch and onto the backyard lawn, which was wet with morning dew. The cool wetness sent a shock through me, and I felt an even sharper sense of rawness than I had before. Night was slipping away, birds were beginning to sing, and the stars were fading into the approaching light.

I was no longer in the abyss. I was on the threshold of something white, blank, and new. The journey had ended. It was finished.

The dawn was breaking free all around me. In every direction I looked, everything looked new. I watched in silence as the sun peeled back the night and then broke across a cloudless, blue sky.

A cloudless, blue sky.

The new day had begun.

PART TWO

Kate

18

$\mathcal{S}$ ometimes when the house is quiet, when there's no sound except for the ticking of the grandfather clock in the hall, when Michael is so still next to me that it feels like I am alone in our bed, I sneak outside—careful not to make any noises that would awaken Olivia or Bennett from their childish dreams— and resume my ongoing rendezvous with the night sky.

If it's a wintry night, I wrap myself in one of Grandma's quilts. If it's an airless night in July, I slip out in only a thin nightgown. Draped or not, I take my place on the north side of the porch and watch the stars shimmer in their appointed places. And I imagine I'm watching that same sky from the railing of a New York high rise or from a bungalow porch on a Carolina beach or from a cabin deck in the damp woods of the Pacific Northwest.

I stay for as short as a minute or as long as it takes for dawn to find me and chase me back to my bed. When the sun comes up, the sky no longer holds my interest. It no longer beckons me to imagine any life other than the one I am living.

I can paint almost anything except the sky at night. I have tried. The depth of the velvet expanse always eludes my brush and my brain. I simply cannot capture starlight on any canvas.

On those nights when I escape to the porch at midnight, I absorb the image as one memorizing lines for a play, and in the morning, after Olivia and Michael are at school and while Bennett watches cartoons or pesters my mother at our shop, I try to transpose the image onto my easel. I just haven't been able to duplicate it.

And I can't seem to stop wondering what it must be like to look at that same unharnessed, starlit sky from somewhere else, though I am learning not to dwell on that.

It's not that I am unhappy with my life. I am happy. But the sheer vastness of the heavens suggests—every time I look at it—that the world is bigger than what I have seen of it.

When I was a little girl—when we still lived in Minneapolis—I used to dream that one day I would live in New York City or San Francisco and wear gloves and hats that matched and be married to a concert pianist who would make little old ladies weep when he played, and we would have twin girls we would name Kristin and Megan. I never pictured myself staying in Minnesota, certainly never imagined living on an acreage that disappears into drifts every time it snows, and it never crossed my mind that I would go into business with my mother.

I've never been to New York or San Francisco. I own no dress gloves. The only hats I wear are made of polar fleece. My husband teaches agricultural science at the high school we both graduated from.

Michael can't read a note of music, but I love him anyway.

We don't have twin daughters, but I'm crazy about Olivia and Bennett, the kids we *do* have.

And I don't mind being in business with my mom. We're actually doing quite well. Between her knack for books and literature, my talents as an artist, and Michael's mom, Nicole's flair for culinary masterpieces, we have a highly successful book, coffee, and art shop.

Minnesota has always been my home, so I cannot truly miss living in other places, because I have lived nowhere else.

I have a beautiful home. A husband who loves me. Two amazingly wonderful kids. A successful business. It doesn't seem thinkable that I could be discontent. And yet I am haunted by the night sky. And by all the possibilities it conjures in my mind.

～ ～ ～

It started long before I married Michael.

I suppose my attraction to the stars began when we moved from Minneapolis to the country when I was twelve and I really saw the night sky for the first time, completely unpolluted by city lights. It was so dark and heavy with stars that I felt for the first time that the universe above me was bigger and grander than the world surrounding me. Until then the world only seemed huge and expansive to my right and left and in front of me. That first night, when I really saw the heavens for the first time, I realized it stretched endlessly *above* me.

I was getting my first glimpse of God as bigger than I had imagined.

That first year in our new home in Blue Prairie was unremarkable. It was neither good nor bad. My parents assured me I would make new friends, and I did. They assured me I would love living on a hobby farm and getting my own horse, which I did. They assured me that time would heal our collective wounds, that the pain over losing Lara, my half-sister, would diminish a little more each day.

And I suppose it did.

For my brother, Spencer, who was seven back then, that pain diminished so easily and quickly that within a year's time he quite forgot why we moved there. He barely remembered that Mom had been attacked and that she had borne a baby that wasn't truly ours.

My father never said Lara's name again until by circumstance sixteen years later he had to. I know he felt badly for my mom; he often spent quiet moments holding her when she gave in to the temptation to grieve over the child she had given away. They both tried to conceal those moments, but they couldn't hide them all from me. I saw my mother's suffering. She was terrible at hiding it. And I honestly don't know when the pain of losing Lara diminished into something my mother could live with. Because the whole thing—the attack, the pregnancy, the adoption, Lara, her adoptive parents—all of it became a great mass called That Which We Do Not Discuss.

Those few occasions when I did bring up Lara's name or even her adoptive parents, Ed and Rosemary Prentiss, my parents would nervously try to shift the conversation away from what was to what is. I don't know how many times I heard them say they did what was best for everyone, but I got ridiculously tired of hearing it every time I mentioned my sister's name. I wasn't asking them to defend their actions; I just wanted someone to talk with me about how I was feeling.

There was no friend to bounce anything off of. My new friends didn't know my mother just had a baby and gave it up for adoption, and I was told that's how it should stay. My old friends knew, but I saw them so infrequently in the beginning and then not at all.

Occasionally, I would call and unload on my grandparents in Ann Arbor. I figured they would understand since Lara was their granddaughter. I spent a couple of weeks with them the following summer and then every summer after that. They did indeed understand, but they never quite knew what to say. I think they were hoping I would outgrow my curiosity about Lara and leave the whole matter alone.

The older I got, the more I realized pretending Lara didn't exist was my parents' and my grandparents' way of not reopening old wounds. It took a few years, but I eventually fell into pretending as smoothly as they did.

As far as I knew growing up, my parents never spoke again to Ed and Rosemary after the adoption was final. The Prentisses left for Ecuador when Lara was five months old. They sent us a postcard with their new address before they left just in case my parents changed their minds about keeping in touch. When I was doing my household chores one day, I found the postcard in the upstairs bathroom trash, folded neatly and shoved to the bottom. I took it out and placed it in my diary where it stayed between pages eighty-two and eighty-three for more than a year.

One day, when I was feeling particularly brave and daring and very much fourteen, I wrote to the Prentisses in Ecuador and asked about Lara. I told them to use my friend Carly's address to write me back because I didn't know if my parents would like my writing to them. I told Carly the Prentisses were friends that had a falling out with my parents, but that I still liked them. I asked Rosemary to send me a picture of Lara, who would have been two then.

Rosemary's letter arrived at Carly's house about a month later. Carly called me as soon as I got off the bus to tell me the letter had arrived, and I had to beg and cajole my mom into taking me back into town so Carly and I could "study together."

I don't recall everything Rosemary said in her letter, I do remember feeling guilty after reading it for going behind my parents' back in writing to her, and yet none of Rosemary's words were accusatory.

She did not send a picture, but she did describe Lara to me in such specific detail that it may as well have been a picture. She also told me what a good daughter Lara was, so eager to please, so easy to correct, so willing to be taught. Right about there is when I began to feel bad. Rosemary also told me that she prayed for me and my family every day and that I could do the same for her and Ed and Lara but that I should not write again unless my parents gave their blessing. She concluded by telling me that someday we would all meet again, if not here on earth, then surely in heaven, and then Lara and I would truly be sisters in every sense of the word.

I kept that letter for a long time, stuffed in my Bible between the pages of Hosea—as safe a place to hide something as any, I thought.

And I did what Rosemary said. I prayed for them. For a while. And I never wrote them again without my parents' blessing, which, of course, means I never wrote them again at all.

I met Michael the first day we moved to Blue Prairie. He was fifteen and incredibly tall and handsome. I fell for him right then and there, even though I was only twelve and a half. My dad's new partner at the veterinary clinic, Wes Gerrity, and his wife, Nicole, who would be my mom's business partner several years before she was my mother-in-law, came with a pan of lasagna the day we moved in. They also brought Michael and Andrew, their sons. Andrew was ten, and though Spencer was three years younger, they found plenty to do together, leaving Michael to me whenever our parents got together, which was often.

I don't know when he fell in love with me. I am sure it was not the day we moved in. But by the time he graduated from high school three years later, we had secretly betrothed ourselves to each other.

The day he left for South Dakota to go to college, my mom sat down with me and told me that a lot could happen while Michael was away at college, that it might be wise if I dated other people. I was only a sophomore; I had my best high school years ahead of me, she said. And Michael would be facing new situations of his own.

I knew she meant well, but I was mad at her for weeks after that. She was suggesting Michael would want to date other girls. Unthinkable!

As it turned out, Michael did date other girls. That spring, in his second semester of college, he broke up with me, telling me we needed time to make sure we were meant to be together. That summer when he came home to work for our fathers at the vet clinic, he told me he had made a mistake, that I was the only one for him. Would I take him back?

I made him wait a week before I told him "yes."

That was the end of my dream of big city life, matching hats and gloves, and a pianist husband. When I graduated in 1992, I went to college in South Dakota too, only because Michael was there and it was his senior year. I took a year's worth of generals, and then we got married. He came back to Blue Prairie to teach ag at the high school. And I came back with him, of course.

By then, my mom and Nicole had this great little business going. Their little shop started out as an idea for a small used-book store that my mom wanted to open. She wanted to call it Tennyson's Table. She has always been crazy about Tennyson.

She bought this little nineteenth-century writing table at an estate sale once, and a box of old books came with it. By the time she came home with her purchases, she already had this idea in her mind.

The table wasn't really Alfred, Lord Tennyson's but it looked like it could have been. It was old enough to have been his, was English, and was definitely a writing table. My mom started buying old and antiquated books everywhere she went, and just about the time she was ready to open her bookshop, Nicole offered to go in with her and make it a book and coffee shop. Nicole is an incredible cook, can make anything from scratch, and never needs a recipe. They bought and cleaned out an old Victorian house right next to Blue Prairie's renowned twin bed-and-breakfast inns and opened Tennyson's Table on August 5, 1989, which would have been the celebrated poet's one-hundred-and-eightieth birthday.

They placed the writing table in a bay window overlooking a butterfly garden that Nicole dreamed up. Anyone who wants to use the table to write at can do so, and they get all the coffee they want for free. But they have to be writing something to qualify, even if it's just a letter to a friend. It was a great idea, my mom's, of course—ever the teacher. All the downstairs rooms except for the kitchen and formal dining room are devoted to rare, old, or out-of-print books. The upstairs bedrooms were turned into rooms for book clubs and writing groups to meet. When I was a senior in high school, there were four clubs meeting. There are ten these days. Nicole also started offering cooking and gardening classes.

When Michael and I returned to Blue Prairie in 1993 and set up our own house, I was a little overwhelmed with my new life as a wife with no other dreams to catch. It was actually Nicole who, after watching me mess around with cheap watercolors, encouraged me to take art classes at the state college an hour's drive away.

I joined my mom and Nicole as a third partner in Tennyson's Table two years later. My dad, my father-in-law, Michael, and Andrew added a studio at the back of the shop for me to paint in and teach painting. We began to decorate the walls of Tennyson's Table with my watercolor paintings and an occasional chalk or charcoal piece. As they sell, I paint more.

Olivia, our daughter, was born in 1996, followed by Bennett, our son, in 1999.

Sometimes on those nights when I was in awe of the enigmatic night sky, I felt a little guilty over feeling restless when I had so much. I seemed to already have more than I deserved. And then I'd think to myself, *But there are no paintings of a starry night on the walls of Tennyson's Table. Something is missing.*

For a long time I thought I knew what it was, but I was wrong.

I am not easily surprised.

I knew when I met Michael—even at the age of twelve—that I was going to marry him. I was not surprised to realize this, but I was smart enough to know it would certainly have surprised everyone else, especially my parents, so I told no one. Naturally when Michael broke up with me that first year he went away to college, I honestly thought something terrible had rocked the universe. It wasn't supposed to be this way. I was supposed to marry Michael.

Naturally everyone thought my initial shock was the visible sign of a typical, broken teenage heart. I didn't feel like my heart was broken. It was more like something was wrong, not something was shattered. The way it appeared couldn't possibly be the way it was.

Since I grew up keeping most of my thoughts and feelings to myself, I didn't share this with anyone—certainly not with my mom, who thought I was "moody." That was the exact word she used one day when she thought I wasn't listening to her and my grandmother talking about me.

So while my family eyed me carefully and walked around on eggshells after Michael's announcement, I eventually shook off the disappointment and just stepped wherever I pleased. I knew he would come back to me. And he did.

I am not easily surprised because I don't participate in surprises. You'd be amazed how few surprises come your way when you choose not to take part in them.

I don't participate in them because I don't like not knowing what is reasonable for me to know. Surprises are surprises because you suddenly learn something you should have already known. You either should have been told it, or you should have guessed it. Surprises are fine for people who like toying with the unknown, but I don't care for intrigue.

I thought it was rather silly that my doctor wanted to keep me from knowing the sexes of my unborn children, like I would love them more if I was surprised by their gender. Or that I would love them less, if that were possible. Either way, I resented the inference. Michael didn't care, so we found out both times.

I don't like being astonished. It makes me feel weak, and I don't like feeling weak. Michael says it's because I'm a typical, take-charge firstborn who must be in control of everything, which, he is always quick to add, he finds very alluring.

I don't think I am a control freak. I don't demand that I be the potter. I'm okay with being clay. I just don't want to be molded into something in secret. I don't want to be surprised by anything, least of all by who I am.

Which is why, about a year ago, I found myself disagreeably stunned by Rosemary's letter.

I know I shouldn't have opened it. I so wish I hadn't. But I did.

My parents and in-laws had been gone for four days to an equine endoscopy conference in Atlanta. They were due back on the fifth day, and I had sole responsibility for the Table while they were gone. It was a little chaotic on Monday, the first day. The cappuccino machines were acting up, and neither I nor our hired help, Trish, knew how to straighten them out. The pastries Nicole had made in advance took longer to thaw than we thought, and the man who was supposed to deliver our fruit juices at eight o'clock that first morning didn't show up until noon.

But by the time Thursday rolled around, Trish and I had settled into a routine. I hadn't painted a thing all week, but I expected that would happen.

That particular morning, I dropped Bennett off at our church's daycare center and drove Olivia to school before going to the post office to get the mail for the shop as well as our personal mail and my parents' mail.

There was a lot in all three boxes, and I struggled to get back out to my car without losing any of it. At the Table, the morning crowd was far bigger than usual, and Trish and Ellie, a morning-only worker, were struggling to fill all the orders. I dropped the mail into a box behind the cash register and then helped them until almost noon. I spent the rest of the afternoon looking on the Internet for books my mom was interested in and watching her eBay accounts where she acquired and sold most of her books. When school got out, I called Michael to remind him that Olivia had an after-school activity that day and wouldn't be walking over to the high school side until four o'clock. I must have sounded a little frazzled, because he offered to pick up Bennett for me so I could stay a little later if I wanted to.

Just when I was about to take care of the mail, Seth, Michael's seventeen-year-old cousin, walked into the shop with a look on his face that I had seen many times before. Seth, Nicole's sister's child, had been living with Wes and Nicole for several months as they attempted to redirect his life and get away from the destructive crowd he was running around with in Minneapolis. He's an alcoholic, among other things, and desperately in need of guidance. For some reason he took to me and liked talking with me. He was staying with us while Wes and Nicole were gone, but I still didn't expect to see him at the shop that afternoon. Most days I didn't mind his spontaneous visits. But that day I was so busy, and yet he looked so dejected.

In spite of my workload, I mixed up two mochas, and we headed to the quietest corner of my studio where big south-facing windows let in the calming, afternoon sun. There were only two weeks left in the school year, and Seth was afraid he was going to fail all his classes, wouldn't be able to pass the eleventh grade, and was going to be stuck in high school forever.

It was a conversation we'd had before.

It was close to five o'clock before he felt energized enough to go home to my house and work on his current assignments. I promised I would call the school to see if he could work on completing his junior requirements during the summer break. I would help him. I volunteered my mother's time too. My mom had already told Seth on a number of occasions that she would help him with his English classes.

When he finally left, I told him to tell Michael I would be a little late, that I needed to finish a few things. The shop had already closed at four o'clock, and the place was calm and quiet when Seth left and I locked the door behind him. I finished tracking my mom's eBay accounts for that day and counted the day's receipts. I left a note upstairs for the Thursday-night book-club leader to call me if they had any trouble with the cappuccino machines, adding that my mom and Nicole were still out of town.

Then I sat down on the floor of the main room with Dickens and Longfellow and Steinbeck all around me and sorted the mail. The three bundles had all merged together in the box under the register, so I began making three new piles on the floor—one for Michael and me, one for my parents, and one for Tennyson's Table.

I was nearly done when I came across the letter in the pale blue envelope. It was addressed to my mother: Claire Holland, General Delivery, Blue Prairie. My eyes immediately traveled to the return address, and as they did, the room and everything around me seemed to start spinning. Or to cease spinning. Everything seemed different.

In the left-hand corner, on a small, white, return-address label with a black monogrammed letter P, was a name I had not seen printed or heard with my ears in more than a dozen years:

Rosemary Prentiss

I probably looked quite strange, sitting there on the floor with three piles of mail around me, holding an envelope and staring at it as if I were willing it to speak to me. I can't adequately describe how I felt. I certainly felt surprised, a feeling I hated. I also felt betrayed. If Rosemary was indeed breaking her vow of silence, she ought to have broken it with me. I was the only one who had ever tried to contact her, not my mother. At least I thought I was the only one. What if she and my mother had secretly been in contact all these years?

The letter had come from Two Harbors. I remembered suddenly that the Prentisses had family near Duluth, that they had stayed there when they were home from Ecuador the year Lara was born. Two Harbors was a twenty-five minute drive from Duluth.

Why was Rosemary writing my mother? She had been asked not to. Maybe she ought not have. Maybe I was destined to intercept the letter so my mother would never have to see it. This was ridiculous, of course, but I was already trying to rationalize why I should open my mother's letter and read what Rosemary had to say.

I stood up with the letter and walked into the dining room where we had several tables set up for customers. I sat down at one of them, placed the letter on the linen cloth, and stared at it.

I knew I would regret it, but I also knew my mother would forgive me.

I opened the letter and read it.

May 12, 2002

Dear Claire,

I am writing to you after having prayed as earnestly as I have ever prayed about anything. I believe God has directed me to write to you, but if I have misunderstood His prompting, please forgive me. I would never intentionally hurt you, my dear sister.

I am dying, Claire. Ed has already been gone for four years. He had a heart attack in 1998 when we were still in Ecuador. He survived it, but when we came home a month later, he had another one. This one took him home to Jesus. Lara and I have been living in Ed's mother's house in Two Harbors since then.

I was diagnosed with breast cancer last year. I have had surgery twice, but it keeps coming back. The cancer has now settled into my bones, and no radiation or chemotherapy can stop it now. My doctor doesn't expect I will live to see another autumn.

Claire, you gave Lara to me when your life was at its darkest moment. I am now giving her back to you at mine, if you will take her. She has just one year left of high school as she is a grade ahead of other kids her age. But besides needing a home for her last year of high school, she needs a family.

There are kind people here in Two Harbors who have offered to take her in, but when I go, I want her to have a family for the rest of her life, not just friends to see her through one phase of it. My brother in Florida, whom Lara has never met, said he would take her if need be, but he is unmarried, is not a Christian, and has made it clear he is not thrilled with taking Lara. He is the only family I have left.

I know how hard it was for you to give Lara up those many years ago. I now feel the same way. It pains me to leave her. I know you loved her once. I pray that you still do, because I want her to be with you and Dan.

Again, please, please forgive me if I have erred in writing to you. If I have, you do not need to write me back. I will understand.

Your sister in Christ,

Rosemary

I read it a dozen times.

Then I picked up the letter and my own pile of mail and left.

I walked into our two-story farmhouse with our mail in my arms and Rosemary's letter in my jeans pocket. Bennett, my three-year-old, had a bucket of plastic soldiers spread out over the kitchen floor, and six-year-old Olivia was yelling at him to pick them up. Seth had the television on in the family room, the volume up seemingly as high as it would go. A textbook and notepad sat untouched by his side. Michael was nowhere to be seen.

"Where's Daddy?" I said, without even pretending to sound polite.

"In the barn with Muffy," Olivia said. "He told me to tell Bennett to put these soldiers away, and he's not doing it!"

"I'm not!" Bennett yelled. I have no idea what he meant by this. But I wasn't going to try and figure it out.

"Bennett, take the soldiers into the family room instead. Olivia, you can help him," I said, leaving the room before they could argue. I headed outside to the relative quiet of the yard. Bogart, our black Lab, followed me into the barn where I found Michael kneeling by his prized ewe.

"I think she's better today," he said, barely looking at me. "That stuff your dad came across is really making a difference."

"That's good," I said absently.

He looked up then, with those blue-black eyes that I loved.

"Tough day at the shop?" he said.

"Yeah," I said. "You could say that."

"Something happen?" he continued.

I wanted to tell him then. I wanted to tell him about Rosemary's letter, but I dreaded the thought of admitting I opened my mom's mail. Plus, it had been a long time since I told Michael about Lara; we were both still teenagers back then. I wasn't even sure he would remember her.

"I don't know," I said instead, which didn't answer his question, but answered some of mine.

"Well, the folks get home tomorrow, love," he said reassuringly. "You only have one more day flying solo." He stood up then, brushed straw off his jeans, and stepped out of Muffy's pen. "I'll make you supper," he said, slipping his arm around me.

"Hot dogs on the grill, right?" I said, easing into his side.

"My specialty," he replied.

After supper I bathed Bennett, read to Olivia, and put them both to bed. Then I helped Seth with an American History assignment until well after ten o'clock. Exhausted, I climbed the stairs and got ready for bed. I dozed while Michael graded papers and was asleep when he turned off the light. At some point I snapped awake when all was quiet and dark in the house. I looked at the clock on my bedside table. Twelve thirty. I had been asleep for less than two hours, and I felt wide awake.

And I knew why.

Rising from the bed as quietly as I could, I grabbed a robe and Rosemary's letter. I crept downstairs, past Seth, who had fallen asleep on the living room couch, and tiptoed into the kitchen. I stepped out onto the porch and let the familiar night sky envelope me. The moon was full and bright, and I probably could have read Rosemary's letter again by its light if I had wanted to, but I practically had the thing memorized. One line in particular kept replaying itself in my head: *You gave Lara to me when your life was at its darkest moment. I am now giving her back to you at mine, if you will take her.*

If you will take her.

It was something I never dreamed would happen. I had let go of Lara ages ago. In tears and in sorrow I had let her go. I never expected to see her or hear from her ever again. I never for a moment imagined that she would find her way back to me.

It came as a complete and utter surprise.

So of course, I didn't like it.

20

*I*t was a long while before I slipped back into bed, and I awoke the next morning groggy and in a bad mood. Michael, sensing I was having a rough start to my day, took the kids and Seth under his wing, leaving the house for school with all of them in tow. He even dropped Bennett off at daycare for me.

I arrived at Tennyson's Table late. I had wanted to get there in time for the busiest hour of the day, from seven thirty to eight thirty, but it was a quarter to nine before I arrived. Trish said nothing, but I could tell she and Ellie had needed my help.

"I'm sorry," I said as I rushed in.

"It's all right," Trish said, handing me a latte. "Go ahead. You look like you could use it."

"That bad?" I said.

"You've looked better."

Leave it to Trish to be completely honest.

I took the latte into the little office by the main room and sat down to sip it and consider my options.

My parents would be arriving in Minneapolis later that morning. It would take them a little over two hours to drive home. Knowing my mother, she would want to come straight to the shop to see me even though we had communicated by e-mail every morning they had been away except that one.

That meant I had until three o'clock or so to decide what I was going to tell her.

I felt completely awkward praying about what to do since I had blown it so badly by being dishonest in the first place. God would certainly want me to tell the truth.

So what was the truth?

I wanted the truth to be that I was worried for my mother, that I was concerned that a letter from Rosemary—which would certainly be a letter about Lara—would be painful for her to read.

But, actually, the truth was that I was worried about me. I was concerned that something important regarding my sister was taking place and I was going to be in the dark about it. Just like I was when my parents decided to give her away.

That was the truth, even though we never spoke of it to one another. I had been left out of everything that happened to Lara. I had to beg to see her before they gave her away. I wasn't even allowed to have a picture of her.

If God wanted me to be truthful, so be it.

I had opened the letter because I didn't trust my mother.

At noon she called me from the airport.

"We're going to spend a few hours with Spence and Natalie and the baby before we come home," she told me. "Is that okay?"

Like I was the mother.

I didn't care if she wanted to see Spencer, Natalie, and their new baby, but I was all mentally prepared to see her at three o'clock. Now she and Dad wouldn't be home until after five.

"So Wes and Nicole are still with you?" I said.

"They don't mind," Mom said right away. "It's on the way, anyway."

Spencer and Natalie live in Apple Valley where Spencer is a youth pastor at a large church. He and Natalie have been married for two years. Their first child was a baby boy they named Noah.

"Okay. Fine," I said, trying to sound nonchalant. Guess it didn't work.

"What's wrong?" she said.

"Everything's fine, Mom. Really," I said.

"Olivia and Bennett are all right?" she said, probing for more assurance.

"Mom, you have only been gone five days," I said.

"I know, but…but I had this funny feeling when I woke up today that…that something wasn't quite right," she said.

What was I supposed to say to that?

"Mom, the kids are fine, okay?" That was true.

"Well, we'll see you later today," she said after a pause.

"Right," I said. "Drive carefully."

I hung up.

The afternoon dragged by. I went to the school at three to get Olivia and invited her to come back to the shop with me. On the way, we picked up Bennett. When the shop wasn't busy, I liked having my kids with me. Michael had fixed up a room in the basement for them to play in. Sometimes Trish brought her daughter Alex, who was Olivia's age, to play with my kids.

Trish offered to get the place ready for the Friday-night book clubs and writer's group so that I could leave at four. All four upper rooms would be used that night. We had three high school girls running the kitchen and the coffeemakers for the thirty people who would be coming to the Table for Friday club meetings. We also had a jazz coffee bar on Friday nights that began at eight and ended at midnight. Michael and I often liked to come and host those evenings.

But we weren't going to be there that evening. My mom was coming home, and I wanted to talk with her.

I made sure when I left the Table that afternoon that I had Rosemary's letter with me.

My parents pulled into our driveway about six thirty. They had been home already—our acreage is just a few miles away from theirs—and had also dropped off Wes and Nicole, whom we would see the next day for brunch. Nicole's brunches are a Saturday tradition. It's how she tests all the new things she wants to try out at the Table. Nobody likes missing them.

Olivia and Bennett ran out to meet Mom and Dad with Bogart dancing at their heels. I watched as my parents made their way onto the porch where I stood. It's hard to believe my parents are in their midfifties. They both still look like they can take on the world. I was reminded of the time when that was just about what they had to do.

The letter almost felt warm in my pocket.

They had brought pizza from town with them—an unexpected treat—and little gifts for the kids from Atlanta. We sat outside in the May sunshine, and I let Olivia and Bennett have as much of my parents' time and attention as they wanted. Later, my mom helped me get them into bed, and then we headed downstairs. Dad and Michael were watching a baseball game, and I asked my mom if she wanted to join me on the porch.

I suddenly felt very nervous. I was also glad this conversation had not taken place at the bookstore that afternoon, but that we were having it on my front porch at twilight, where the blue sky of the day was melting into the diamond-laced sky of the night.

"Mom, I need to tell you something," I began, instantly getting her attention. "A letter came in the mail for you yesterday. And…I opened it."

"A letter? Who from?" she said, not concerned at all.

I swallowed. "From Rosemary," I said.

She merely blinked at me, like she was waiting for the last name to roll off my lips. "Rosemary Prentiss?" she said softly, like she had been expecting it all along.

"Yes." I said and looked away. "I'm really sorry I opened it, Mom. I just couldn't let it sit there unopened. I just had to read it."

She didn't seem to care at all that I had intruded—and for some dumb reason I wanted her to. "What did she say?" My mother's voice was barely a whisper.

I looked over at her and could see that she had already imagined the worst—that Lara had been killed. I could not bear to have her think that even for a second. "Lara's okay, Mom." I said. "But Rosemary isn't. Here. You should read it for yourself."

I pulled out the letter from my pocket and held it out to her. She just looked at it but didn't take it.

"Read it to me," she said, looking at the letter, not at me.

As I read it, I began to cry, even though I had read it so many times already without shedding a tear. Mom began to cry too. When I was done, neither one of us said anything. I folded the letter, put it in its envelope, and placed it in her hand.

Then a light breeze skipped across the yard, drying our faces as we sat there in silence.

"I don't know what to do," she finally said, shaking her head. And though she said it out loud, I don't really think she was saying it to me. It was like she was saying it to herself. Or to God.

"What am I supposed to do?" she said a few seconds later, like they were two different questions, and I guess they were.

"Oh, God…" she whispered and dropped her head. The letter made a crinkly sound in her hand.

"You don't have to decide anything today, Mom," I said.

She raised her head and looked past me, into the shadowy horizon. "Decide?" she said. "I thought I did that already. I never thought I would be asked to decide again."

"You shouldn't have to," I said, a jab at God, I guess.

"You don't think we should take her?" my mom said, her brow furrowed.

"I don't know what I think," I said after a moment's pause.

"You were the one who wanted to keep her," she said thoughtfully.

"You were the one who said we couldn't," I replied. I didn't mean for it to feel like a barb, but I'm sure it must have. But there was no return volley. My mother just sat there. I began to regret what I'd said. But she had a faraway look in her eyes like she had long since moved on to another thought.

"How can I not take her?" she said.

"You can write Rosemary and tell her you won't," I said.

But I didn't really want her to do that. And she knew it.

Neither of us really knew what we wanted.

It was like being right back where the whole thing started. The only difference was, this time I was in the loop.

〜 〜 〜

By the time the baseball game was over, my mom and I recovered enough to appear to our husbands as if we had merely enjoyed a long, woman-to-woman chat under the stars. She and I agreed to say nothing to anyone about the letter for the moment. She wanted time to think, and she needed to consider what my dad's response would be.

The next two weeks were awkward for us. At the shop we acted as if there were nothing unusual on our minds, but every time our eyes met, we were both reminded of the letter. Sometimes I would catch my mom staring off into space, completely absorbed in thoughts that had nothing to do with old books. At home, I would find myself likewise distracted. Michael asked me on more than one occasion if I was all right. I hated lying to him.

School was let out, and Seth amazingly passed all but one course. It was an algebra class that I really couldn't help him with. But Michael is good in math, so Seth starting coming to the house in the evenings for tutoring so he could pass the class in summer school. Michael had also given Seth a lamb to raise for the upcoming county fair, and Seth couldn't keep it in town where Wes and Nicole lived, so Spock lived in our barn. I think Seth liked having Spock at our place because it gave him reason to come over.

On Friday of the first week in June, my mom came to me in the studio. I was working on a commissioned piece for City Hall. She stood there admiring my rendition of Blue Prairie's main street, saying not a word. I could tell she had something on her mind.

"You've decided something," I said.

"Yes."

"What are you going to do?" I asked, apprehension quickly filling my mind.

"I'm going up there. I want to see her."

I knew my mother would not travel all that way to see Lara and then decide to let her be shipped off to Uncle Unbeliever. She was going up there because she wanted her and just needed to find a way to convince my dad they should take her.

"That means you want to bring her here," I said.

My mom continued to look at the painting.

"I suppose it does," she finally said.

"I want to come with you," I said, expecting her to protest. But she didn't.

"All right," she said. "But I can't tell your dad. Not yet."

"I don't know if that's a good idea, Mom."

"This is just like before," she said to me. "There are no good ideas."

Then she started to walk away.

"I will tell him when the time is right," she said. "I have to see Lara first, or I won't have the courage to ask him."

*T*elling Michael my mom and I were going away for the weekend was easy; she and I had done it a few times before when she wanted to go to outlying estate sales where books were listed on the sale bill. But this trip had nothing to do with Tennyson's Table, and I simply couldn't let Michael think that it did. I didn't feel good about Mom's not being completely honest with Dad, and I felt no compulsion to deceive Michael in the same way.

"There's something my mom wants to do," I told him. "Something I will explain when we get home."

He smiled when I said that, but it was a puzzled smile.

"What are you two up to?" he said.

"I promise I will tell you everything when we come home," I replied.

It must have occurred to him then that my mom was terribly sick and that we were on a journey to get a second opinion.

"Your mom's okay, isn't she?" he said, concern whisking away the smile on his face.

"She's fine," I said quickly. "Really."

"So you're not going to tell me what's in Duluth?" he said.

"It's actually Two Harbors, and I will tell you," I assured him. "When I get home."

~~~

Bennett and Olivia were a little upset about my leaving them for the weekend, but I promised them both a little surprise for helping their daddy take care of things while I was away.

Mom and I left on a Friday morning a little before eleven o'clock on a day that would later blossom into a scorcher. I don't know what my mom told Nicole about our trip. She just told me not to worry about our shop while we were gone, that Nicole had it all under control.

We were on the highway for a little while when I asked Mom if she called Rosemary or made hotel reservations. She told me she had done neither.

"I just want to take this one moment at a time," she said.

"So we're just going to show up at her door?" I said, somewhat nervously.

"Maybe. I don't know," she said, watching the road but clearly distracted.

"Don't you think we should call first?" I asked a few minutes later.

"I don't want any of this to take place by phone. When I see the house, I will decide what to do."

I just left it at that.

We drove a few more minutes in silence, and then I asked her what she had told my dad about where we were going. She didn't answer right away; it was like she was still trying to decide if she did the right thing.

"I told him you and I had a special little mission to accomplish and that I would explain what it was when we got home," she said.

That sounded vaguely familiar.

"Did you tell him we were going to Duluth?" I said.

"We're not going to Duluth. We're going to Two Harbors."

"Okay, did you tell him we were going to Two Harbors?"

She paused.

"Yes."

"You did?"

"Yes, I did."

"What did he say?" I asked.

"He asked if we knew anybody in Two Harbors."

"And you said…"

"I said it didn't matter if we did or didn't, that we were going to stay in a hotel."

So she had answered his question without outright lying to him.

We had just passed the Twin Cities when I realized I had finally been given an incredible opportunity to discuss That Which We Do Not Discuss. We were on our way to see Lara. I could ask anything I wanted, and my mom couldn't possibly ignore it or redirect the conversation. With every mile, we were drawing nearer to Lara, and I had a ton of questions on my mind; some that I had carried with me since the day we moved to Blue Prairie. I had my mother captive in a car for the next two hours. I couldn't let the opportunity pass. There was so much I wanted to know and so much I forgot I wanted to know, until that moment. I hardly knew where to begin.

"Whatever happened to the man who attacked you?" I asked first.

My mom sighed and shrugged her shoulders. "He's sitting in a Stillwater prison cell, I suppose."

"Does he know? About Lara?"

"I don't know. And I really don't care," Mom said, adjusting the rearview mirror, though I am sure it was positioned just fine.

"Do you hate him for what he did?" I asked, getting bolder by the minute.

She didn't answer right away. I guessed she hadn't thought about it in a long time and had to consider how she felt about Philip Wells.

"I used to hate him for his part in giving me a child I wanted and couldn't have," she finally said. "But I don't hate him anymore. I have no feelings whatsoever for him. I don't even know what he looks like."

"You never remembered any of it, did you?" I asked. "You never remembered what happened the night he hurt you."

"That was the one splendid thing God did for me," she said, a little irreverently for her. "He swept away any memory of that awful night. Sometimes I forget to be thankful for that."

I moved on.

"Do you think about Lara? I mean, before this letter, did you ever think about her or wonder about her?" I asked.

My mom glanced at me, a weak smile forming on her lips.

"Of course I did," she said, turning her eyes back to the road. "She was born on Memorial Day, Kate, a day already set aside for remembering."

"Is that the only time you think about her?"

Mom shook her head.

"In the beginning I imagined every milestone. I wondered about her first step and her first tooth and her first day of school. But over the years it became easier not to give in to the desire to imagine. And that made it easier to live with what happened and what we had to do," she said.

As she said this, I remembered sitting by her hospital bed on that long-ago day, Lara in my arms, just twelve hours old. My mother asked me then if I understood why she and my dad were giving Lara up for adoption. I told her I understood her reasons but didn't agree with them. I wondered if that was still how I felt. I really wasn't sure.

"Do you still think you did the right thing?" I asked. "Do you ever wish you had kept her?"

Mom thought for a moment and then answered without looking at me.

"Yes, we did the right thing. And, yes, I wish we had kept her."

In Duluth, we stopped at a Hampton Inn near the shore of Lake Superior and got a room for the next two nights. Mom decided she didn't want to stay in the little town of Two Harbors; I think she wanted to be able to escape from time to time, if need be. Though stiff from the long drive, we got back in the car and headed toward Two Harbors, about twenty-five miles away. I pulled out the map we had made using the Internet, which would lead us to Rosemary's house. It was a little after four thirty in the afternoon when we entered Two Harbor's city limits. The little highway just blended into the town's main thoroughfare. In some ways it looked a lot like Blue Prairie. The red lighthouse on its hill above the North Shore was unlike anything in our little agricultural town. But the people, the shops, the cars—they all looked the same. My heart was pounding. I'm sure Mom's was too.

We found Rosemary's street quickly enough and began to search the house numbers, both of us fidgeting in our seats. Finally, the last house on the corner came into view. Rosemary's house. With a For Sale sign in front and the word *Sold* plastered across it.

It looked empty.

I cannot describe the despair of that moment. Neither of us could believe it.

"We're too late," my mom said, in a voice that was half a wail and half a whisper. "Rosemary's dead and Lara's gone!"

I refused to believe it. I was the queen of No Surprises. This could not be happening.

"No way," I said. "Pull into the driveway."

She did, and I got out of the car. It was still hot and sticky outside, but I hardly cared. I went up to the front door and knocked. There was no answer. I peered in the front-room window. Mom joined me, worry creasing her face like a mask.

"Look, there's furniture still inside," I said.

She looked in as well.

But something wasn't quite right. There was indeed a couch and a coffee table and a bookcase visible, but there were no books on the bookshelves, no pictures on the wall, nothing to indicate who lived there and what they loved.

"If you want to buy that house, you're too late," someone said from behind us.

We turned. A woman in her midsixties, I'd say, wearing a flowered dress and walking a little dog stood by our car.

"It's been sold," she said.

"Where's Rosemary?" I asked, closing the gap between us. Her little dog yapped at me, but I barely noticed.

"Are you family?" she said, cocking her head.

"Oh, dear God, is she gone?" my mother said.

"Yep, she's gone. They're both gone." Clearly this woman had not understood what my mother meant.

"Where are they?" I asked impatiently.

"At Cleo and Ben's two doors down," she said, frowning. "Who are you people?"

"We're family," I said. "Why is their furniture still in the house?"

" 'Cause she and Lara sold it all with the house. If you wanted some of it, you shoulda come before. Now it's too late. All that stuff belongs to the new owners," she said, obviously pleased with herself for knowing so much.

"Which house is Cleo and Ben's?" I asked, approaching the end of my patience.

"That one," she said, pointing to a blue-and-cream house two houses away. "But I'm telling you, you're too late for that furniture."

"I don't care about the stupid furniture!" I said.

"Kate, it's okay," Mom said. "Let's go."

Mom thanked the woman for her information, and we got back in the car.

The woman stepped aside, watching us back out of the driveway while her little dog barked wildly, like he was personally chasing us off the property.

Mom slowly pulled up to the blue-and-cream house, put the car in park but left the engine idling. She sat there just looking at the house. The woman in the flowered dress, who I could see in the mirror on my side, was still looking at us.

"Don't you want to stop the car?" I said.

"I need to calm down a minute," she replied. "And so do you."

We sat there for a few seconds, just breathing in and breathing out. Then she turned off the ignition.

"Are you ready?" I asked.

"Why are they at this house?" Mom suddenly asked. "Why didn't Rosemary give me this address?"

"Mom, she wrote you three weeks ago. They probably still lived at the other house then," I said. "Besides, she probably thought you would write to her first and the letter would have been forwarded to her here."

"Maybe I *should* have written first," Mom said, staring at the house as if it were a fortress of stone.

"We're here now, Mom. Don't you think we should do what we came here to do?"

She nodded, and I took that as a cue to open my door and get out. She slowly did the same.

"I don't know what to say if Lara answers the door," she said as she closed her car door.

"You may not even know if it's Lara who answers the door," I said as I waited for her to join me on the sidewalk.

"Yes, I will," she said softly.

"I can do the talking," I offered.

She again just nodded her head.

We went up the curved walkway to the front door and stepped onto the porch. I rang the bell. The lady with the yapping dog was still standing there watching the whole thing like it was a movie. I waved to her. She yanked on her dog's leash and started to walk away, but her eyes never left us.

The door began to open, and both Mom and I took a shallow breath as it swung wide. A tall, slender woman in her late fifties or early sixties stood before us with a dish towel in her hand and an apron around her waist. She peered at us through the screen door.

"Yes?" she said, kindly but authoritatively. She probably thought we were peddling something.

"Cleo?" I said tentatively.

"Yes, that's me. What can I do for you?"

"My name is Kate Gerrity, and this is my mother, Claire Holland. We're friends of Rose—"

But I could get nothing else out.

The screen door swung open, almost in our faces.

"You're Claire?" she said to my mother, her eyes suddenly alight with something like fear or anticipation. I wasn't sure which.

"Yes," my mother said.

"For heaven's sake why didn't you write or call her first? Are you out of your mind?" Cleo said, with as much venom but as little volume as she could.

It was on my lips to ask her if she was out of hers, but Mom spoke up right away, absorbing the reprimand like she deserved it, which she didn't.

"I know I should have, Cleo, but this has been very difficult for me, and I was hoping Rosemary would understand."

Cleo just stood there glaring at us.

"She waited *days* for you to write back to her," Cleo finally said, saying the word "days" like it had a life of its own. "She had all but given up."

"I am sorry. I had much to consider. I'm sure you must know that."

I was proud of my mom for standing up to this woman, but she didn't deserve this kind of treatment. I had had enough.

"Is Rosemary here? We'd like to talk to her," I said as civilly as I could.

Cleo stood there for a moment and then stepped aside, motioning for us to come in.

"I'll tell her you're here," she said, leaving us to stand there in the entryway, where at least it was cool.

She disappeared down a hallway, then we heard her open a door and close it. Within seconds she reappeared.

"She wants to see you," Cleo said. "But don't you dare cause her any more grief, do you hear me? She cannot bear any more pain."

My mother just nodded.

"Kate, come with me," Mom said, and together we followed the Accuser down the hall.

Cleo opened the door and stepped away so we could enter. Rosemary was in a rented hospital bed surrounded by equipment I didn't recognize. She was propped up with pillows. She looked pale and thin but also completely overjoyed to see us. I turned around to face Cleo, slipped my hand over the doorknob, and shut the door so the three of us could be alone.

My mother ran to Rosemary and wrapped her arms around her. For several minutes there was no sound in the room but the aching cries of two sobbing women who had loved and lost so much.

*W*hen their tears subsided, Mom and Rosemary began to giggle like they had just shared a little joke.

Then Mom whispered something to Rosemary, and I heard Ed's name. Rosemary closed her eyes and nodded.

"It was so hard to let him go," Rosemary said, fresh tears welling in her eyes.

"And what about Lara?" my mom asked.

"She was so brave for me, but I know it broke her heart," Rosemary said. "She and Ed were so close. Sometimes I was a little jealous of them. But we were doing okay. And then this happened, and I..."

Rosemary stopped then, noticing me for the first time. I don't think Madame Cleo told her I had also come calling.

"Oh, my goodness, it's Katie, isn't it?" she said, breaking into a smile and reaching for me.

"It's just Kate these days," I said. I went to her and hugged her small body. Within her embrace I could tell both breasts were gone. She felt like all bones, tiny and weightless, like she was slowly disappearing. I winced at the thought I might be hurting her and gently pulled away. Her long braid was gone, replaced by a cropped haircut just beginning to curl at the edges. I guessed she had lost her long hair during treatment for the cancer.

"Katie, I'm so glad you've come too. So glad," she said, leaning back on her pillows. She looked exhausted.

"I'm glad too, Rosemary," I said.

"You are so beautiful," she continued, looking at me. "You're married?"

"Yes, to a wonderful man named Michael. We have two children. Olivia and Bennett."

"Olivia and Bennett. What beautiful names," she said, looking past me to see if anyone else had come into the room with us.

"Is...Is Dan here?" she asked

Mom paused for just a second as she sat in the only chair in the room, next to the bed. "It's just Kate and me today," she said.

"Oh...," Rosemary said, worry creeping into her voice. Perhaps she wondered what that meant, that only my mom and I were there and my dad wasn't. She sounded very tired and weak.

I could tell Mom sensed this as well. I didn't think we'd be able to stay much longer, and there was still so much to talk about.

"Rosemary, is Lara here?" my mom said gently.

"No, she doesn't get home from the library until after five," Rosemary said. "She has a job there."

I looked at my watch. It was ten minutes to five.

"But you will stay until she comes home, won't you?" she said, blinking hard as a wave of pain gripped her.

"Will that be okay with Cleo?" I said, motioning with my head.

Rosemary smiled in spite of her suffering.

"I suppose Cleo wasn't too happy to see you two on our doorstep, was she?" she said in a low voice.

"That's putting it mildly," I replied.

Rosemary's smile grew wider.

"Cleo is as tough as nails sometimes, but she protects those she loves with all her heart," Rosemary said. "She is my closest friend here and gracious enough to let me die in peace in her spare bedroom rather than at a hospital. So I put up with her rough edges. It's how she shows her love."

I suddenly remembered this about Rosemary, how she could see through to the very soul of someone. I recalled the day I met her. She sat with me on our freezing deck and listened to me complain about how nobody cared what I thought. She told me it was hard for my parents to decide what to do when so much lay in the balance. She told me my parents cared very much what I thought. It only seemed like they didn't because they were trying so hard to protect me from getting hurt, from feeling the pain they were feeling.

"Please stay until she comes," Rosemary said, looking first at my mom and then me.

"Of course we will," Mom said, reaching for Rosemary's hand.

"I want to move into the living room," Rosemary said suddenly. "Get that chair over there, will you, Katie."

She motioned to a wheelchair in the corner.

"Are you sure we should do this?" I said. "Maybe I should get Cleo."

"No, no," Rosemary said, pushing back her covers and grimacing. "We can do it."

I got the chair, and Mom helped Rosemary into it. It didn't take much effort. Rosemary hardly weighed anything. I fetched an afghan from the foot of her bed and wrapped it around her.

"Thank you, dear," she said. "Let's go. I want to be settled when Lara comes in the door."

I opened the door, and Mom pushed Rosemary out into the hall where Cleo stood, aghast at the parade.

"What on earth are you people doing to her?" she said, hands on her hips.

"Cleo, I asked Claire and Katie to help me come out here," Rosemary said. "I want us all to be able to sit down together and talk about what we need to do. There's more room out here."

"You know I'm supposed to go visit with Ben as soon as Lara gets here," she said stiffly, like we couldn't have a conversation without her.

"Of course you can go on and have supper with Ben," Rosemary said to Cleo. "Ben's living at the nursing home these days," she said to us, then added, "We'll be fine, Cleo. Please don't worry."

Cleo leaned down close to Rosemary but said loud enough for all of us to hear: "I didn't put in enough chicken for four."

"Oh, I'm sure we'll manage," Rosemary whispered.

"We aren't planning on staying very long," Mom said.

Rosemary looked quickly over at my mom and then back at Cleo.

"Cleo, why don't you go on now to the nursing home," she said. "I'll be fine here with Claire and Katie. And Lara will be here in a few minutes. And…and we really need some time alone. You do understand, don't you?"

Cleo straightened and sniffed. Then she untied her apron and laid it over a chair back. She walked over to a coat closet and took out a black purse, reaching inside for a set of car keys.

"I'll be back by eight," she said, and I half expected her to add "and *they* had better be gone."

"Say hello to Ben for me," Rosemary said.

Cleo stood there for a moment.

"Nice to have met you," she said to my mother and me, nearly through her teeth. Then she turned on her heel and walked into the kitchen and then into the garage. We heard a car start and the garage door open. Then through the living room window we saw her drive away.

"I apologize for her," Rosemary said. "This has been a tough year for her. Ben has Alzheimer's real bad. She can't look after him at home anymore. She will also miss me terribly when I…when I am gone. And she has asked me repeatedly to let Lara stay and live with her."

That seemed like a sentence far too stiff for a young, grieving girl, but I said nothing.

"But I don't think that is what's best for either of them," Rosemary said, turning to look at my mother.

"Does Lara know that you wrote me?" Mom asked.

"I told her I was going to ask you and Dan to take her in," Rosemary said.

"What did she say when you told her that?"

"She asked me if I thought that would make you and Dan happy."

My mom was quiet for a moment.

"What does she think of me, Rosemary?"

Rosemary leaned over and took my mom's hand in hers.

"She thinks you are very brave," she said.

We heard another car then, one pulling into the open garage. My mom's breathing quickened as did mine. She held tighter to Rosemary's hand, and I wished I had somebody's hand to hold. The door to the kitchen opened, and we heard the sound of someone entering it mixed with the sound of a cat meowing.

"Hello, kitty," a gentle voice said.

Lara.

Then we heard the sound of keys hitting the kitchen counter.

"Cleo?" Lara said.

"Lara, I'm in the living room, dear," Rosemary said, holding my mom's hand tight. "There are some friends here I'd like you to meet."

My mom stole a glance at me and then quickly turned her head back toward the doorway to the kitchen.

Lara stood framed in it.

She was slender and petite, maybe five foot five. Her dark brown hair fell loosely to her shoulders. She had soft brown eyes, a nose like my mom's, and a mole on her left cheek. She was wearing a pale blue sleeveless top that complemented her fair complexion.

"Hello," she said, smiling and revealing a perfect set of white teeth.

My mom just looked at her, unable to speak.

She came closer, choosing my mom to approach first, and held out her hand.

"My name is Lara," she said politely.

Tears filled my mother's eyes, and still she could say nothing.

"Lara," Rosemary said softly, "this is Claire."

Lara turned back to my mom as understanding came over her. She seemed to be frozen, like she was unable to decide what to do, like she didn't know if she should run from the room or lean over and embrace my mother. It was as if she was simply studying my mom, gauging what it was our mother *wanted* her to do. She waited until she was sure and then bent down and wrapped her arms around my mom in a hug that she was so right about. Mom desperately wanted it.

Mom stood with Lara's arms around her and enveloped her in her own arms. Rosemary was crying. I was crying. Lara and my mother were crying. If Cleo had been there, I'm sure she would have stormed out of the room in disgust to find a box of tissues.

Finally Mom stepped back and looked over every feature of the little girl she had given away. She touched her hair, her cheek, studied her hands.

"You are as beautiful today as the first time I laid eyes on you," Mom said.

Lara smiled.

"Lara, this is your sister, Katie," Rosemary said, motioning toward me.

Suddenly she was looking at me, and I felt weak and exposed. She stepped toward me and hugged me also.

"My mom has told me so much about you," she said.

I tried to hug her back. I wanted to. And yet I didn't. She seemed to sense none of this as she hugged me.

I don't know what it was—the beginning of jealousy or a wish to turn back the clock or just simply fear of letting her back into my life. I had a hard time absorbing the moment: We were in the same room with Lara. She was no longer relegated to the deepest, darkest corners of our memories where no one was allowed to go. I could speak her name again. She ceased to be the subject of a tragic circumstance that no one ever wanted to talk about.

She was suddenly real to me again.

And I could not reconcile that in my head.

We didn't stay long after that. It was obvious our visit had been physically draining on Rosemary. Lara told us that a hospice nurse was coming at seven to get Rosemary prepared for the night ahead, and she needed to try and eat something before then. She also asked us to stay and share their evening meal with them, out of tremendous courtesy, I am sure, since Cleo had made it pretty clear there was only enough chicken for two.

We declined, of course, and got ready to leave.

"Will you come back tomorrow?" Rosemary said, her eyes imploring my mother.

"Yes, Rosemary," Mom said, and I could tell by the way she said it and the way she looked at Rosemary that she was saying, "Yes, we'll take her."

Rosemary could tell too.

She rested her head against the back of her wheelchair and smiled in a way that I can only describe as relief.

23

The next morning I awoke to the sound of Olivia crying. My eyes snapped open as I realized that was impossible: I was in a hotel room three hundred miles away from my daughter.

The room was dark, like it was still night. The cries that awakened me stopped, leading me to believe I had dreamt them. But as I looked over at my mother's bed, I noticed it was empty, and then I heard the sound again.

It was a stifled sob coming from behind the closed bathroom door. I glanced at the clock glowing on the table beside me. It was a few minutes before six.

I was trying to decide if I should get up and offer to console my mother or let her grieve in private when another sob escaped her, followed by these words—every other one punctuated by a choked-back cry.

"I am so sorry…I don't know what I was thinking…"

I assumed she was praying, but there was a pause followed by, "But I should have told you, Dan."

She was talking to my dad.

I sat up in bed, uncertain what to do next. I didn't feel right listening; it felt like eavesdropping. But I couldn't help hearing everything she said.

"No…it wasn't that. I just…I was stupid. I was afraid you wouldn't understand."

My dad must have said something next as Mom ripped a length of toilet paper off the roll, sniffling loudly.

"I know. I am sorry. You don't know how sorry I am," my mom said next. "But I don't want to make any more mistakes, Dan. I want you here. Please, Dan. Please come."

I didn't like hearing my mother sound so broken and insistent. I wasn't used to it. I had never heard my mom plead with my dad for anything. Even when she was pregnant with Lara, even when I knew she wanted to keep her, I never heard her beg him to reconsider. There were times back then when I couldn't decide who I was mad at the most—him for refusing to acknowledge my sister or her for allowing it. I realize now it was a complicated situation, but at twelve, I thought she should have fought for Lara.

I heard her ask him again to come.

There were several moments of silence, broken by a sniffle here and there.

"We'll be here," she finally said, relief clear in her voice.

I heard the sound of her cell phone going off as she pressed the button to end the call. She blew her nose and ran some water into the sink. Then she emerged from the bathroom but hesitated when she saw that I was sitting up in bed.

"I'm sorry I woke you," she said and then came and sat on the edge of my bed.

She seemed to be sorry for a lot of things that morning.

"You called Dad," I said.

"I tossed and turned all night, Kate. You were right," she said, shaking her head. "I should have told him about the letter. I should have asked him to come with us. I should have asked him first what he thought about Lara's coming to live with us."

She sighed.

"Does he know everything now?" I asked.

Mom nodded.

"What did he say when you told him?"

She shrugged.

"I don't think he knew what to say," she said. "He hardly said anything about Rosemary or Lara. He just talked about us. About him and me. How we needed to be together on whatever happens next."

"And?" I said.

"And I agreed. I asked him to drop everything and come here," she said.

"So that's what he's doing?"

She nodded and rose from the foot of my bed. "I told him we'd be back at the hotel by three o'clock today. I also told him to bring along some extra clothes for me…" She hesitated before adding, "I might stay a little longer."

I didn't know what to say to that. I knew I couldn't stay longer than the weekend, but I kind of wished she would have at least asked me.

"So what are we going to do until then?" I said.

"We'll see what we can do to help Rosemary and Lara," she said.

It was far too early to think about going back to Two Harbors, yet neither one of us felt like going back to sleep. We got dressed, made a pot of rather tasteless coffee, and with our paper cups in hand, went out for a walk along the shore of Lake Superior. To my surprise, it was one of the nicest walks I ever shared with my mother. It was enjoyable because while I fully anticipated it being a walk weighted with talk of Lara, she instead talked to me about me—about how glad she was I was there for her, how dependable I always was, and how much she relied on me.

When we got back to the hotel, we ate a quick complimentary breakfast and then got into the car to head to Two Harbors. On the way we stopped at a grocery store and filled a cart with basic staples. I had a feeling Cleo would resent our bringing several bags of groceries into her house, but if my mom felt any apprehension, it wasn't noticeable. As we checked out, she grabbed a mixed bouquet of daisies, carnations, and tiger lilies sitting in a bucket by the registers and added it to our cart.

By the time we reached Two Harbors, it was almost nine thirty. We both hoped it wasn't too early to ring the doorbell at Cleo's house.

Thankfully, Lara answered the door and welcomed us in. She looked happy to see us but tired. She must have sensed that we noticed.

"Mom had a bad night," she said, trying to sound detached from what she was saying, but not being able to do it. "But she's finally resting now."

Lara's deep, brown eyes were suddenly brimming with tears. My mom hastily set down the two bags of groceries she was carrying and drew her other daughter into her arms. Lara wrapped her arms around my mom and began to shake as she let fall tears that had obviously been kept dammed up for too long.

I felt a little awkward, so I picked up my mom's bags as best I could with my own bags still in my arms and headed into Cleo's kitchen. I opened the fridge and started to put away the cold stuff. My mom was wise in deciding to stop for groceries. There was barely anything on the shelves.

I opened cabinet after cabinet looking for the proper places to put the canned things we had bought, the boxes of cereal, and bakery items. I couldn't find a vase, so I put the flowers in an empty mayonnaise jar I found under the sink. I set the bouquet on the kitchen table. When I was done, I stepped back into the living room. Lara and Mom were sitting on the couch, and Lara was drying her eyes.

"Where's Cleo?" Mom was asking her.

"She's visiting Ben at the nursing home," Lara said. "She wouldn't leave Mom's side all night. When she left, she was exhausted."

"What about you?" Mom said. "Did you get any sleep?"

"A little," Lara replied. "But I'm all right."

"Why don't you rest a little now?" Mom said. "Kate and I can stay in the room with…with your mother."

"I don't know if I could sleep," Lara said. "And she may need her pain medication when she wakes up."

"Tell me what to do, Lara," Mom said.

While Lara told my mother how to start the flow of morphine in Rosemary's IV, I peeked into a linen closet and found what I was looking for: a pillow and a light blanket. We settled Lara on the couch with the pillow and blanket, and then Mom and I tip-toed into Rosemary's room. As we opened the door, Rosemary's imminent appointment with her own mortality was almost palpable.

There were two chairs in the room this time. No doubt one had been Lara's and the other Cleo's during the night. It was depressing to picture them hovering over an agonized Rosemary as they kept their vigil in the dark.

We both sat down. To wait.

It was a little after ten o'clock when Rosemary woke up with her face wrapped in a grimace. When she saw us, she made a heroic effort to chase it away and replace it with a smile.

"Lara's resting, Rosemary," Mom said to her. "But she told me what to do. Do you want your pain medication?"

Rosemary shook her head.

"It's not so bad right now," she said softly. "The medication makes me so sleepy, and we have so much to talk about."

"Why don't we wait until Dan gets here?" Mom said.

"Dan is coming?" Rosemary said, her voice seeming to lift.

"He'll be here late this afternoon. I'll bring him then."

Rosemary nodded.

"There are papers in that desk," Rosemary said, motioning with her head to a little desk by a window. "Top drawer. You and Dan should look at them. I don't mean to rush you, Claire, but I …I feel like there isn't much time…"

Mom nodded, and I could see that her eyes were brimming with tears. She then turned her head to me and nodded. I went and got the papers.

They were legal documents giving my parents legal custody of Lara Claire Prentiss.

I had forgotten Lara's middle name. Seeing it in ink gave me a queer feeling.

I walked back over to the bed with them, but Mom made no move to take them from me. She just sat there holding Rosemary's hand.

"We sold the house…" Rosemary whispered. "The money is in Lara's name. There is enough for her expenses for next year and for her to go to a good college. I already put the car in her name. But she has only had her license for a few weeks, so don't let her drive down to your place alone..."

"I'll drive her down," I said in a spontaneous gesture to make Rosemary remember I was in the room and that I had never forgotten how kind she had always been to me.

"Thank you, Katie," she said, turning her head slowly in my direction.

The phone rang in the kitchen and Mom offered to get it, leaving me alone with Rosemary.

She smiled at me.

"I kept your letter," she said and winked.

"I kept yours," I said. "For a long time I kept it."

"I want you to have it. It's in Ed's Bible, back in the map section. Over there in that basket by the desk," she said.

A worn, leather-bound Bible lay atop a stack of other books, and I quickly found the letter I had written to Rosemary in Ecuador when I was fourteen. It made my heart race a little to handle it. I shoved it into my purse and sat down again by Rosemary.

She reached for my hand, and I met her halfway with it.

"Do you remember what you said in it?" she asked.

I looked to the door wondering if Mom was going to walk through and feeling like I was about to be caught with my hand in the cookie jar.

"Yes."

"You said it didn't matter how far away Ed and I were, Lara was your sister and she always would be."

I nodded.

"She always will be," Rosemary said, squeezing my hand.

We sat in silence for a few minutes as she let this thought envelop me.

My mom opened the door, and I stiffened. Rosemary squeezed my hand again. Mom was carrying a tray with a teapot and three cups on it.

"Rosemary, do you think you could manage a cup of tea?" she said.

Rosemary smiled.

"I'd sure like to try," she replied.

We sipped our tea, and Mom distracted Rosemary from her pain by telling her about Tennyson's Table. I could tell Rosemary was wishing she could see it for herself. When we finished our tea, Rosemary tentatively asked if Cleo was back yet. It didn't appear that she was.

"Do you need something, Rosemary?" my mom asked.

Rosemary wrinkled her brow.

"I need my bedpan," she said, barely above a whisper.

"I can help you with it," Mom said. "I don't mind, Rosemary."

I rose to leave while Rosemary began a series of protests I knew she would not win.

I went to use the bathroom myself and noticed a hamper full of laundry that needed to be done. Anxious to be of use, I grabbed the hamper and began to look for the washer, walking silently past Lara asleep on the couch. I didn't see a washer in the garage or anywhere near the kitchen. I decided to try the basement. Downstairs I found a small family room, another bedroom, and the laundry room. I sorted the clothes and got a load of whites going in the washer. I then gave in to my curiosity. I figured this other bedroom had to be Lara's since I saw no other bedrooms besides Rosemary's and Cleo's upstairs. I peeked inside.

The only light coming into the room was from a small egress window on the north side. I switched on the light. The room was sparsely furnished with boxes lining one entire wall. It looked like someone had just moved in. Or was preparing to move out.

Several of the boxes were marked with Lara's name. *Lara's winter clothes. Lara's books. Lara's camera stuff. Lara's baby things.* Others had been scrawled with labels like "Mom's books," "Dad's journals," and "Ecuador."

The bed wasn't made, evidence that Lara had been called from it in the middle of the night, no doubt. I decided to make it for her. I picked up some clothes in the corner and put them in the empty laundry basket I was holding. As I turned, I noticed that the wall by the door was covered with photographs of all sizes. Some were framed; some were not. Some were in color; some were black-and-white.

There were photos of the black cat I had seen upstairs, photos of Ed and Rosemary, photos of landscapes and seascapes, and photos of Ecuadorian children wearing brightly colored woven capes. They were beautiful photographs. The artist in me couldn't help but stare at them. I didn't even hear Lara come into the room.

I was marveling at a photo of Ed sitting on a rock with surf behind him and a wonderful smile on his face. I jumped when Lara spoke from behind me.

"That's my favorite picture of my dad," she said.

"Lara!" I said sheepishly. "I didn't mean to intrude. I should have asked first…"

But she would hear none of it.

"You're not intruding," she said, like the very idea was laughable. "I wanted you to see my pictures."

"They're beautiful, Lara," I said, looking back at my sister's art and trying to regain my composure. "You took them all?"

She nodded. "I started taking photographs for a monthly newsletter Mom and Dad sent to their supporters. After a while, I found I had a passion for it. That one," she said, pointing to the one of Ed on the beach, "was taken at Galapagos. It's the most wonderful place.

"These are some of my friends in Otavalo," she continued, pointing to three, dark-skinned girls with their arms around each other, their teeth as white as pearls.

"This is my cat, Silhouette," she said, pointing to a photo of the black cat sitting in a pile of autumn leaves.

Looking at such beautiful pictures and realizing they weren't just nicely composed portraits but precious slivers of my sister's life, I began to feel emotionally unhinged. I had to get out of that room.

"They are very nice," I said and quickly moved to the door, banging the laundry basket against one of the frames and nearly knocking it off the wall.

"I'm sorry," I said, wincing. I tried to steady it, making it worse.

Lara reached out to help me.

"It's okay, Kate," she said calmly. "No harm done."

I nearly fled from the room.

We returned to the hotel a little before two to await Dad's arrival. While we waited, I dozed. My mom did not but instead sat at the little desk in our room studying the papers from Rosemary's desk. A few minutes before three, I told Mom I was going for a walk. She must have known I thought she might want a few minutes alone with Dad when he got there.

"Thanks," she said, but then added. "But don't be gone long. I told Rosemary we'd be back before five."

I nodded and left.

When I returned I saw Dad's truck in the hotel parking lot. I made my way up to our room and stopped at the door to listen. I could hear nothing. I had my card key but knocked anyway.

Mom opened the door. She looked remarkably happy. Dad was at the little table, looking at the same papers Mom had been studying when I left. He rose when I came in and hugged me.

"Everything okay?" I said, looking from one to the other.

My dad eased into a smile that I knew didn't come easy, but it was sincere.

"Everything's okay," he said.

But I suspected he had a different view of these new events than Mom had. I doubted he was thinking "We've got her back!" like I believe Mom was.

Just then Mom went into the bathroom to change into some clothes Dad had brought for her, and I took advantage of the opportunity to be alone with him for a few minutes.

"So, what do you really think about all this?" I asked.

He shrugged and looked at the papers in his hand. "Ed and Rosemary were wonderful to Lara," he said. "Now Rosemary needs our help. Her daughter needs a place to live for the coming school year."

Then he looked at me.

"And that's who she is, Kate. She is *her* daughter. She is not ours." Then he looked away.

He was right, of course, but I knew it wasn't that simple. I was sure he knew it too, but I wanted to hear him say it.

"But, Dad...," I asked, as gently as I could. "Don't you think there's more to this than just providing a place for Lara to live for a while?"

He looked back, and I could see the shadow of old wounds in his eyes.

"Right now there isn't more to it," he said, but not unkindly.

Mom emerged from the bathroom. The conversation was over.

But I couldn't take my eyes off my father. I'm sure Dad would have said his primary motivation for agreeing to take Lara in was his compassion and admiration for Ed and Rosemary. But I knew that what really made him do it was love for my mother. He knew Mom had never stopped thinking of Lara, had never stopped loving her, even though she hadn't spoken of her in years.

I was touched by Dad's obvious devotion. He was doing this because he loved Mom and knew it would make her happy, despite his fear of what the future held. I suddenly remembered, as a bitter twelve-year-old, thinking my dad made such selfish choices when it came to Lara. I winced now at those remembered thoughts.

And I could see my dad's reasoning, of course. I could see what gave him the courage to say "yes" this time. It was different than when Lara was born. It was very different. The infant girl who had worn a hospital anklet that bore the name "Holland" was long gone. In her place was a teenager whose last name was Prentiss.

Mom drove us back to Two Harbors in her car, me sitting in the back. Dad was quiet. He asked only one question. Who was handling the details of Rosemary's estate? Neither Mom nor I had even thought of that.

"I am sure we can find that out," Mom said, trying to sound nonchalant.

When we arrived back at Cleo's, Lara was in the garage trying to untangle an extension cord from the top rung of a six-foot stepladder. She stopped when she saw us step out of the car and walked out into the sunshine.

I couldn't help but glance at my dad. He looked kind of sad.

Mom didn't seem to notice.

"Lara, this is Dan," she said brightly, motioning toward my father.

Lara waited a moment and then held out her hand. My dad took it. It seemed like an awkward moment for all of us. No one said anything as they shook hands.

"It's wonderful to meet you," she said.

"We've met before," Dad said softly, almost like he was only reminding himself of it.

"I'm sorry I can't remember it," Lara said with a smile and I could tell she really meant it.

"Can I give you a hand with that ladder?" Dad said after a moment's pause.

"That would be great," Lara answered. "There's a lightbulb out in the basement. It's kind of high."

"You just lead the way," Dad said, pulling the tangled cord free and hoisting the ladder in his grip. "I'll change it for you."

Mom was completely pleased.

We walked through the garage and into the kitchen. Cleo was standing there, hands on her hips.

"Who are you?" she said to my dad.

Mom and I exchanged glances. We had told him about Cleo's house, but we hadn't told him about Cleo.

"I'm Dan Holland," Dad said, eyes a little wide.

"I'm Cleo," she said. "What are you doing with my ladder?"

"Dan's helping me change that bulb in the family room, Cleo," Lara said.

"All right," she said, as if we were all standing there awaiting her permission to proceed.

"It's this way," Lara said, and Dad followed her through the kitchen and into the hallway where the basement stairs were.

"While you're down there, you may as well right the washer," she called after them. "It bounced a corner off its pallet this morning. Someone filled it too full," she added, looking at me.

"How's Rosemary doing?" Mom asked.

"The hospice nurse just left. That woman woke her from a much-needed nap, but at least she upped her pain medication," Cleo said, opening the oven door and checking the meatloaf she was making.

She then mumbled a thank-you to my mother for the groceries we delivered earlier and asked if she could pay us for them. Mom said she would rather Cleo didn't, that it had been our pleasure to get them. Cleo just nodded.

"You can stay for supper," she said. It wasn't quite an invitation, more like a summons, but Mom didn't seem to notice.

"Thank you, Cleo," she said. "We'd love to."

Mom and I started to walk out of the kitchen as Cleo suddenly said, "Nice flowers."

She was looking at the bouquet in the mayonnaise jar. I caught the trace of a smile on her face. Lara told me later that it had been years since anyone had given Cleo flowers.

I hadn't planned on going in to see Rosemary that afternoon, but she insisted I come, and she asked Lara to come too.

Rosemary looked very pale and weak. I couldn't believe the difference one day had made. I wondered if she was starting to let go because she now knew Lara was going to be all right.

"Come in," she said. Her face broke into a smile when she saw my dad. "Dan…"

Dad leaned over and kissed Rosemary on the forehead. She tried to raise an arm to hug him but the pain medication had made her too weak. He held the hand she had tried to raise and squeezed it.

"I almost didn't recognize you without your long braid," Dad said with a smile, but his voice sounded funny.

Rosemary smiled and closed her eyes.

"I see you don't have as much hair as before, either," she said.

Everyone smiled at that, and some of the tension left the room.

"I wanted all of you here because I don't want to miss the opportunity to tell you all how much you mean to me," Rosemary said softly. "Sometimes when I close my eyes, I imagine I will open them in heaven."

Lara drew in a breath next to me but said nothing.

"I want you all to always remember how precious you are to me. Don't forget."

Lara reached for Rosemary's other hand.

"Lara, would you give me a moment with Dan and Claire and Kate?" Rosemary said next. "I promise it won't be long."

Lara nodded, wiped her eyes and left.

"Dan...," Rosemary said softly.

"Right here," my dad said, his voice hoarse.

"I would not have asked such a tremendously big favor of you if I did not believe God wanted me to," she said. "You and your family have such a capacity to love. It was love that motivated you to do what you had to back when Lara was born. Love for your wife and your children and even love for Lara.

"Claire," she said turning to my mother, "I know how hard it was for you to give Lara to me. I know it was your love for her that enabled you to do it. And Katie, I know it hurt you terribly when Ed and I took Lara away. It hurt because you loved her so much."

Rosemary closed her eyes and took a deep breath. I thought for a moment she had dropped off to sleep. My parents and I looked at each other. We all had tears in our eyes.

"Don't you see?" Rosemary said, slowly opening her eyes. "Everything you have ever done for my daughter, my Lara, you have done out of love."

Those few moments I spent with Rosemary that sunny Saturday afternoon were the last. I left the next day in my mother's car to go home to Michael and my children. My parents stayed. Six days later Rosemary died in her sleep.

I don't know what Lara would have done if my parents hadn't been there for her. Rosemary's estate, although there wasn't much to it, was left in a trust for Lara with Rosemary's brother in Florida as the executor. He came to the funeral but left as soon as he politely could. Rosemary's lawyer, a friend of the family, helped take care of the last loose ends regarding my parents becoming Lara's legal guardians, and he also took care of filing for Lara's Social Security benefits. Technically, Lara was an orphan.

The funeral was attended by only a handful of people. Lara and Rosemary had been attending a small church in the country, one that Ed's mother had belonged to when Rosemary and Ed and Lara moved back to Minnesota after Ed's first heart attack. When Ed's mother died, they kept attending there. The congregation numbered less than twenty families. A few church friends came to Rosemary's service, but including my family and Spencer and Natalie, there were less than thirty in attendance. Rosemary deserved a motorcade and a national day of mourning.

Lara sat with her uncle in the front row of the little church, and my parents and I and my family sat right behind them.

Rosemary was buried alongside Ed in a shady spot in the church cemetery. After the interment, we went back inside the church for a light meal in the basement. Lara seemed to be holding up well. My little Olivia never left her side, and I didn't know if that annoyed her or comforted her. My dad and the uncle spent considerable time in a corner going over legal matters. It was so obvious Rosemary's brother was in a hurry to get back to Florida and his own life. I shot him several reproving looks, but I don't think he ever caught on that I thought him to be one of the more callous people I ever had the misfortune of meeting.

Mom offered to stay with Lara and Cleo the night of the funeral, but Lara seemed to want some time to herself. We agreed to come back for her the next morning. I had not forgotten my promise to Rosemary to drive her down to Blue Prairie.

We stayed that night in the same hotel by the lake, and the next morning, Michael, Bennett, Wes, and Nicole left ahead of the rest of us. I tried to convince Olivia to go with them, but she wouldn't do it. She was utterly taken with Lara and wanted to ride with her.

All of Lara's boxes fit in the back of Dad's truck, as did her bicycle and darkroom equipment. We filled the back of my mom's car with Lara's clothes and photographs.

Finally, in Lara's little blue Taurus, we placed Olivia, Lara's cat, Silhouette, and a few miscellaneous items.

Then it was time to go.

"Are there any friends you need to say goodbye to?" Mom asked Lara as she closed the trunk to her car.

"I did that on Sunday," Lara said softly, like it was slightly painful to say.

Mom turned to Cleo who was standing in the driveway. Hands on her hips, of course.

"Cleo, is there anything Dan and I can do for you before we head out?"

"I've gotten along fine for sixty-six years and I don't need any help now," Cleo replied, chin high.

Lara turned to her and threw her arms around her.

"Thank you, Cleo, for everything you have done," she said. "I will never forget how you cared for us."

Cleo, who had not shed a tear up to that point—at least not that I had seen—began to cry.

"You come back and visit me anytime," Cleo finally managed to say.

Lara kissed her cheek and stepped away, getting into the passenger side of her own car. Cleo dried her eyes and turned away for a moment to blow her nose into a handkerchief. Then she turned back toward the three vehicles and placed her hands squarely on her hips. We waved goodbye, and she nodded her head once in response.

The five-hour drive home was long but uneventful. Olivia fell asleep after the first hour, and Lara followed suit after the second. We stopped in Apple Valley at Spencer and Natalie's to stretch our legs before tackling the last hundred miles and so Lara could see Noah.

Spencer and I hadn't had a moment alone since I told him over the phone that Mom and Dad were taking in the daughter they had given up for adoption when he was seven. He barely remembered that time in our lives. He never missed Lara like I did. He always thought our move to Blue Prairie was the most ingenious thing Dad had ever came up with, like it was all done so Spencer could get a big dog and a three-wheeler. Even as an adult, I don't think he sensed the complexity of Lara re-entering our lives. To him, this was all new. There was no history to be reckoned with.

Noah, ever a happy baby, cooed and giggled on Lara's lap, giving her plenty of reasons to smile back. It was nice to see her smile again. Lara said something about wanting to take Noah's picture sometime. Natalie promised to bring him down some day soon.

We finally got home about six thirty. Michael had come over to my parents' house and had steaks on the grill ready for us, and Bennett was scooting around on his toy tractor when we drove up. Wes, Nicole, and Seth were there too. We sat outside on my parents' deck and ate supper, enjoying the summer night and the breeze that blew our napkins out of our laps but kept the mosquitoes from landing and biting.

We brought in Lara's boxes and set them in the dining room until they could be sorted and unpacked. Then my mom and I carried in her clothes and took them up to my old room, which I had made ready the week between my first trip to Two Harbors and my second.

Lara came up a few minutes later with two photographs in her hand. One was the portrait of Ed on Galapagos; the other was of Rosemary with her long braid, holding a little Ecuadorian baby in her arms. She set them on my old dresser.

"This was your old room?" she said.

"Yes, it was," I said.

She turned and smiled at me.

"I'm glad," she said, and then she headed back downstairs.

For the first few days after we arrived home from Two Harbors, I tried to keep what I thought was a respectable distance from my parents and Lara. I went to the Table the day after we got home, not expecting to see Mom or Lara at all.

They came after lunch and stayed the whole afternoon. One of Nicole's kitchen helpers was home sick, so Lara offered to help out. I guess I should have guessed Nicole would eventually offer Lara a job since we all worked at the Table. But it startled me anyway that it happened that very day. One moment Lara was sipping a white chocolate frappaccino, the next she was making one.

She was introduced to everyone she met as a friend of the family whose parents had both passed away and who would be living with my parents for the next school year.

The shop was busy that afternoon. Mom had been away for more than a week, so she had a lot of catching up to do. And since I had to cover for her while she was gone, I was behind on two paintings I was matting for a customer who had bought two watercolors from me on eBay. I also had a beginner's sketching class that afternoon that I had done nothing to prepare for.

In the middle of trying to sort through all this, Seth arrived. He had just gotten off the phone with his social worker. He had been caught drinking two nights before, and his social worker was threatening to place him in a group home if he didn't shape up. Nicole was pretty much at the end of her rope, I think. As she cleaned the glass-fronted bakery case, Seth told her he wanted a new social worker, that the one he had was a "total loser." She told him he had better do whatever the social worker told him, because the group home idea was starting to look pretty good. I knew that would make him angry. And it did. He followed me into the back of my studio and told me Nicole never tried to see his side of things. I asked him if he ever tried to see hers. He shrugged.

I was working on a frame when suddenly he had the urge to help me.

"I bet I could do that," he said.

"Maybe I'll show you sometime," I said.

"It doesn't look that hard," he said as I beveled the mat. "Let me try."

"Another time, okay, Seth?" I just didn't have time for him that day.

He turned and left. I felt bad for him, but he really wasn't my responsibility. By closing time, my mom, Nicole, and I were worn out. As we readied the shop for the end of the day, my mom asked where Lara was. I hadn't seen her, and Nicole didn't know. We looked upstairs in the meeting rooms and in the bathroom, and just about the time Mom started to worry, I spotted Lara and Seth sitting at one of the sidewalk tables out front. Seth was talking a mile a minute, and Lara was sitting there listening to his every word.

Mom and Nicole both froze. On their faces were twin, worried-mother looks.

"Good grief," Nicole said. "Something else to worry about."

"No kidding," Mom said and headed for the front door.

She stepped outside and said as cheerfully as she could, "Hey, Seth. How's it going?"

He had barely said, "It's cool," when Mom asked Lara if she was ready to head home.

I watched Lara rise from the little table and push the chair in. "Bye, Seth," she said.

"See you 'round," he replied, and there was no mistaking the trepidation on my mother's face as she heard his words.

Mom and Lara drove away, and I headed back into the studio to turn the lights off. As I was leaving, Nicole handed Seth a bag of trash to take out, and I heard her tell him to "leave that young girl alone."

"Why?" he asked, obviously challenging her.

"Because, Seth," she answered. "She's just lost her mother. She doesn't need to hear about your problems or *catch* your problems."

"I wasn't telling her about my problems," Seth said, brushing past me, hurt etched into his face.

I hadn't been home more than fifteen minutes when Mom called me and invited us over for spaghetti.

"I thought you might want some time alone with Lara," I said.

"There will be plenty of other evenings alone with her," Mom said in reply. "I was hoping you could...talk to her about Seth."

I was slightly perturbed at realizing the invitation had strings attached. I toyed with saying something like "Tell her yourself," but the truth was, *I* was worried about Lara getting mixed up with Seth. He was trouble with a capital T.

I told her we would come.

Olivia and Bennett monopolized every moment with Lara after we arrived. I wouldn't have gotten a word in at all if my mother hadn't distracted them after supper with news that there were new kittens in the barn. While she showed them the kittens, I volunteered Lara and me to do the dishes. Dad and Michael went outside to tinker with my dad's ailing riding mower.

The table was half-cleared when I finally summoned the courage to advise Lara to be careful developing a friendship with Seth.

"Lara, I think I should tell you that Seth has some pretty significant problems," I said, "and that being his friend can be very…complicated."

"I don't think I understand," Lara said.

"He's had a tough time lately with choices. Maybe he shared some of his frustrations today?"

Lara looked utterly confused.

"He didn't tell you he had a fight with his social worker today or an argument with Nicole?" I asked.

She just shook her head.

"Can I ask what he was talking about when you were sitting out in front of the shop?"

"He was telling me his dreams," Lara said. "He was telling me what he wanted to do with his life."

I was speechless.

"He was?"

"Well, yes. He wants to design and build houses," Lara said.

I couldn't believe Seth had never shared this with Michael or me before, but I tried to shake it off. She still needed to know Seth was dangerous.

"Look, Lara. Seth has a problem with alcohol and a problem with authority," I said. "He has some pretty tough friends who tend to bring him down. That's why a friendship with him can be complicated. I just don't want to see you get hurt."

Lara smiled at me. "Thanks, Kate. I promise I will be careful."

And I knew at that moment that Lara had no intention of avoiding a friendship with Seth, like my mother was hoping for, and was instead intending to cautiously yet conscientiously rescue Seth from self-destruction.

The phone rang then, and I answered it. It was my grandmother in Ann Arbor.

"Is she there?" Grandma asked me.

I looked over at Lara as she wiped down the place mats. "Yes, she's here."

Lara looked up and I winked.

"Do you want to talk to her?" I asked.

"Yes!" Grandma said.

I brought the phone over to Lara.

"It's Mom's mother," I said, with my hand over the mouthpiece. "Her name is Sophia. She really wants to talk with you."

Lara smiled and took the phone.

"Hello?" she said and strolled into the living room. I stepped outside to see the kittens for myself.

The barn was warm and sweet smelling, and the kittens were nestled with their mother in an unused sheep pen. The kids were still gushing over them as I approached.

"Well?" Mom asked.

"I told her Seth has a lot of problems and to be careful."

Mom nodded, like that was the end of it, but I knew it wasn't.

"But I have this feeling she will want to befriend him *because* of his problems, Mom," I said.

She looked up at me like I had failed, and yet I could tell she quickly realized how stupid that was. Lara was so much like Rosemary. Rosemary could never let a needy person pass her by.

"What's she doing now?"

"Talking to Grandma," I said.

"On the phone? Right now?"

"Yeah," I said.

"Good heavens," and she headed for the kitchen door.

"Grandma said we could have ice cream," Olivia said to me.

"Well, then let's go get it," I said.

I wanted to hear the conversation in the kitchen too.

Lara was sitting on the floor of the living room, her back against the sofa and her feet pointing toward the kitchen. She saw us come in and smiled.

"That sounds great," she was saying.

Then there was a pause as Grandma said something.

"Well, actually, my mom's parents died before I was born. I did live with my Grandma Prentiss for a while, but she passed away a few years ago," Lara said.

And then, "Well, maybe."

I knew what Grandma was asking her. She was asking Lara if she wanted to call her "Grandma." And if she wanted to come visit her and Grandpa Stuart in Ann Arbor. Mom could tell too. It was a little awkward.

"Okay," Lara was saying. "Here's Claire." And she handed the phone to my mom. Mom took the phone into the adjoining study.

"So she asked you to call her Grandma, huh?" I said to Lara.

"She did," Lara said. "But I don't know that Claire would like that… "

"And she asked you to come to Ann Arbor this summer?" Lara smiled. "Yes. How did you know?"

"She always liked having us kids out there for the summer."

"Are you and Spencer her only grandchildren?" Lara asked.

"Yep. My Uncle Matt didn't get married until he was forty. He and Marta never had kids. I'm not sure if they couldn't or if they just decided not to. They're both history professors and travel a lot," I answered.

"I see," Lara said. Then after a pause she asked, "Do you think I should go visit them?"

I felt a peculiar sense of envy at the thought of Lara spending a week or two at Grandma and Grandpa's, doing all the things with them that I used to do. I knew once they met Lara, they would be crazy about her. That bothered me too. It was a weird feeling. Like I was proud of my little sister and I wanted my grandparents to meet her and like her, but I also didn't want them to because it would mean sharing them with her. I didn't know what to tell her. I didn't know what was true and what was just jealousy.

"I guess that's for you and Mom to decide," I finally said. "But I always had a great time at their house."

Both statements were true.

That weekend at Nicole's Saturday brunch, she and Mom decided to throw a big Fourth of July party/family reunion at my parents' house. It didn't surprise me at all that Nicole would think of throwing a huge party with less than two weeks' notice.

She was always coming up with grandiose ideas on the spur of the moment. I was a little amazed Mom jumped on the wagon with her, though. Mom's a planner. She likes everything to be perfect at her parties.

But then I realized Mom just wanted the family to meet Lara, especially the family members who really knew who Lara was, including both sets of grandparents, Matt and Marta, Karin and Kent, and my mom's Aunt Elizabeth. She wanted to show her off.

The two of them fell into a crazed, party-planning-in-a-hurry mode. I felt a little left out and got up from the table to start the dishes. Olivia and Bennett disappeared into the TV room, and the men went out into Wes's shop to see his new fishing rod. Lara started to help me, but I was grumpy and wanted to be alone. I told her to just relax, that I'd take care of the dishes. She hesitated and then stepped outside, unsure of where to go or what to do.

I rinsed a dish and looked out the window to see if she had decided to follow the men into the shed, which I thought would be rather pointless.

But she hadn't.

She had been joined on the porch.

I watched as she and Seth strolled out to a bench under a cottonwood in the backyard and sat on it. Seth was talking; she was listening.

I turned back to the dishes and didn't look out the window again after that.

26

The day of the big party dawned hot and sticky, but by afternoon the humidity had tapered off some, and a nice breeze had kicked in. It turned out to be a perfect day for an outdoor party. Mom and Nicole did pretty much all the planning for the big event, and I just went along with their ideas. They asked me to take care of the dessert because they wanted a decorated sheet cake, saying it was the perfect thing for me to do since I was "so artistic."

Whatever.

It was my token responsibility so I wouldn't feel left out. It bothered me then. I have since gotten over it.

But I did what I was told. I made a cake to beat all cakes. It was a white cake layered with blueberry and strawberry filling and decorated with blue stars, silver stripes, and red roses for the kids to fight over.

My grandparents from Michigan—retired and free to do pretty much what they pleased—decided to drive out with my mother's Aunt Elizabeth who had moved in with them the year Bennett was born. They allowed my Uncle Matt and Aunt Marta to drive them, which I was very glad about. I didn't like the idea of my eighty-something grandparents driving out alone, though both were still mentally as sharp as tacks. They arrived on the third of July.

I knew Grandma Sophie, my mom's mother, would fall in love with Lara the moment she saw her. I was right. Grandma was as bad as Olivia. She barely left Lara's side the whole day. It was sickening and comical at the same time. The two of them, Olivia and Grandma, were all over Lara until Spencer and Natalie arrived with Noah, and then they took turns smothering first one and then the other.

My other grandparents, Grandma and Grandpa Holland, drove down from Red Wing with my Aunt Karin and Uncle Kent, arriving around two in the afternoon. My cousin Allison, her husband, Tim, and their two-year-old daughter, Kaitlin, followed them, bringing with them my cousin Jennifer and her fiancé, Jared.

Michael's brother, Andrew, arrived from Minneapolis an hour late, as was customary for him, but bringing a date—a quiet girl named Tara, who did not seem to like family reunions very much. Wes, Nicole, and Seth arrived early that morning to set up tables and chairs and returned later wearing matching red, white, and blue tie-dyed T-shirts. So very Nicole.

Dad and Michael butchered a hog for the occasion and roasted the best parts over an open flame. The aroma of the roast pork brought out all the barn cats, who were quite undaunted by Bogart, who had tagged along for the party.

It was actually a nice get-together. The kids did great—no one got hurt or mad—and everyone seemed to have a great time. Lara initially appeared at ease, though I could sense having an extended family for the first time in her life was a bit much to absorb all at once.

Not long after the party got going, however, she watched most of it from behind the lens of her camera. She took pictures of everyone and everything, as if making sense of her world through her art. I understood this about her—because it's exactly the way I am too.

Throughout the day, I found myself wondering what people thought about Lara. For me, I had no trouble thinking of her as my half-sister. And I knew Grandma Sophie was dying to call Lara her granddaughter; maybe to her friends back in Michigan she already was calling her that. But I wasn't sure what Grandma and Grandpa Holland thought of Lara, aside from believing her to be a nice, polite teenager who took incredible photographs. Lara was not Grandma Holland's granddaughter, and Grandma Holland didn't act like Lara was. My cousin Jennifer seemed to take a tremendous liking to Lara. After seeing Lara's pictures, Jennifer asked her if she would take pictures at her upcoming August wedding. It appeared to me that Jennifer was making a fast friend in Lara. But not a fast cousin.

Again, I had no alone time with my brother. I had no idea what he really thought about Lara. Did he think of her as his little sister? I was both unnerved and delighted, if that makes any sense at all, to notice that almost everyone treated Lara like she was a foreign-exchange student my parents were hosting for the year.

All that day whenever Lara spoke to our mother, she called her Claire. I liked it and hated it at the same time. It drove me crazy that I couldn't decide how I felt about it, or that perhaps I really did feel both ways.

When it got dark, Dad passed out sparklers, and we stood around the farmyard singing "Yankee Doodle Dandy" at Olivia's request.

July nights in Minnesota take their time in arriving, so by the time the sparklers ran out, it was close to ten o'clock. My kids were exhausted as was Kaitlin. Noah had long since fallen asleep in Grandpa Stuart's lap.

Our Red Wing and Minneapolis relatives packed up their cars and their sleepy kids and headed for home. We would see them all in a few weeks' time for Jennifer and Jared's wedding.

There were a few things left to clean up in the yard, but Mom insisted what was left could be taken care of in the morning. Wes and Nicole began getting ready to leave and looked for Seth. He was nowhere in sight. Neither was Lara.

Nicole and Mom exchanged the same look I had seen before at the shop, and Nicole called Seth's name. Mom went to see if Lara was in the house with my grandparents and Aunt Elizabeth. As Michael and I put our kids in our car, Seth and Lara appeared from behind the barn, walking slowly and looking like they hadn't a care in the world. Lara stopped as they neared the open area where all the cars were and peered behind a couple of planks of wood leaning against the side of the barn. Seth stopped too.

Nicole gave Wes a look of exasperation. Mom stepped onto the porch and saw them too. Wes called out to his nephew.

"Seth, come on. Let's go."

I couldn't hear what Seth said to Lara, but he said something, and she nodded. He started to walk away, turned and said something else to her, and she looked toward the barn doors. She nodded again.

Nobody said anything as Seth, Nicole, and Wes got into Wes's car.

"Great party, Claire," Nicole said, through the open car window. "I'm not opening until ten tomorrow, okay?"

"Fine by me," Mom said. But she wasn't looking at Nicole. She was looking at Lara who was slowly making her way toward the rest of us.

"We'd better go too," Michael said to me. He thanked my parents, shouted a goodbye to Lara, and got in the driver's side.

I called Bogart, who came bounding out of the machine shed, and let him into the back of the car with the kids.

"See you tomorrow," I said to my parents, waving to Lara, who was still somewhat in the shadows.

She smiled and waved back.

Later that night, Michael asked me in the quiet darkness of our bedroom if I was okay with Lara being here in Blue Prairie.

I said something dumb like, "What do you mean?"

"You seem a little...edgy."

No woman likes to be told she's edgy. Even if it's true.

"It's like you're apprehensive about her being here," he continued.

"It's just a big change for me, that's all."

"Are you sure that's all it is?"

"What's that supposed to mean?"

Then he said something that I could tell he had been wanting to say for days, probably since Lara arrived. He told me I was acting a little jealous. A little childish. I could handle being told I was acting jealous. That would make sense, as uncharitable as it was. I had always been the only daughter. Now the long-lost and dearly loved other daughter was back. Of course I might feel a little jealous.

But acting a little childish?

It was like being told to grow up, something no one had ever said to me. I was the take-charge firstborn who grew up too fast. I had never been thought of as immature. Michael didn't exactly say he thought I was acting immature, but he may as well have. To me, it meant the same thing. And I could not recall any other time in my life when someone accused me of behaving like a child, not even when I *was* a child.

I honestly didn't know what to say to him. My silence bothered him; I guess he thought I would defend myself or accuse him of something worse or at least get angry, but I didn't do any of those things. I didn't say it to him, but I suddenly felt like he had hit the nail right on the head. I didn't know if I really was acting like a child, but I knew he had one thing right—I really did feel like one.

He began to apologize.

I told him not to worry about it.

But he kept saying he was sorry and asking me to forgive him, which I said I did, but I didn't feel any forgiveness, because I didn't feel any injury.

It was a while before he fell asleep. Until he did, I laid very still to make him think I had drifted off so he would give in and do the same. When his breathing became steady and slow, I inched my way out of our bed and tiptoed downstairs. Bogart wagged his tail as I stepped into the moonlit kitchen, and he followed me out onto the porch.

My beloved constellations greeted me.

The sky was shimmering with starlight, and the sheer splendor of its size amazed me once again. I sat down and leaned against a post. Bogart curled up beside me to wait out my contemplations.

As I sat there, it occurred to me that I was looking at the same July sky as when I first moved to Blue Prairie, when my losses were painfully fresh. I was a child then. I was only twelve. Every-thing I felt back then—about what happened to me, my family, and my sister, Lara—I buried deep within me while encircled by a night like this one. No wonder I felt like a child. I was exhuming dreams and desires I had buried when I *was* a child. Now I was twenty-nine, and my buried dreams were being unearthed all around me, without my consent, without my blessing, without my permission.

It didn't matter that I was getting what I wanted all along—a relationship with my sister. It was the way it was happening that troubled me. It was all happening outside of my control—just like before, when I wanted to love Lara and no one would let me.

I began to pray to God that He would help me let go of the part of my past that still hurt and hang on to the part that loved Lara, but I kept remembering what I said that day Lara was taken from my young arms.

I don't want to see her anymore.

I wanted to erase the fact that I ever said it, ever thought it, ever wanted it. But I didn't know how. I didn't know how to dis-regard the reality that I wanted to let her go, that I agreed with my mother that loving her was too hard, forgetting her was easier.

I don't know how long I sat there under my stars, pleading with the One who made them. When I felt like I said all I could say, I rose to return to my bed, feeling no better.

As I took one last look at the heavens, I almost felt like God was whispering something to me, but when I stood completely still to listen, I realized it was only the wind in the elms.

My grandparents and Uncle Matt and Aunt Marta stayed two more days and then left Sunday for the long drive back to Ann Arbor. After church, Mom invited Michael and the kids and me to join them for lunch before everyone left.

Grandma seemed particularly sad when it was time to go. Uncle Matt and my dad began loading the car as soon as the meal was over as almost everyone stepped outside for goodbyes. While taking Bennett inside to use the bathroom, I caught the tail end of a conversation Grandma was having with Mom about Lara.

"Just let her come for a week, Claire," Grandma was saying. "That's not such a long time."

"I don't know, Mom," my mother said in return. "Maybe it's too soon for her."

"You mean maybe it's too soon for you," Grandma said, but not in an unkind way.

"Maybe it is," Mom said. "Maybe it's too soon for both of us."

"But she wants to come," Grandma said.

"She's too kind to tell you otherwise," Mom said next. "Who knows what she really wants. Lara would never tell anyone she doesn't want to be with them."

There was a pause.

"Just a week," Grandma finally said. "She's my granddaughter, Claire."

I guess it wasn't until that moment that I realized Grandma completed the trio of women who had loved Lara and let her go: my mother, my grandmother, and me. She probably had done what both my mother and I did with the affection we held for that little baby girl with the dark hair: pressed it into a tight space where no light would shine. But the walls of that tight space had been bulldozed for her just like they had been for Mom and me, and light was now pouring in on all sides.

"The wedding's coming up," my mom said rather absently.

"That's not until the tenth of August," Grandma said. "That's more than a month away. She could come week after next, stay a week, and still be back in plenty of time."

Bennett was finished using the toilet and was asking loudly if he could have another brownie. The voices in the kitchen became suddenly hushed.

I took my son back outside. Lara was pushing Olivia in the tire swing, and the adults were standing by the car, waiting for Mom and Grandma. They soon came out. Grandma was smiling from ear to ear. She headed straight for the tire swing.

"How does week after next sound?" Grandma said to Lara.

Lara looked over at my mother like any child would look to its mother for permission or advice. It was the unmistakable gesture of a daughter seeking a parent's blessing.

This did not go unnoticed by Mom, either. She seemed to relax as Lara looked her way and waited. My mom smiled and nodded. Lara turned back to my grandmother.

"That sounds great," she said.

"I'll take care of making the airline reservation," my grand-mother said, giving Lara a hug goodbye. "We'll have such a good time."

"I am sure we will," Lara said.

"I want to come, too, Gamma," Olivia said.

"Well!" my grandmother said, "Wouldn't that be fun!"

"Maybe next time, Livvy," I interjected.

"I want to go this time!" she said, and I could sense a battle brewing.

"Let's talk about it later and see what's best," I said.

"I'm coming with you!" Olivia said to Lara, looking up at her from the swing.

Mom came to my rescue.

"Olivia, can you get Aunt Elizabeth's sweater for her? I left it on the kitchen counter."

Olivia bounded off the swing to fetch the sweater as I gave Mom a look of gratitude that I knew she understood.

We said goodbye and watched the car drive away; then Michael and I ushered our own kids into our car to go home.

Lara stood there between my parents as we drove off, and I suddenly saw the irony of her being between my parents. I won-dered what it was like in that house with just the three of them: the mother, the daughter, and the man who loves his wife.

On Monday, as another workweek began, I found myself itching to get away from the tedious routine of my job, even though it was work I loved. I brought Olivia and Bennett with me to play in the basement at the Table that morning. Michael was doing livestock judging in another town all that week, so the kids had to be with me or spend their days in daycare. That probably also colored my mood. One day was fine in the basement of the shop, but I knew they would balk at five days of it, and they didn't particularly enjoy daycare in the summer. I wasn't looking forward to the week.

Mom and Lara were already at the Table when we arrived. Mom was on the phone in the office, and Lara was making lattes behind the counter with Nicole and Trish. I sent the kids downstairs to play since it was my day to run the front rooms where we sold the books, my paintings, and a few other gift items.

It was one of those mornings where nothing went right for me as a mother. The kids were up and down the stairs, constantly needing my attention or my refereeing skills. By lunchtime I had a monstrous headache. I was swallowing two Advil when Lara came up to me.

"I'm off at noon every day this week," she said. "I can take Olivia and Bennett home with me, and you can come get them when the shop closes."

"That's too much to ask of you," I said, holding my head.

"You didn't ask," she said softly. "I offered. I want to do this. It will help you, it will be fun for me, and hopefully they'll enjoy it too."

I looked up at her, searching for some ulterior motive, which was ludicrous. Lara never seemed to do anything with a concealed purpose. And she was right, it would be a tremendous help to me.

"You sure?" I said.

"We'll have a great time," she said. "I love your kids."

Then she disappeared down the basement stairs.

When I drove up my parents' driveway at four thirty, Olivia and Bennett were sitting in a plastic wading pool that I hadn't seen since Spencer was a kid. I didn't even know my parents still had it. They had spoons, measuring cups, and Cool Whip containers, and they were having a great time filling the cups and containers with water and splashing each other. Lara was at the side of the pool with my parents' cell phone tucked under her ear, deep in conversation, as she filled the pool with more water. She must have stopped at my house to get the kids' swimsuits.

I got out of my car to the sound of laughter.

"Mommy! Look! I can blow bubbles!" Olivia screwed up her eyes, stuck her face in the water, and blew air out of her nose. Then she lifted her face. "Lara said she can teach me how to swim!"

I looked over at Lara, who smiled sheepishly.

"Yes, Cleo, I will," she was saying. "I miss you, too. Say hello to Ben for me. Bye-bye."

She threw the hose away from the pool onto the grass and stood up, pressing the off button on the phone as she stood.

"Cleo says hi," she said.

"Does she really?" I said, probably sounding more cynical that I intended.

"Yes, she does," Lara answered, meeting my gaze and slipping the phone into her pocket.

"Lara is a light guard!" Olivia announced. "She can teach me to swim!"

"I can blow!" Bennett said, putting his face in the water and blowing bubbles as well.

"You're a lifeguard?" I said to Lara.

She nodded.

"I just finished the last level in March. I taught a preschool swimming class in April," she said. "It was a lot of fun."

"We want to go to the big pool," Olivia said.

"We need to ask Mom first," Lara said to Olivia.

My daughter looked up at me, hope shining on her wet face.

"We can probably do that," I said.

"Can we go *now?*" Olivia said, hopping out of the wading pool.

"How about tomorrow?" Lara said, handing her a towel and looking at me.

"Sure, you can go tomorrow," I said.

I got my kids dried off and changed into dry clothes and then helped them get into the car.

"The swimming thing was just an idea," Lara said to me. "If you have made other arrangements for swimming lessons…"

"No, I haven't," I said, feeling strangely at ease and yet apprehensive about Lara teaching Olivia how to swim. "Maybe tomorrow I can leave a little early and take Bennett off your hands when you take her."

"All right," Lara said smiling.

On the short drive home Olivia held up one of her Barbie dolls and told me her name wasn't Barbie anymore. It was Lara.

On Tuesday and Thursday of that week, Lara took Olivia to the pool in town in the late afternoon, and the two of them spent more than an hour in the water both times. On Thursday I came to watch the last few minutes before the pool closed for the supper hour.

Olivia was completely relaxed in Lara's care and didn't seem the least bit afraid of being in the water. It was so unlike the year before when I couldn't get Olivia anywhere near the pool. I was both amazed and irritated that Olivia could lavish such trust upon a teenage girl she had known for only a month.

I took Bennett outside to wait while the girls changed into dry clothes. We sat on a bench by a bunch of kids waiting for rides or for friends and siblings still inside. I was anxious to get home, and Lara and Olivia seemed to be taking forever. I kept looking at my watch like it would hurry them along. Finally they emerged.

I stood up as they approached us. I didn't even bother to try to hide my impatience, but neither of them seemed to notice.

In fact, Lara's attention was drawn to two nearby children fighting about who knows what. The older one, a boy, said something in Spanish to the other one, a younger girl. He was angry. He said something else and then laughed. Then he got on a bike and pedaled away. The little girl began to cry.

Lara walked over to her, knelt down, and said something to the little girl in perfect Spanish. I had forgotten she lived in Ecuador for twelve years.

I took French in high school, not Spanish, so I had no idea what she was saying. I heard Lara say "Mama," and the little girl answered her.

Lara said something else to the little girl, then stood up and held out her hand. The little girl took it, and they began to walk toward the pool admission window.

"I'll be right back," she called to me.

I watched as Lara led the little girl to the office window. She explained something, and then the pool cashier handed Lara the handset of a phone. She talked into the phone for a few minutes, speaking Spanish the whole time. Then she handed the phone back, knelt down, and told the little girl something.

The two of them walked back out to where we stood.

"You guys can go on ahead," she said. "I have my car here. I'm just going to wait until this little girl's grandmother comes to get her."

"What's up?" I said.

"It seems her bicycle was stolen," Lara said. "She's not sure of the way home without her brother to show her the way. And he took off."

"We can wait," I said, hardly knowing why. Lara did have her own car. I was going home after this, and so was she. But we waited.

About ten minutes later an aging, gray sedan pulled into the parking lot, and an older woman stepped out of it.

"*Mi abuela*," the little girl said softly.

Lara and the child walked over to the car, and Lara chatted with the woman in Spanish for a few minutes, stroking the back of the little girl's head the whole time. Then the little girl got into the car, and Lara waved as they drove away.

"What were you talking about?" I asked Lara when she walked back to where we waited.

"I told her I could call the police for her, that her granddaughter's bike had been stolen," Lara said. "But she said she has a nephew who speaks English who can call for her."

I shook my head.

"Where are that little girl's parents?" I said gruffly, making my way to where our cars were parked side by side.

"They're in heaven," Lara answered.

On Friday, my kids wanted to be at their own house while Lara watched them. So at noon, Lara took them home.

When I arrived later that afternoon, I was a little perturbed to see Seth's car in the driveway alongside Lara's.

Nobody was in the yard or the house. As I headed toward the barn I heard Olivia and Bennett's voices.

The two of them were in the pen where Seth kept the lamb he was raising for the county fair. They were brushing it while the lamb ate. Seth and Lara were seated side by side on a hay bale.

"Hi, Mommy," Olivia said. "We're brushing Spock."

"He's eating," Bennett chimed in.

"I wasn't sure where everybody was," I said. "Hey, Seth. I didn't expect to see you here."

He just looked at me.

"I always come on Friday afternoons to take care of Spock," he said.

He had me there.

"I guess it is Friday, isn't it?" I said.

"Yeah, it is," he said, standing.

"I should probably go," Lara said, as she rose also.

"Can Lara sleep over?" Olivia said, handing the brush over to Seth.

"Maybe another time, Olivia," Lara said right away. "I'm going to help your Grandma Gerrity at the shop tonight, okay?"

It was Friday. Jazz Night at Tennyson's Table.

I found out later Seth spent the evening there as well.

The next day at Nicole's brunch Seth and Lara disappeared as soon as the cheese soufflé was eaten. Mom gave me a look a few minutes later, and I went to see where they had gone.

I found them on the deck in the backyard. She was sitting. He was pacing. I was indoors, and the air conditioner was humming merrily, so I had no idea what they were talking about. I didn't know what else to do now that I'd found them, so I headed back to the kitchen.

Mom and Nicole both looked at me when I came back.

"Well?" Nicole said.

"I'll talk to Lara later," I said.

I came over to my parents' house later that day with the kids and an old bookcase I bought some weeks earlier and was going to refinish at my parents' place. It was a good enough reason to go over and talk to Lara.

I asked her to help me bring the bookcase into the machine shed, which she cheerfully did. When we had set it down, I asked her if there was anything going on between her and Seth.

"Going on?" she asked.

"You know what I mean," I said. And I was sure she did.

She paused for a moment.

"It's not what you think," she said. "Seth doesn't need a girl-friend right now. He needs a friend. And he needs God."

"And you think you're the one to lead him to God?" I said.

She shrugged. "It doesn't have to be me."

"What? But no one else is doing it?" I said, a little miffed. I had spent countless hours trying to help Seth make sense of his life.

"I don't know what anyone else is doing, Kate. I don't presume to know," she said. "He just asked me about God. And he keeps asking me. He's searching for answers."

"What were you two doing the night of the party when no one could find you?" I suddenly asked.

She looked puzzled.

"The night of the party?" she repeated.

"When everyone was leaving, you and Seth came walking up from behind the barn."

Her eyes got wide as she realized what I was hinting at.

"I was looking for Silhouette," she said, clearly hurt. "He was just helping me."

So they were looking for her cat. I'm sure *she* was, but I had my doubts about Seth.

"Look, Lara," I said. "I've spent a lot of time with Seth. He is a born manipulator. He may just be using every opportunity to get you to fall for him."

Lara looked away. A tear slipped from one eye. She didn't say anything for a few seconds.

"I know you mean well, Kate," she said softly. "And I know Seth has a lot of respect for you, but you will never get anywhere with him until you see him as more than just the sum of his faults."

I was speechless.

"Inside that tough guy is a little boy who was abandoned by his father, whose mother has pretty much given up on him, and who believes he isn't worth the air he breathes," she said, softer still. "God chooses to perfectly love the unlovely and the lovely alike, without hesitation," she said, wiping the tear away. "Seth needs to know that. He *has* to know that, or he will destroy himself."

She turned and walked back toward the house.

28

*L*ara and Mom left for the Twin Cities on Monday morning so Lara could catch a noon flight to Detroit. Mom asked me if I wanted to go with them, inviting me to do a little shopping with her and her friend Becky after Lara was safely on her flight, but I decided not to go. I told her I didn't want to leave Nicole with the shop all to herself on a Monday, usually a busy day. But that wasn't the real reason.

The real reason was I felt uncomfortable around Lara, because part of me felt I owed her an apology. I hadn't been alone with her since the episode in the machine shed at my parents' house. She wasn't mad at me, and I thought it would make a lot more sense if she were. It made me feel worse that she didn't treat me differently. It was like we never had that conversation in the machine shed. In truth, I was kind of mad at her for accusing me of missing the boat with Seth. I wanted her to be mad at me for accusing her of having romantic feelings for him. But she wasn't.

Every day that week Olivia told me how much she missed Lara, and even Bennett started to moan about her not being around. I tried to keep up with Olivia's swimming lessons at the community pool. I tried twice. But I "didn't do it right." Olivia didn't want me to try and show her anything about swimming while Lara was away. And Michael started getting things ready for the county fair, an event many of his agriculture students were involved with, so I didn't see him much that week.

Everything seemed wrong while Lara was away, not "back to normal" like I thought it would be. And that aggravated me. Mom was moody at the shop, and even Dad, the few times I saw him, seemed quiet and deep in thought. By Sunday, the day Lara was to return, everyone seemed anxious and distracted, like she was returning home from a year's absence, not just a week's.

After Lara came home from Ann Arbor, the rest of July slipped away without incident, and August arrived, as hot and humid as ever. Lara seemed to have enjoyed her time with my grandparents, but I didn't ask her much about it, and she didn't volunteer any information. I asked her if she had a good time. She said she did. End of conversation.

The county fair came and went, and Seth sold his blue-ribbon ewe to a local breeder. He kept the ribbon. I think it was the first time Seth had ever gotten an award for anything. He hung it over the rearview mirror of his car like a pair of furry dice.

The Friday before Jennifer's wedding, Mom, Dad, and Lara, together with Michael, our kids, and me, drove up to Red Wing to practice for the wedding and attend the rehearsal dinner. I was a little nervous about the whole thing. Jennifer was adamant from the beginning of her wedding plans that Olivia and Bennett should be the flower girl and ring bearer for the ceremony. I figured Olivia would do okay, but I wasn't sure about Bennett. Not knowing for sure what he would do that Saturday—the day of the wedding—kept me from enjoying Friday.

The rehearsal went okay, and the dinner, which was held at an old inn, was nice, but it was late when the kids got to bed, and I feared lack of sleep would just make things worse for me.

On Saturday, Olivia was at the beauty salon by ten in the morning. She wanted Lara to take her. Part of me was slightly offended that she didn't insist I come, and part of me was glad I could concentrate solely on keeping Bennett fed and rested.

Pictures with the photographer began at noon and became rather tedious. The photographer came across as somewhat of a perfectionist, every pose seeming to take forever. I felt Lara was doing a much better job just taking candids. Everyone seemed to be relaxed and comfortable in front of her lens.

At one o'clock, two hours before the wedding, I found a quiet place in the church's nursery and rocked Bennett to sleep. I wanted him to have one nap under his belt before the ceremony began, even if it was just a short one. It took a while, but he finally gave in, and after he was sleeping soundly, I tiptoed out to see if I could find a Diet Coke.

Being unfamiliar with Karin and Kent's church, I got lost looking for the kitchen. But I did come across Lara and Olivia sitting in a little alcove. Olivia was in Lara's lap, with her blonde curls nestled against the cornflower blue of Lara's dress. Olivia's white tulle skirt was spread across Lara's knees, and she was clicking her shiny white heels together. Neither one saw me approach.

"Do you like my dress?" she was saying to Lara.

"It's a very beautiful dress," Lara answered.

"I have a crown, too," Olivia said, pointing to the tiny tiara poking through the ringlets on the top of her head.

"Yes, you do," Lara said. "You look just like a princess."

"I might be too scared to throw the petals," Olivia said after a pause.

Lara looked out the window for a moment.

"Sometimes being in a big place where there's lots of people can seem a little scary," Lara said. "But just remember whose big place this is, Olivia. This is like God's house, so you can feel safe here. And you can just look at your mommy and daddy as you're walking. Don't look at anyone else if you think it might be too scary. Your mommy and daddy will be right up front by the tall flowers. They will be looking at you walking toward them and thinking how beautiful and grown-up you look."

"What if I forget to throw the petals?" Olivia said.

"It will be okay if you don't throw them, sweetie. Nobody will mind."

I loved seeing Olivia becoming so relaxed, but I wished I was the one setting her at ease.

"Do you have any brothers or sisters?" Olivia asked Lara, and I felt myself lean forward to hear her answer. I wondered what Lara would say. It amazed me how much I wanted to know what she thought of Spencer and me. But what could Lara possibly say to Olivia? I couldn't picture Lara lying, but to Olivia, Lara was just a friend of the family. What was she going to tell her?

"Well, when I was growing up, it was just me and my mom and my dad," Lara said. "But where we lived in Ecuador, there were lots of other children, so I felt like I had many brothers and sisters."

"Did you ever wish you had a real sister?" Olivia said, clicking her heels.

I felt my breath catch in my throat.

"Yes, I did," Lara said softly, looking out the window. "Many times."

"Me, too," Olivia chimed in, not giving me a moment to absorb what I was hearing.

"How about if *you* be my sister?" Olivia said, looking up at Lara and smiling widely.

Lara smiled down at her.

"We sort of already are," Lara said. "We both love Jesus, and we are both in God's family—that makes us sisters in Jesus. Pretty cool, huh?"

Olivia looked back down at her shoes, smiling.

I decided it was time to emerge from the shadows.

"Can I use your camera a moment, Lara?" I said, motioning to the Canon sitting next to her.

"Sure," Lara answered, a bit surprised to see me.

I took the camera and stepped back from them, angling the camera so it picked up the sunlight through the window, which splashed their beautiful faces with natural light.

"Say cheese," I said and pressed the shutter button.

Jennifer's wedding was beautiful, and my kids did everything they were supposed to do. Olivia walked down the aisle with Bennett at her side, stopping every other step to throw a tiny handful of petals. It seemed to take a long time for the kids to reach the bridal party at the front of the church. Every time Olivia stopped, Bennett stopped. And if a petal landed off the white satin runner, Olivia bent down, picked it up, and placed it where it belonged. She watched over Bennett like a mother hen, making sure the rings he carried in between the pages of an open Bible didn't fall off.

As soon as they made it to the front of the church, Olivia and Bennett came and sat down by Michael and me. Mission accomplished.

The rest of the day was pleasant enough. My kids found other kids to pal around with at the reception, which was held in the fellowship hall of the church. Lara stayed at our table for the most part, as did my parents. At one point I heard Mom introduce Lara to a wedding guest.

"This is Lara Prentiss," she said to the woman. "Lara's mother just recently passed away. She was a very dear friend. Lara is spending her senior year in high school with Dan and me."

The woman said something like, "Oh, I am so sorry," to Lara but I didn't hear the rest. Bennett was suddenly at my side, doing what I call the potty dance.

I took him to the toilet, but my mind was elsewhere. I knew Lara wouldn't just be "spending her senior year of high school" with us like my mother told that woman. It wasn't going to be just nine months of having her and then letting her go. That's what happened the last time. But I knew it wouldn't be that way this time. I knew that Mom would never let her go again.

I brought Bennett back out, and he scampered away to rejoin his new friends. I walked toward my parents' table and saw that Mom and Lara had left it, leaving Spencer sitting alone. Natalie must have found a quiet place to nurse Noah. I couldn't immediately see where Mom and Lara were, but I decided I would take advantage of even a few minutes alone with Spencer.

"Having a good time?" I asked him as I reached the table and took the chair I had sat in earlier.

"Yeah, it was a nice wedding," he said.

"Yes, it was," I replied.

"Olivia and Bennett were as cute as can be," he said. "They nearly stole the show."

"I guess I worried for nothing," I said. "I was so afraid it would end up a disaster."

"How come?" he said smiling.

"Wait until Noah is older," I said. "Then you'll know how unpredictable kids can be."

"You're doing a great job with your kids, Kate," he said. "I'm sure they don't surprise you with disasters too often."

"No, but when it happens, run for cover," I said half-grinning and ignoring that we weren't talking about what I wanted to talk about at all. "Olivia has a temper you wouldn't believe. Sometimes it amazes me how quickly she can get angry. Bennett is following right along in her footsteps. And then of course when they get angry, I get angry, and I usually say and do things I regret."

"It happens to all parents," Spencer said. "None of us is perfect."

"Being a parent sure brings out the worst in us sometimes," I replied.

"And sometimes the best," Spencer said, looking me straight in the eye.

I think he knew then why I had come back to the empty table to talk with him. Even though the conversation seemed to be about my kids and my being a mother, I could sense in that moment that Spencer was really talking about Lara and our own mother. I felt like he was telling me with his eyes that there was no cause for regrets when it came to Lara, that terrible circumstances had actually brought out the best in our mother. And even in our father.

And if I let it, it could bring out the best in me.

~~~

We stayed another night in Red Wing and then drove home on Sunday. On Monday, Michael and Mom registered Lara for classes at the same high school where Michael teaches. I think Mom was hoping that Lara wouldn't really be academically ready for her senior year. But there was no getting past the fact that her school records showed she was way ahead of most sixteen-year-olds.

Just before school started, Michael, the kids, and I prepared for our family vacation—a week in northern Minnesota at a lakeside resort. Olivia begged us to bring Lara along. I almost wished she hadn't, because for some reason I wanted it to be my idea that she come with us. I was starting to become aware of new feelings for Lara that made me feel good inside, not anxious. I wanted them to grow.

The week at the lake was very relaxing in many ways. We didn't have a schedule from day to day; we just woke up every morning and said to one another, "What do you want to do today?" We would decide, and then we would do it.

One morning late in the week, Michael took Bennett and Olivia out in a canoe. Lara and I sat on the dock with our bare feet hanging over the side. I was finally starting to feel comfortable around her—not completely at ease, but certainly less apprehensive.

We chatted about trivial things: the weather, food, and traveling. Somehow Rosemary's name came up.

"Do you miss her?" I asked, realizing that, of course, any child misses a parent who has just died.

Lara looked out over the water and said nothing for the first few seconds.

"I miss her more than I thought I would," she finally said. "I was so ready for her to be free of pain that in the end I wanted her to go home. I guess I thought I wouldn't miss her as much because she would be in heaven and would never know pain again. But I do miss her."

"Rosemary was an amazing person," I said, looking out over the water as well.

"Yes, she was," Lara said.

"You're a lot like her, Lara," I said, looking at her.

She looked up at me and smiled.

"I think that's one of the nicest things anyone has ever said to me," she said.

We were quiet for a moment, each of us kind of lost in our own thoughts.

I didn't know what Lara was thinking, but I was wondering what it would be like to be compared to someone as matchless as Rosemary. I couldn't imagine it ever happening to me. I was nothing like Rosemary, nothing like Lara.

"Did you ever get into trouble when you were little?" I suddenly asked.

Lara looked over at me and smiled. "Didn't you?" she said.

"Of course," I replied, like it was a silly question for her to ask. It occurred to me she must have thought the same thing or she wouldn't have turned the question on me.

"I have a hard time picturing you being defiant," I said honestly.

Lara's smile didn't fade. She kicked at the water that covered her feet.

"I spent my share of time in the corner," she said, laughing a little.

"Well, you seem to have now mastered the knack of always doing the right thing at the right time," I said. "You haven't been in the corner in a long, long time, I'm sure."

It sounded like an indictment. I hadn't meant for it to sound that way, but it did.

Lara looked thoughtful for a moment.

"I think we all struggle with trying to always do the right thing at the right time," Lara said. "I know I struggle sometimes with even *wanting* to do the right thing."

"But you always seem to win that struggle," I said.

Lara looked surprised. Worried.

"Well, I don't," she said.

"Lara, you are annoyingly perfect!" I said, turning my face to her. "I've watched you. I have *seen* how you respond to people."

I immediately wished I hadn't said "annoyingly."

But Lara just looked out over the water.

"My dad told me once that people usually see what they want to see," she said, and then she cocked her head and looked back at me.

I wanted to believe I had no idea what she was talking about, but the funny thing was, I did. Somehow she knew I had only seen the part of her I wanted to see—the lovely, perfect, tender part—because it proved to God and to everyone else that I had been right all along about Lara. She wasn't haunting evidence of the existence of evil in the world, though I was only just beginning to realize no one had ever really thought that about her. To me, Lara was simply a beautiful girl whose life began the way all human life begins—in the mind of God. This was the reason I had so desperately wanted my parents to keep her. I had not really understood the horribleness of the offense that had been commited against my parents. I had only understood my own twelve year old wonder of finally having a sister. And the frustration of having her for only one May morning.

There were several long minutes of silence between us. I wondered if Lara was thinking she had said too much.

I knew Lara couldn't know what I was thinking at that moment, but she rightly guessed I was again pondering our common past, the little of it that we shared.

"Kate, I'm sorry so much had to change for you because of me," she said.

I honestly didn't know what to say to her. I hadn't been aware that part of me held her accountable for the life I was now leading. Certainly it wasn't her fault; she was an innocent victim. And while on the one hand she was tangible proof of the tragedy that had reshaped our family life, on the other hand if there had been no Lara, we likely never would have moved to Blue Prairie. I wouldn't have met Michael. I wouldn't have Olivia and Bennett. And I couldn't bear to consider that.

"You have nothing to be sorry for," I finally said. "You never had a say in any of this, Lara. And I can't suppose my life would be better had I stayed in Minneapolis. Most of my dreams have come true in Blue Prairie."

"Which ones haven't?" she asked in a voice that sounded a little shaky.

"Just little ones that don't really matter, Lara," I said. "I'd like to see New York sometime. Or San Francisco."

"Me, too," she said. "I have always wanted to take pictures of busy New York sidewalks."

"Maybe someday we'll have to do that," I said.

She smiled at me.

"Do you have any other dreams waiting to come true?" she asked.

I had never told anyone—not even Michael—of my unfulfilled desire to paint the sky at night. I guess I didn't think anyone else would understand. I wasn't sure if even I understood why that mattered to me. But while sitting on the dock on that hot August afternoon, I told Lara.

She just nodded her head like she knew exactly what I meant.

"And I can't photograph it," she said. "Not enough light. And it's so frustrating because the midnight sky is so incredibly beautiful."

"Yes, it is," I said, amazed that we had this in common.

"But I know one day you will do it," she said. "It's too hard to remember the next day what the sky really looked like. You just have to bring your canvas out to where the stars are."

At that moment I began to understand something about myself that I am still learning. I'm afraid to bring my canvas out to where the stars are, afraid to paint alone in the dark with no one but God for company. I'm not sure why. But I was beginning to understand that somehow it was tied in with my fear of bringing my love out to where Lara was.

School started a few days after our return from the lake, and a new routine developed. I would drop the kids off at school and daycare in the morning, and Lara would pick them up in the afternoon. From three to five o'clock, the three of them would do "fun things all the time," as Olivia liked to say. Sometimes they went swimming at the community pool—Olivia could now dog paddle from one side of the pool to the other. Other times they went to the library or the park.

Sometimes they had tea and stories with Edith and Elaine, the sisters who owned the side-by-side Victorian bed-and-breakfast inns next to Tennyson's Table. This was Lara's idea. She began helping the sisters get their yards ready for the winter and developed a friendship with them. Olivia and Bennett loved going over to the inns with Lara. I could look out a side window of the Table to the porch of the East House and see my kids, each in a lap of one of the sisters, and Lara reading to all of them. Most of the books she borrowed from the Table.

On Fridays, Lara would bring Bennett and Olivia to the Table just before closing. I would take them home, and Lara would stay and get the place ready for Jazz Night. She also worked Saturdays at the shop and hosted the Tuesday-night book clubs.

That September was one of the least stressful months I had experienced in who knows how long.

There was only one day in that month that was not at all "routine." In fact, it was unlike any day I have ever experienced.

It was a Monday near the beginning of the month. I arrived at the shop early to find my mother sitting at the little writing table by the bay window—the writing table that had given the shop its name.

She had a cup of coffee in her hands and was looking out the window, quite unaware of my presence. I couldn't remember the last time she had sat at that table. And the look on her face was one I did not recognize. It scared me a little.

"You know you can only have free coffee at that table if you're writing," I said, wanting her to know I was there and, more importantly to me, wanting her to come out from under that spell.

She jumped a little as a weak smile broke across her face.

"Is it nine o'clock already?" she asked.

I came over to her.

"No, I'm just here a little early," I said, and then added, "You looked like you were off in another world when I came in. Is everything all right?"

She looked out the window again and then up at me.

"Everything is all right," she said, like she meant every word, but she turned to look out the window again like everything wasn't.

"What is it, Mom?" I said, pulling up a chair.

She sort of smiled and sort of sighed.

"It's the ninth of September," she said.

It took me a few seconds to understand what she meant. But I finally clued in. It was the anniversary, the seventeenth anniversary in fact, of the attack that had changed everything for us.

"It's been a long time since this day has mattered to me," she continued, almost like she was talking to herself. "When we moved here, I taught myself to forget it was a day that mattered. But it's different this year."

"Because Lara is here with you?" I asked.

She nodded.

We were silent for a moment.

"Do you remember when we were driving up to Two Harbors and you asked me if I knew what had become of Philip Wells?" she asked.

"Yes."

"And I told you I didn't know or care?"

"Yes."

"He died in a fight with another prisoner six years ago. They were arguing over cigarettes."

She said it like she was telling me the forecast called for rain. Without emotion or engagement.

"How did you find out?" I asked.

"I thought Lara might want to know some day," she said. "I thought she might ask me, and I didn't want her to go looking for the answers. I wanted to have them ready for her so she wouldn't have to. So I called the prison and asked."

"Does Lara know?" I asked.

My mom nodded and her eyes got misty.

"You mean she asked about him already?" I thought that was pretty heartless, and I struggled to believe the Lara I knew would do it after living here only three months.

Mom shook her head.

"She didn't ask about *him*, she asked about herself," Mom said, starting to cry.

I didn't understand.

My mom cleared her throat and sat up straight, trying to regain her composure.

"She asked me if it was painful for me and Dan to have her here because of... because of how she was conceived. She told me if it was, to just tell her, and she would call her uncle. She wanted to make sure Dan and I didn't take her in just because Rosemary begged us. Lara said she would understand if it was too difficult for us to have her."

"What did you tell her?" I said.

"I told her the truth," Mom said, looking at me. "That it has always been difficult *not* having her, even when I pretended it was easy."

I said nothing.

"Then I told her I didn't even remember that night, that I didn't even know what Philip Wells looked like," Mom continued. "And then I told her what had happened to him in prison."

Mom hung her head like she was ashamed she had told Lara, like maybe she had tried to use the news to her own advantage.

"What did she say?" I asked.

Mom shrugged.

"She said she hoped he had come to faith before he died."

Now it was my turn to look out the window.

"I don't think she ever thought of Philip Wells as her father in any sense other than simple biology," Mom said, as a tear slipped down her left cheek.

I hated to ask it, but I needed to.

"So where does that leave you?" I said.

My mom dabbed at her eyes with her shirtsleeve.

"I asked Lara that same question," she said, smiling nervously.

I waited to hear the answer.

"She said Rosemary was her mom, but she also always thought of me as her mother, even when she didn't know me," Mom said. "I gave her life, and I gave her a family. She said she always thought I had been a good mother to her in the short time I had her."

We were both quiet for a moment. I wondered when this conversation had taken place. I asked my mom, thinking maybe it was just after the wedding. They had actually had the discussion the day before the July Fourth party—more than two months ago.

"Why didn't you tell me this before?" I asked. "I mean, about Philip Wells."

Mom turned to look at me.

"I didn't say anything because until just recently you seemed like you were…I don't know…like you were distancing yourself from Lara," she said. "Like you already had more than you could mentally deal with. I didn't want to intrude."

"It was that obvious?" I asked quietly, not looking at her.

"It was to me," she said. "But I understood why. I even expected it."

I looked up at her.

"You were so young when you had to give Lara up," Mom said to me. "And you wanted a sister so badly. You loved her before she was even born, just like I did. You loved her because of who she was—your sister—not because of how she came to be, just like I loved her because she was my daughter. Then you had to let her go. And that hurt you *because* you loved her. Loving Lara had been painful for you, Kate. Now she's back in your life, and you have to decide how much you will allow yourself to love her again. I think that's why you've kept her at a distance."

I now found that my own cheeks were wet but didn't raise a hand to wipe the tears away. It was almost as if I didn't want to admit I was crying and that everything my mother was saying was true. I asked her in an unsteady voice how she so easily let Lara back into her affections.

"I decided loving her completely was worth the risk of getting hurt because I wanted the joy of it," she said.

"So it's that easy?" I said curtly, finally wiping my cheeks.

"No, it's that wonderful," she said.

"Why is God doing this?" I said after a moment's pause. "Why did He give her to us in such a terrible way, then take her away for years only to give her back?"

"I don't know," Mom said, looking out the window to a cloudless, blue sky. "I'm not sure I will ever know."

Then she turned back toward me.

"Grandma told me once, when I was still pretty young, that sometimes God's reasons for allowing certain things to happen are too complex for us to fully appreciate," she continued. "What He doesn't tell us, I think He wants us to trust Him for, because He is good and He cares for us. But I think I do finally understand something God has been trying to tell me, ever since I was a little girl."

She paused.

"What?" I asked. "What has He been trying to tell you?"

My mom shifted in her chair, like she was sure of what she knew but unsure of how to explain it to me. She took my hands in her own.

"I haven't told very many people this, Kate," she said. "But I awoke the morning I found out my real father had been killed with a voice in my ear, a voice I was sure was...God's voice. It was like He whispered something to me just as I was waking, something terribly important. Kate, He whispered the same thing to me three decades later on the day I knew I was pregnant with Lara. And I heard Him say it again the day we came home from Atlanta and I called you to see if everything was all right. Do you remember that day, Kate? You had just read Rosemary's letter the day before. I was going to be reading it that night."

I felt a shiver come over me. Mom held my hands tighter.

"What did God whisper to you?" I said, whispering myself.

"He told me not to be afraid."

"Not to be afraid of what?"

"I have never really understood that until now."

I waited.

"Not to be afraid to love," she said.

I knew what she meant. She was telling me that the risk of giving love and receiving love is better than the safety of not loving at all.

Deep down I knew she was right, but I wasn't ready to admit it. Not to her and not to myself.

*T*hat fifteen-minute conversation I had with my mother on the ninth of September would end up weaving itself in and out of my mind for weeks afterward. My doubts about trusting God and loving my sister filtered their way into every private moment, whether I was doing the dishes, painting a bowl of fruit, or staring at the sky at two o'clock in the morning.

I tried praying for wisdom, reassuring myself that the Bible promises that whoever prays for wisdom will get it. If I really was becoming wiser, I wasn't aware of it. It seemed to me that the more I tried to reconcile my conflicting thoughts, the more I realized I had no real desire to trim back the hedge of protection I had built around my heart. I wasn't going to trust God fully, and I wasn't going to love Lara fully. That's just the way I was, and I didn't think I was capable of changing.

Most of my waking hours I spent in the company of others, so I wasn't forced to wrestle with my private thoughts at every turn. The shop stayed busy during the autumn months. A new book club for young girls began—Lara's idea—and I began helping the mental health clinic in the next county with some kids who seemed to reveal their troubled thoughts only while painting in my studio. As November eased into December, Lara and Nicole fell into a decorating frenzy and turned the Table into a scene from A Christmas Carol. It was quite festive. Mom found all kinds of old editions of the Dickens classic and placed them on all the tables in the coffee shop. We turned off all the electric lights downstairs and instead used kerosene lamps all month. Nicole changed the whole menu in the coffee shop to include only nineteenth-century English delicacies. She and Trish and Lara decided to speak with an English accent whenever waiting on anybody. The contemporary Christmas CDs we usually had piped into all the rooms were replaced with music that would have been around in Ebenezer Scrooge's day.

Lara still kept the kids for me every afternoon. She and Seth did a lot of outdoor activities with them. They went sledding and ice skating, built snow forts, and shoveled the walks of elderly neighbors. Mom still worried about Lara and Seth spending so much time together, even after I told her about my conversation with Lara back in July. Lara had even told Mom she had no romantic feelings for Seth, that they were just good friends.

But Mom and I both feared that Seth was developing deeper feelings for Lara. How could he not? Lara was attractive, smart, fun to be with, and exceptionally compassionate. If Seth fell in love with Lara but she didn't return that love, it could prove to be disastrous. Seth had already been rejected—many times. He seemed to have tackled his drinking problem at that moment; at least there were no calls from the school or his social worker. But I worried that it could all come crashing down around him if Lara continued to want only his friendship.

For my birthday, just a few days before Christmas, Lara, Seth, and the kids decorated the house with balloons and streamers and baked me a cake. It was probably the sorriest looking cake ever made—Lara and Seth gave Olivia and Bennett free rein in decorating it—but it was special nonetheless because they had made it just for me.

Two days before Christmas Mom called me at home and asked if I could do her a favor. She was going to be tied up at a retailers' meeting in another town and wanted me to go with Lara to pick someone up at the bus station.

"Sure," I said. "But who's coming here on a bus?" I said. I had almost forgotten the bus even made a stop in Blue Prairie.

Mom paused for a moment.

"Cleo," she said.

I could hardly believe it.

"Cleo is coming here? For Christmas?" I said.

"It means a lot to Lara," Mom said, and I could tell she had rehearsed this speech. She had probably already used it on my dad. "Cleo has no one to spend the holidays with, Kate. Her only son and his family live in Texas, and they're spending Christmas with his wife's family."

I let out a little sigh.

"So you will go with Lara?" she said. "I don't want Cleo to think we're not happy that she's coming. I want one of us to be there with Lara when the bus drops her off."

"What are we supposed to do with her?" I said.

Mom paused for a moment.

"Just bring her back to the shop. I'll try and get back there as soon as I can."

At ten minutes to two, Lara and I pulled into the service station just off the highway where the bus from the Twin Cities stops every afternoon at two o'clock. Every day, that is, when someone wants to get off in Blue Prairie. I don't think that happens very often.

The bus arrived a few minutes early. The doors opened, and one solitary figure got off the bus. Cleo looked as tall as ever and carried her two black bags like they were filled with government secrets.

Lara ran to her, and Cleo hugged her with her bags still in her hands.

"Merry Christmas, Cleo," I said as cheerfully as I could.

"Thank you, Kate," she said, politely.

"Can I help you with those?" I mistakenly asked, reaching for a bag.

"I've got them," she said, whipping the bags from my reach.

Lara slipped her arm through Cleo's, and we walked toward the car as the bus pulled away. During the five-minute ride to the Table, Lara chattered about her new school, the new friends she had made, and the colleges she was interested in.

I drove in silence like a professional chauffeur. I dropped them off at the Table and then went to get Olivia from a friend's house. On the way I stopped at the grocery store to get a few last minute things for Christmas, taking my time because I wasn't too anxious to get back to the Table.

When we finally got back to the shop, Olivia and I came in through the back, hoping to avoid being noticed. I was hoping Cleo was sitting in one of the front rooms, drinking a cup of hot cider, and waiting for my mother, and that I could sneak back to the studio and put things away for the four days we would be closed.

But Cleo wasn't in one of the front rooms. She was wearing an apron, standing over a trio of elderly ladies at a little table in the dining room and was serving tea from a Royal Doulton teapot.

"What's going on?" I whispered to Nicole, motioning toward Cleo.

"Lara put her to work," she said casually.

"And you just let her?" I said, laughing, but not in a humorous way.

Nicole shrugged and opened a bag of whole coffee beans.

"She makes good tea," she said.

"Anybody can make good tea," I whispered, taking off Olivia's heavy coat. "You just put boiling water into a cup and put a teabag in it."

"Cleo makes hers in a teapot with loose leaves and an infuser," Nicole said, pouring the beans into the grinder.

"What? She just happened to bring tea leaves and an infuser with her?" I asked, pulling off my own coat and watching Olivia scamper off to find Lara.

"Yep," Nicole said. "Orange pekoe."

I shook my head.

"You don't know her like I do, Nicole," I whispered. "She's as crotchety as they come."

"Maybe, but she sure has made fast friends in those three," Nicole said, winking at me and motioning with her head to the three women with whom Cleo was chatting. Hands on her hips, of course. "They're having a wonderful time talking about their grandchildren, amaryllis bulbs, and health ailments."

When Mom arrived a few minutes later, rushed and thinking she was terribly late, Cleo had made a fresh pot of her magical tea and was serving it to a second set of older women. Lara and Nicole stayed busy behind the counter, trying out a Cockney accent while serving up scones and clotted cream.

Before we knew it, it was time to clean up and close for the four-day break. Cleo insisted on scrubbing the tile floor in the dining room, saying, "It looks like it hasn't been done correctly in a month of Sundays."

Nicole gave her a mop and bucket and whispered to me as she walked past, "I like her!"

In no time at all the shop was sparkling clean, and everyone was sent to a different room to extinguish all the kerosene lamps. I overheard Cleo muttering that if people would take more care to pay their utility bills on time, they could avoid such trouble.

Nicole had to excuse herself to giggle in private. I followed her.

"We'll have to find a way to keep her," she said, wiping her eyes.

A gentle snowfall greeted us on Christmas morning—a beautiful beginning to the day. Michael, the kids, and I spent a quiet morning alone—just the four of us—opening gifts and putting together new toys. That afternoon we bundled up the kids and went to my parents' house for Christmas dinner with the family. My grandparents from Ann Arbor had flown in a few days before, and I wasn't surprised to see that Cleo and my grandmother hit it off rather well.

Grandpa sat in a leather chair by the fireplace most of the afternoon. He seemed to have aged considerably over the autumn months. It shouldn't have surprised me, but it did anyway. I began to have the queer and unpleasant sense that this would be the last Christmas he would spend with us.

My mom seemed to think this too. She hovered over him and spent more time tending to his comfort than anyone else's. I overheard her and my grandmother talking in hushed tones as I helped Bennett get a drink.

"It's his heart," Grandma was saying, but I didn't want to hear any more.

When we began opening gifts around my parents' tree, I was pleased to see so many gifts for Lara. She truly was one of the family. Olivia gave her a necklace of beads she made with modeling clay. Lara slipped it around her neck and gave Olivia a hug.

"I will treasure this always," I heard her say to my daughter. Then Lara stood up and approached the tree.

From the back, she pulled out a pile of like-sized presents. They were all wrapped in brown paper she presumably stenciled herself using half an apple and brick-red paint. Each was tied with a plaid ribbon. She began to hand them out.

Inside each was a framed eight by ten black-and-white photograph that Lara had taken, most of them shot either at the Fourth of July party or at Jennifer's wedding. My parents' photo was of the two of them sitting on their own porch steps. Mom had her arm through Dad's and her head rested on his shoulder. They were looking off to the west, unaware of any camera being focused on them, thinking about something known only to them. In my grandparents' photo, the two of them were making over Noah, who lay in Grandma's arms. Noah had one of Grandpa's fingers in his grasp. Each one, including Noah, had a look of awe and adoration on their faces. Lara had taken Olivia and Bennett's pictures in the barn with the new kittens. The looks on their childish faces were precious. Lara gave Michael and me a photo of the two of us looking at each other against the backdrop of the setting sun with our kids in the far background playing with our dog. It was a beautifully composed photo. She even had a photo for Cleo; a wonderful picture of Cleo and Rosemary taken the previous year when Rosemary's cancer was thought to be in remission.

Everyone was in awe of Lara's photos. Mom said she should start selling her work at the Table, and I wondered why we hadn't thought of that before.

As we started to clear away the wrapping paper and prepare for supper, Lara bent down and asked me quietly if I could come upstairs with her for a moment. I nodded and followed her upstairs to my old room.

When we got there, she smiled and handed me another present.

"I didn't want to give this to you downstairs because…well, because it's kind of a special photo that really isn't mine to give," she said, clearly a little uncomfortable.

Interest piqued, I opened the gift. The framed black-and-white photo was the one I had taken of Lara and Olivia on the day of the wedding. It is hard for me to describe the beauty of that photo. Lara's dark hair, Olivia's blonde curls, their smiling faces, the sunlight framing them both in a halo of radiance—it all combined to create a photograph unlike any I have ever seen. I could hardly believe I had taken it.

I stood there completely transfixed by it, displaying neither awe nor gratitude, but somehow Lara knew I loved it.

"It's beautiful, isn't it?" she said. "I am so glad you took it."

"Yes," I said, not taking my eyes off it.

We stood there for several moments in a silence that might have seemed awkward to someone else. But I was rather unaware of both the silence and the long moments, and Lara didn't seem to mind either.

The sound of Olivia calling for Lara broke the spell, and Lara called down to her, telling her she would be right there. She started to walk past me.

I reached out and stopped her. She turned to look at me.

"Thank you," I said, longing to communicate how much I was coming to appreciate her and wishing there was nothing to hold me back from returning her love completely.

As always, she seemed to understand it anyway.

"You're welcome," she said, wrapping me in a hug.

We spent the next day with Wes, Nicole, and Seth. They had returned late that morning from a four-day stay in Iowa where Nicole's parents lived. Nicole tried out a table full of new recipes, including several dishes that the kids flat-out refused to try.

Seth seemed moody and quiet, and when it seemed like a good time, I asked him how things were going.

He shrugged his shoulders.

"Is there anything you want to talk about?" I said.

"No," he answered quickly and left the room.

I asked Nicole about it later when we were alone in the kitchen with the dishes.

"My sister doesn't want him to come home yet," Nicole said with a sigh. "He had always been under the impression that after the first of the year he'd be able to go back. He saw her on Christmas Eve, and she told him she's not ready."

"What's the deal?" I said.

"I don't think *he's* ready to go back there myself," Nicole said. "But I could strangle my sister for telling Seth she doesn't want him back yet. You don't tell a kid who is already down on himself that he isn't wanted."

"Is she afraid he will go back to his old ways?" I said.

"She should be," Nicole said bitterly, scraping a plate into the sink. "But that's not what's bothering her. She has a new boyfriend, and she's afraid her needy son will get in the way."

"She didn't say that to him, did she?" I said.

Nicole threw a sponge into soapy water.

"She didn't have to."

We had a quiet New Year's Eve at my parents' house. Mom convinced Cleo to stay until the second of January so she wouldn't have to spend the New Year's holiday alone. At the shop a couple of days after Christmas, I asked my mom if Cleo was fretting over being away from Ben or if she thought Ben was having a tough time without her being there.

"Ben doesn't even know who she is anymore," Mom said. "It's been a little difficult on Cleo to be away from him, but she knows Ben hasn't missed her. That makes it both easy and hard for her."

I also asked my mom what it was like to have Cleo as a house-guest.

"She is a little brusque," Mom said with a smile. "But Kate, she really does have a heart of gold. Rosemary saw that in her. Lara does too. And now I can. I guess sometimes you have to look deep to see what someone is really like."

Yes. That was something I was beginning to understand.

On the second of January, Dad drove my grandparents and Cleo up to the Twin Cities, Cleo to catch a bus to Two Harbors, and my grandparents to catch a flight to Detroit where my Uncle Matt would be picking them up.

Saying goodbye to my grandparents was hard. I again had that horrible feeling that time was running out for my grandpa. When my mom hugged him goodbye, she held him for a long time.

"You have been the best father in the whole world," she said to him, quietly, but I could hear it.

"And you have been the best daughter," he returned.

"Goodbye, Dad," Mom said softly as they parted.

It was the first time I ever heard her call him that.

*F*ebruary arrived, and Mom, Lara, and I began spending cold and blustery nights looking through the pile of college brochures Lara accumulated in the six months she had lived with us. Somehow it didn't seem right that we had to plan for Lara's move to college so soon after bringing her here. Mom had of course told Lara she could live at home if she wanted and commute each day to the state college an hour away. I had done that and knew what a pain in the neck that was. Lara was genuinely appreciative of the offer, but I knew she probably wouldn't go that route.

Both Mom and I thought Lara had the talent to be a professional photographer, but Lara never seemed to think of her skill as anything more than just a hobby.

"I want to do something that really matters," she said to me one day at the Table, when we were in between customers.

"Like what?" I said.

"I'd like to do what my parents did," she said quietly, watching me for my response.

"You want to be a missionary?" I said, a little surprised.

She looked away and nodded.

"I loved what we did, Kate," she said. "It's the most meaningful thing I have ever done, and I was just a little kid."

"Where do you think you would want to go?" I asked, instantly remembering how I felt when I was twelve and Mom told me the Prentisses were taking Lara to Ecuador.

"Somewhere in South America," she said. "It doesn't have to be Ecuador, but I do miss it."

I wasn't sure what to say next. I knew what I wanted to say. I just wasn't sure if I should say it. Then I suddenly felt a burst of boldness.

"You might want to consider how that would affect my mother," I said. Should I have said *our* mother? I wasn't sure.

She nodded, and I could tell I touched on something she had already labored over in her head and heart.

"I keep praying about it and wondering if I'm being selfish, Kate," she said, almost whispering the words. "I'm just not sure what I should do."

"She loves you so much, Lara," I said, knowing it was true and unexpectedly feeling okay about it.

"And I love her," Lara said, turning her head toward me. "I do."

In that moment—I don't know if it was God prompting me or not, but it sure felt like it—I suddenly knew what I should say to her.

I looked her in the eye, waited until I had her full attention, and then told her what Rosemary had said to me on a similarly cold day.

"You know, there was a time in my life when things seemed pretty cloudy and I was very confused," I said. "You weren't born yet and my parents were making decisions about you and our family, and I didn't think they were the right ones. Rosemary told me something one day that really helped me, Lara. I've never forgotten it."

Hearing her mother's name pricked her heart, I think, but she never took her eyes off me.

"What did she say?" Lara asked.

I looked away for a moment. I was only just beginning to understand how sometimes love leads you down paths you never expected to travel. It seemed I was the least qualified at that moment to give advice about making wise choices. But I told her anyway.

"That everything usually turns out for the best if you let love lead the way," I said.

Seth continued on his depressing downward spiral in those first two months of the new year. His grades, which had risen remarkably in the fall, began to plummet again. It seemed even Lara couldn't bring him out of his blue mood. He didn't spend as much time at our place as he did before Lara came. And at first I was a little put out. But he was a grouch most of the time and constantly had to be told to watch his language. I didn't want Olivia and Bennett to be around him.

He spent many evenings over at my parents' house. I think it was my mom and Lara who kept him from failing his second semester classes. Between the two of them they managed to motivate him enough to keep his grades at just below a C average, not a pretty sight, but enough to keep him in line for graduation.

When Lara and he first became friends, he went with her to every youth group event at our church and seemed to really enjoy being around kids his age who had fun and didn't drink. I think it was a first for him. But he stopped going to those youth events after the first of the year. Wes and Nicole insisted he attend Sunday morning services with them, but he sat in the pew and scowled the whole time.

It was depressing for all of us to watch.

Lara and I talked about it several times, but neither of us could put a finger on what had really sent Seth on this horrible spin into despondency. It seemed to be more than just his mother's decision to have him continue living with Wes and Nicole.

If I could have seen the future, I would have tried harder to figure him out, because in the end it mattered a great deal. But I don't suppose anyone could have predicted what was going to happen on one chilly night in March.

I came home from the Table at about four-thirty in the afternoon on that crucial day and found Olivia and Bennett wide-eyed and clinging to Lara when I walked into my kitchen.

Both of my kids ran to me. I looked up at Lara for an explanation.

"Seth just left," Lara said and I could tell she had been crying.

"What happened?" I said, anger and fear mixing together in my head and voice.

"Lara told him to leave because he was being naughty!" Olivia told me.

"He yelled," Bennett said. "He said bad words."

I needed to talk to Lara alone. I sent Olivia and Bennett upstairs to watch television in my room—a special treat usually only reserved for times when we had company.

"What happened?" I asked again when the kids were safely out of earshot.

"He came over here when we were outside playing with Bogart," Lara said, wiping her eyes. "And he was angry about something. He wanted to talk to me alone, but I told him I couldn't leave the kids, that it would have to wait until I was fin-ished babysitting. He just got angrier and started saying...saying things he shouldn't have said in front of the kids."

"Had he been drinking?" I said.

"I don't know," Lara said, choking back a sob. "Maybe."

"Go ahead and go on home, Lara," I said as gently as I could, because I didn't want her to think I was mad at her. But I *was* mad. I was mad at Seth. "I'll call Nicole."

She nodded and picked up her backpack.

"Will you tell the kids goodbye for me?" she said, tears welling in her eyes.

I told her I would and then watched as she drove away. I checked on the kids without their seeing me and then came back downstairs to call Nicole. I got the answering machine. I didn't know if Seth was there and listening to my message so I just said I wanted Nicole to call me back when she got home.

Then I hung up.

I went upstairs to reassure my kids that all was well.

I really thought all was well.

I was so very wrong.

It was about nine thirty that night when Mom called. The kids had been in bed for an hour, and Michael and I were eating a bowl of popcorn, watching television, and unwinding from the long day.

When the phone rang, I thought it was Nicole finally returning my call.

"Can you send Lara home?" Mom said after we had exchanged greetings.

I paused for the slightest moment.

"Lara's not here," I said. "She left hours ago."

"She's not there?"

"No," I said. "Have you been out?"

"We had a farewell dinner for that veterinary assistant who's moving to Des Moines. We just got in. When did you say she left?"

"Mom, were Wes and Nicole with you?" I could feel that my voice had risen in pitch.

"Well, yes," Mom said, sensing it. "Kate, what's wrong?"

I told her what had happened that afternoon. Even as I told her, I knew. I knew something bad was happening. Or had happened. I knew that Seth had waited for Lara until she left our house. That he had followed her or convinced her to follow him. That was five hours ago.

"Hang up. I am going to call the sheriff," Mom said.

"I'll call Nicole. Then I'm coming over, Mom."

She clicked off.

Before I could dial Wes and Nicole's number, the phone rang. It was Nicole.

"Hey, it's me," she said. "What's up?"

"Nicole," I said urgently. "Is Seth there?"

"Well, we just got home. I think he is. His car is here," she said.

"Is Lara's car there?" I asked.

"No," she said. "Why?"

I quickly told Nicole that Seth had come to my house earlier that day, presumably drunk, and been verbally abusive to the kids and Lara, and that Lara had left the house at four-thirty but apparently never made it home.

"Please go see if they're in the house somewhere," I pleaded.

I heard the sound of the phone handset being lowered and Nicole yelling Seth's name. Her voice got farther away and then came nearer again.

"Oh, God, no!" I heard her say, and I felt my heart fluttering inside me.

"What? What?" I screamed into the phone, willing her to tell me what she had seen.

"We need to call the police," I heard Wes say.

It seemed to take forever for Nicole to lift the phone back to her mouth.

"I have to hang up, Kate," she said, her voice quivering. "Seth and Lara aren't here. One of Wes's guns is missing. And some bullets."

I suddenly felt very nauseous.

"Call me at my parents'!" I yelled and clicked off.

I raced over to my shoes by the back door and yelled to Michael what Nicole had told me.

"You're in no condition to drive!" he said as I grabbed my car keys. "Let me take you over there."

"We can't leave the kids, Michael!" I said. "And we can't bring them over there. We don't know...we don't know what has happened!"

I promised Michael I would call him the minute I knew something.

Then I fled into the night, utterly oblivious to the brilliance of the starlit sky.

32

When I look back on that night, I feel as though I came to a crossroads in almost every area of my life. All those hours while we waited for news of Lara, I felt like I was teetering on the edge of all that I was and all I wanted to be: like there was just a thin plate of glass between the two, and I was not on one side or the other but somewhere in between.

I knew I loved my husband and my children, but I also knew I still yearned to know what kind of life I would be leading if my mother had not gone shopping that night seventeen years ago. I knew I loved my art and my job. And I even loved Blue Prairie. But I felt like I didn't choose any of it. If I could have chosen, would I have chosen this? I loved my parents, but they had made decisions that I would not have made. I wanted to love Lara, and yet I feared loving her.

But I stumbled upon the deepest truth as I began pacing the floor for the third hour after my mother's call. Tracing my steps over and over between the living room and kitchen—in the house where we tried to forget all our sorrows—I realized I trusted God only to a point. And realizing this made me stop dead in my tracks because it explained everything else.

My doubts about my life's direction, the uncertainty regarding the choices I had made, the fear that kept me from loving my sister completely—they all hinged on trust. And the truth was, I was afraid to trust God with the things that mattered most to me.

As my parents and I waited out the long hours, I found myself silently asking God over and over, "Can I trust You?" And I kept hearing the words my mother told me she had heard Him whisper to her: *Do not be afraid.*

But I was afraid. And I didn't know how not to be.

At a little after midnight the phone rang, and the three of us jumped.

"I can't answer it, Dan," my mom said, fear twisting itself around her words.

Dad nodded and answered the phone.

"Yes?" he said, instead of "Hello."

We waited.

"No, Nicole. We haven't heard anything," Dad said.

Mom and I slumped onto the couch.

"No, the sheriff's department said they would let the other counties know," Dad continued. "I don't think so. They told us to wait here at the house in case the kids come here. Yes. We will. Bye."

He hung up and fell onto the couch next to my mother. Several long moments passed without a word between us.

Then my dad turned to Mom and took her hand. He seemed to forget completely that I was right there in the room with them. Or maybe he didn't care.

"Sometimes I think I made a horrible mistake, Claire," he said.

When she looked at him in wonder, he continued.

"Sometimes when I look at her, when I see how she loves people, when I see how much she reminds me of you, I think we should have kept her," he said, emotion thick in his voice.

Mom laid her head on his chest, and he folded her into his arms.

"We did what we did because we loved her," Mom said. "And she is who she is because she has been loved. Don't you see?" she continued when he said nothing. "It's all been worth it. It's all been worth it, Dan. Even if she's in heaven right at this moment, it's all been worth it. Because we loved her."

I guess they had come to a crossroads of their own that terrible night.

It was a little after one in the morning when the phone rang a second time. Dad answered it again.

"Yes?" he said. "Yes, I am Dan Holland."

It had to be the sheriff's department. I could hardly breathe.

"Yes, my wife and I are her legal guardians."

I looked at Mom. Her eyes were closed and her hands were folded in her lap. I don't think I will ever forget how she looked at that moment. It was like she was already imagining living in peace without Lara. I could not imagine it.

"Oh, thank God!" my dad said next, and we both turned to him. He covered the mouthpiece and whispered, "She's okay."

I sat down next to Mom and put my arms around her. She probably thought I was offering reassurance to her, but I was really seeking it. She hugged me back, and we anxiously waited to hear what Dad would say next. There was a long pause while he listened.

"Oh, is he okay?" Dad said. "Oh. I see. Have you called his aunt and uncle? Okay. Can we come and get her? Okay. We'll be right there."

He hung up and joined us on the couch.

"She's okay, she's okay," he said softly as Mom cried softly onto his shoulder.

"What happened? Where has she been?" she asked when she could.

"They were in her car," Dad said. "I guess she followed Seth to Wes and Nicole's place when she left Kate's. Something happened there. It's not clear yet. But Seth broke into Wes's gun case and took a revolver and some ammunition. He forced Lara to drive out to the edge of a slough about twenty miles from here. That's where they've been this whole time."

"Did he...did he hurt her?" Mom asked.

"They said she was fine. They said she was okay," Dad said. "He turned himself in, Claire. Lara drove him to the sheriff's station, and he turned himself in."

"Can we bring her home?" Mom said, wiping her eyes.

"We can leave right now. You want to come, Kate?"

"Yes, just let me call Michael," I said.

We were out the door in two minutes.

The county jail was quiet. There were only a handful of cars in the parking lot. One of them was Wes and Nicole's. One of them was Lara's.

The quiet lobby didn't seem to match our circumstances at all. We were tense and jumpy. There was no one in the waiting area and only one lady dispatcher behind the glass.

"I'm Dan Holland," Dad said to her. "I'm here for Lara Prentiss."

She spoke into a phone and then hung up.

"It will be a few minutes," she said.

We sat down to wait.

Perhaps half an hour later, she buzzed the three of us in. We entered a hallway where a deputy met us and took us to where Lara was waiting. There was no sign of Seth or Wes or Nicole.

Mom flew to her and hugged her close. Dad hurried to her as well and put his arms around both of them.

"Are you okay?" Mom said through her tears. "Are you hurt?"

"I'm okay," Lara said softly. She sounded exhausted.

"What happened? Why didn't you come home?" Mom said. "Did Seth have a gun?"

Lara looked very tired. She saw me in the background and managed a tiny smile.

"He didn't fire it," she said.

The deputy came forward.

"You should be very proud of this young lady," he said. "She not only saved her own life tonight, she saved the life of that young man."

Mom turned to look at the deputy.

"Is Seth okay?" Mom said to him.

"He's getting the care he needs," the deputy said. "This young gal has had a pretty rough night, so why don't you take her on home and let her get some rest. Okay?"

We filed out of the room into the hallway and through the heavy, leaded door. A Blue Prairie police officer was coming through the door as we were walking through it.

"So, you're the big hero," he said to Lara.

She just smiled and said nothing, and in silence we made our way to the parking lot.

"I can drive Lara's car back to the house," I offered and Lara handed me her keys without a word.

I followed my parents' car back to their house in kind of a daze. When we got to the house, Lara stepped slowly onto the porch, leaning on Dad the whole time. I followed them in with her keys and backpack and set them on the kitchen counter.

"Can I just sleep on the couch?" she said sleepily. "I don't want to try and make it up the stairs."

Without waiting for an answer she headed for the couch in the living room and collapsed onto it.

"I'll get a pillow and some blankets," Mom said, disappearing.

I pulled off Lara's shoes, and she mumbled a thank-you. Dad reached down and turned out the light next to her and brushed away a few stray hairs from across her face. It was an unmistakable fatherly gesture.

"Kate?" Lara said softly.

"Yes?"

"Are the kids okay? Did they get to sleep okay?"

"They're fine, Lara. Don't worry about them," I said.

"He said such awful things," she mumbled.

"I don't think they remembered them," I said honestly.

"That's good. Because he didn't mean them."

And then she was asleep.

*I*n the weeks that followed it was difficult to go about the mundane and ordinary things of life. We all felt like we had traveled an incredibly dangerous journey and made it back safely by just the skin of our teeth. Going back to the routine of everyday life seemed to mock the danger and tempt it to return.

The morning after the episode with Seth, Lara revealed a nightmare that few of us adults could imagine dealing with. Seth had in fact waited for Lara in the driveway of my parents' house after he left my place that day, and he convinced her to come back with him to Wes and Nicole's. He told her he wasn't drunk, but Lara said she didn't believe him and refused to get into his car. She drove in her own car back to Wes and Nicole's, where Seth proceeded to lambaste his social worker, his mother, Wes and Nicole, every teacher at the school, Michael and me, my parents, and just about everyone else who had ever tried to help him.

Lara said they were at the house for a couple of hours. Most of the time, Seth was yelling and complaining. She said she waited until she thought the alcohol had worn off and then tried to help him see past his pain. She told him he would never find peace in his relationships with people until he had peace in his relationship with God. Lara said he listened to everything she said for quite a while without saying a word. She thought she almost had him convinced of his need to turn to God.

"But then it was like he just snapped," Lara said. "He broke into the gun case and grabbed the gun and some bullets. The whole time he was loading it, he was shaking like he had a fever."

Lara said she begged him to put the gun down. She said she told him over and over that God loved him, that He cared about him. And that she cared about him too. Hearing those things was apparently more than he could handle. He told Lara nobody loved him, and he didn't think anyone should.

Lara said he told her to get into the car. She refused. He threatened to kill her and then himself. She didn't believe him. He flipped off the safety and pointed the gun at her.

"Get in the car," he said.

She did.

Lara said she had no idea where they were headed, and she didn't think he did either. When they finally stopped at the slough, it was close to eight o'clock and pitch dark. Lara believed Seth had picked the place where he planned to shoot them both. First her, then himself.

I asked Lara if she was scared, thinking immediately it was a dumb question—of course she was scared. But she said the strangest feeling came over her as they sat in the car and talked—she, about life and love; he, about death and hate. The feeling was that when it all came down to this—to your last moments on earth—all that matters is how much you loved.

"I loved much," she told me. "I loved two incredible parents, plus Dan and Claire, you and Michael and the kids, Cleo, the grandparents, Wes and Nicole, and even Seth."

"I wasn't as afraid for me as I was for Seth," she continued. "I didn't want him dying without knowing what it is like to love and be loved."

For several hours, Lara kept Seth from pulling the trigger. It was another hour after she talked him into giving her the gun—which Lara threw into the slough—before he agreed to let her drive him to the sheriff's department where he turned himself in.

~~~

I haven't seen Seth since that night, though I hear he is doing well at the regional treatment center where he is now living. Wes and Nicole seem to have recovered from the ordeal, although Nicole has not been able to make the trip up to see Seth. Wes has gone twice.

My parents seem different to me in the aftermath, like they finally see eye-to-eye again on the matter of Lara. Then again, I'm not sure if they ever did before this. Maybe this is the first time they have ever both felt the same way about her. It's like Lara is their bright, shining reminder that God can forge beauty from tragedy. The wall of denial they had lived under for the past seventeen years has crumbled. Lara is no longer someone no one is allowed to discuss. She is someone they both love.

Michael says I seem different too. When I asked him not long ago how I seem different, he shrugged his shoulders and said it's like I've grown up, and then he winked at me. I knew what he meant. He means I'm not acting—what was the word he used?—childish regarding Lara anymore. He attributes it to the scare of almost losing her. But that's not it actually. It's attributable to finally understanding where my problem with my discontentment started. It didn't start with my fear of loving something or the fear of losing it. It started with my preference for only trusting God halfway.

In spite of the intense drama we experienced as a family in March, April flew by. Winter gave way to a quiet spring, typical for Minnesota. Spring arrives gradually here, not all at once. There is no riot of new color or burst of green to herald its arrival. It arrived like it usually does—subtly, slowly, and without fanfare.

Lara went to the prom with a fellow senior from church— whom Dad said couldn't be all bad because he raises award-winning heifers. She also got acceptance letters from every college and university she applied to. No surprise there. Her college entrance exam scores were off the charts. By the end of April, she had decided to attend a small, private Christian college in Saint Paul, only a little over two hours away. Mom was pretty pleased with that decision. Olivia didn't like the idea of Lara going to any college, anywhere. But she is learning, just like the rest of us, to flow with change, not resist it.

Lara told me not long ago when we were both at the Table that she's decided on an education major, that being with my kids the past nine months has really shown her how much she enjoys children and watching them learn.

"What about the mission field?" I asked her when she told me this.

"There will always be a need for teachers on the mission field," she said. "And there will always be a mission field."

She didn't say it word for word, but I took that to mean she felt no immediate urgency to pursue a life thousands of miles away from home.

And this *was* home. She felt it. And I was glad she did.

It is now nearing the end of May. Nearly a year has come and gone since Lara came back to us. Earlier this month, Nicole began planning Lara's graduation open house which will be held at Tennyson's Table. On her birthday. It will be a beautiful party. Nicole never does anything less.

Grandma and Grandpa arrived yesterday from Michigan to attend Lara's graduation on Friday night and to help celebrate at the open house on Monday. Grandpa looks so fragile. His doctor didn't want him to come, and I think the airline wished he hadn't. I hate to think that he isn't long for this world. But I am learning that this is how it is. We spend our lives saying hello, we spend our lives loving, and we spend our lives saying goodbye. It is the way it is. To refuse to acknowledge this is to miss out on all the beauty and wonder of life.

Lara will spend the summer here in Blue Prairie, working at the Table, playing with my children, and working her way deeper into my heart. Come September, she will head off to college, and life will sort of seem like it did before she came. But it really won't be like that at all.

Because in the meantime I am on a quest of my own. I now have three goals I am anxious to pursue, and as I sit here at the writing table in my shop, I find that I can't wait to get started. The first, taught to me so many years ago by Rosemary, is to fully learn to let love lead the way—and to enjoy its leading. I feel I have made some headway here, and that progress is helping to fuel my second goal—prompted by my mother though she does not know it: I want to learn how to look deep to see what people are really like. I want to be the kind of person who plunges past the surface and seeks to know the inner thoughts of the people I am around. I want to see the beauty in people like Cleo from the moment I meet them.

Lastly, and this will be the hardest goal for me to reach, but it is also the one I want the most to reach: I want to paint the night sky as God created it.

I know now I can't do it on my terms—that is, in my own studio, where all that I have created surrounds me. I have to do it on God's terms.

I must be willing to meet with God alone under His vast canopy of stars and see where the level of my trust starts and where it stops. If I am going to love people completely and at the heart of who they are, I am going to need to trust that God will watch over them in the way He sees as best. Because loving people will cost me, and I need to be able to meet that price with trust so that I can enjoy love's best moments and endure the worst.

It will take time, and it will take commitment.

It starts tonight. With me. And I know what I have to do to begin.

I just have to bring my canvas out to where the stars are.

Epilogue

October 21, 2003

Dear Cleo,

Thanks for the wonderful cookies you sent! My roommates and I ate them all in one sitting! They all want to know if they can have the recipe so they can send it to their moms.

My classes are going well, and I really like my professors. It's hard to believe it is almost time for the fall break. Time has gone by so quickly.

I am sorry you couldn't make it out for Grandpa Stuart's funeral. It was really beautiful. He reminded me so much of my dad. I wonder if maybe they have found each other in heaven! Perhaps they are right now having a wonderful time chatting about all the things they had in common.

Claire tells me you are thinking of moving to Blue Prairie and sharing a house with my grandma and Aunt Elizabeth! I think it's a great idea, Cleo. And you wouldn't have to worry about Ben; both nursing homes there are really wonderful. I think he would make a very smooth transition. And Nicole could really use you at the Table. No one can make a pot of tea as terrific as you can!

It would be wonderful if you could move there by Thanksgiving. I would love to just sit and chat with you and show you my pictures from Kate's and my trip to New York this summer. We had such a great time. We bought matching hats and gloves in Manhattan at Bloomingdales!

Guess what? I think I have convinced Claire and Dan to come with me on a short-term mission trip to Brazil next summer. It's a three-week trip to this farming community that could really use Dan's skills as a vet and Mom's talents as a teacher. I'm not sure yet if all is a go, but Claire told me she found a good deal on a book and tape set for learning basic Portuguese, and she bought it. That's a good sign!

I really do have to run. I have class soon, and I want to write a letter to Seth before it starts.

Tons of hugs,

Lara

P.S. I am praying that you will come to Blue Prairie for good! I don't like your being up in Two Harbors all by yourself, Cleo. I love my new family, and they love me. And I really think they love you too. I know how much you worried about my coming to live with them because you were afraid they wouldn't love me for who I really was. But they do! Remember that quote my mom liked, Cleo? "Love is not blind—it sees more, not less. But because it sees more, it is willing to see less."

XOXOXO
L.